THE RULES
O F
WAR

XENIA MELZER

DSP PUBLICATIONS

Published by

DSP PUBLICATIONS

5032 Capital Circle SW, Suite 2, PMB# 279, Tallahassee, FL 32305-7886 USA
www.dsppublications.com

The Rules of War
© 2021 Xenia Melzer

Cover Art
© 2021 L.C. Chase
http://www.lcchase.com
Cover content is for illustrative purposes only and any person depicted on the cover is a model.

Trade Paperback ISBN: 978-1-64405-967-8
Digital ISBN: 978-1-64405-966-1
Trade Paperback published November 2021
v. 1.0

Printed in the United States of America
(∞)

This paper meets the requirements of
ANSI/NISO Z39.48-1992 (Permanence of Paper).

By Xenia Melzer

ANDI HAYES MURDER MYSTERIES
Arthropoda

GODS OF WAR
Casto
Love and the Stubborn
Ummana
Braving the Storm
The Rules of War

Published by DSP Publications
www.dsppublications.com

For Aquamarin – even after two years, I still miss you like crazy.

ACKNOWLEDGMENTS

THIS IS the fifth book in the Gods of War series and without the help and support of a lot of people, I wouldn't have gotten so far. First of all, I want to thank my readers, who kept inquiring about what's going to happen next in the series. You guys rock and you really helped me going when I thought about dropping the series. I also have to thank Dreamspinner for keeping the series on even though it's not a bestseller. Knowing your publisher is behind you on a project is what every author needs. The biggest thanks go to my editors, Gus Li, Brian, and Yv, who see every logical mistake, every spelling error, every grammatical monstrosity my non-native speaker mind has constructed, and who sometimes know my story better than I do. Thank you for seeing everything and still having some kind comments for me!

PREVIOUSLY IN THE GODS OF WAR SERIES

A LOT has happened in the lives of Casto and Renaldo so far. After being taken prisoner by Renaldo, Casto fought his master at every turn. Their explosive relationship has seen many ups and downs that would have broken weaker men. The worst came when Renaldo fell for the schemes of Damon, a priest of the Good Mother, who convinced him that Casto had been unfaithful. In a fit of rage, Renaldo sent Casto to the mines in order to kill him. But thanks to Sic's courage, the scheme was revealed and the magic spell clouding the divine brothers' sight broken. Casto returned to his master's side, no longer as a slave but as his lover, heart, and future husband.

To bring Casto down, Damon had used Sic by blackmailing him into bringing Damon a cloak pin that would prove Casto's guilt. When Sic finally found the courage to tell Renaldo what happened, he was punished for his treason. Noran wished to see his apprentice dead, and it was only thanks to Casto's interference that Sic was allowed to live. Deeply hurt by Sic's deed, Noran lost control of himself and tortured Sic cruelly by using the young man's love to force him into absolute subservience.

Daran, on the other hand, was more than happy with his two masters. He overcame his shock after Kalad was almost killed during the battle of Ki't and knew without a doubt that he belonged to Aegid and Kalad for the rest of his life.

The divine brothers found out that the followers of the Good Mother, who had infiltrated the Valley, had been trained in Medelina. Because of that the Wolf of War wished to get his revenge on the city.

They decided to go to Ummana, where Casto claimed the throne and became king, not only of the Twin Cities, but also of the Alliance. That way, Canubis and Renaldo get their revenge on Medelina and Casto his on the council of elders and his father. Before he left, Casto installed his sister Anesha as queen of Ummana.

But their mission also claimed sacrifices. When Noran was poisoned, Sic offered his own life to save his master, only to find out that he is a Luksari, a creature of pure magic. After he was rescued, Noran gave Sic his freedom and Sic found a family and happiness with Jago, the master of the royal smithy, his wife, Cassia, and their little daughter, Heljia. He decided to stay in Ummana, although parting with Casto almost broke his heart.

After the barbarians left Ummana, Sic was visited by Ana-Isara and she marked him as the last Emeris, thus forcing him to follow his gods into the North.

In a foolish attempt to impress his masters and express his gratitude toward them, Daran became a spy for Casto. This dangerous game almost cost him his life and it was only thanks to Casto's foresight that he survived.

After their campaign in Ummana, the Gods of War returned to the Valley with their ranks finally completed. Sic was the eighth Emeris to join Renaldo and Canubis in their war against the Good Mother. Even though they are complete now, the Gods of War still had to wait until their powers and those of the Emeris manifest. Until then, they faced various trials.

Aegid and Kalad lost Daran to death and it was only thanks to Sic's abilities as a Luksari that the thief returned to them. Daran was then no longer a simple mortal but Echend'dim, the first of Canubis and Renaldo's eternal guard. But before he could truly embrace his new status and get used to it, he was kidnapped during a fight with highwaymen and brought to a brothel. There, the owners of the brothel and his kidnapper sold Daran's body and life to the highest bidder. He died twice before Aegid and Kalad found and rescued him.

As a result of the trauma Daran suffered, he started doubting his relationship with Aegid and Kalad. It is Casto who helped him gain focus again and make peace not only with his past but also with all the wrong assumptions he has made about his lovers. In a bloody act of violence, Daran claimed his rank as first of the Echend'dim and lover of Aegid and Kalad.

The desert brothers proposed to Daran and married him in early winter. Sic's relationship with Noran slowly matured while Renaldo and Casto still struggled for a suitable balance in theirs. During the Spring Ceremony, Casto was confronted with Renaldo's true power after Ana-Aruna and Ana-Isara have left Ana-Darasa to their sons. Horrified and furious, he left his mate together with Lys.

THE RULES

O F

WAR

XENIA MELZER

WHERE LOVE ENDS

1. ALONE

"How is he doing?"

Hulda regarded Canubis with worry in her lavender eyes. The Wolf of War sat down, wiping his face in a tired gesture.

"Still staring at the wall. Well, at least he answered my questions today. Just yes and no, but he's talking again."

"Damn, Casto! Why did you have to leave again?"

Hulda had spoken to the room in general, not expecting an answer at all. Still, Canubis's fist came crashing down on the armrest of his chair.

"Because he's a bloody nuisance! I'm almost inclined to believe he was just waiting for something like this incident to happen so he could turn his back on us!"

Hulda shook her head. She had known Canubis long enough to know his violent outburst was fueled by his worry about his little brother. They all were deeply worried.

Two weeks had passed since Casto had left the Valley and told Renaldo farewell and fuck yourself in a dream. Since then, there had been no contact. No dreams, no use of Renaldo's fire, just a big, ominous nothing. At the moment, it seemed as if Casto was really gone. Going after him was not an option, what with the upcoming campaign in the Dark Forest and the fact that Casto could be anywhere by now. The storm Lys had called upon the mountains had washed away all traces the wolves could have followed, and not even Renaldo was desperate enough yet to dash around blindly in the meager hope of finding Casto by chance. All they could do was carry on with their tasks, hoping that the capricious blond would let off enough steam to consider returning.

"I really think you're giving him more credit than he deserves. Casto may be devious and calculating, but not even he can plan so far ahead. Besides, he truly loves Renaldo. So whatever happened, it was bad enough to drive him away."

Hulda raised an eyebrow meaningfully, while Canubis tried to avert his gaze. She had him finally cornered and wouldn't let go until she knew all the details. The Wolf of War sighed. Perhaps it was a good idea to tell Hulda about what had happened during the Spring Ceremony. Until now, this had been a secret between him, Noemi, Renaldo, and Casto.

"I'm not sure if I'm able to explain it properly. A lot is rather blurry."

"Just try. You know how understanding I can be."

So there really was no escaping it. Canubis leaned back in his chair.

"As you may already have guessed, this year's Spring Ceremony was a little different from the ones before. When you all started to sacrifice your blood and then honor the Mothers, we could feel the power practically drowning us. It was unbelievable, like the worst storm you've ever been in. And now we know what Noemi and Casto really are for—they transform all that raw energy we suck up from our followers and turn it into power. Without them, we would be consumed by it and probably die. Catch is, to transform the energy, Noemi and Casto must submit to us completely. Not only with their bodies, but also with their minds and souls."

Hulda winced. There was no need for Canubis to speak on. Casto's motive for leaving was absolutely clear. He hated nothing more than being forced. Even worse, during the Spring Ceremony in front of all the mercenaries. Not that any of them had noticed. They all had been too caught up in their own lust, but for Casto it must have been like a slap in the face. No wonder he had cut himself off completely.

"He's going to need a lot of time to get over this shock. And since Lys is shielding him, there's not much you can do. This is really bad indeed."

Canubis huffed.

"I don't get why he's making such a fuss. I mean, yes, I know him, but still, Noemi took it more or less in stride."

Hulda only stared at Canubis.

"Well, perhaps not in stride. There may have been a small—okay, okay, a *big* argument about my lack of restraint, but she understood. She has forgiven me."

"First of all, you and Noemi have quite a mature relationship compared to that of Renaldo and Casto. Second, your wife is a very levelheaded person who had over a century to get used to all the surprises you can throw her way. Third, I'm convinced that Casto understands as well. He just doesn't like it, and that's the crux, as you well know."

Canubis rose from his chair to pace the room.

"So what do I do now?"

Hulda shrugged.

"You don't have much choice. You have an important campaign starting in two weeks. So you will see to it that your brother gets his act together until then, because we're going to need him. And like all of us, you will pray to the Mothers that nothing happens to Casto while he cools his head and makes up his mind. He will return, of that I am sure. He just needs time."

Knowing Hulda was right, Canubis showed her a weak smile.

"May the goddesses hear you, Hulda. If I think about all the things that could happen to Casto, I want to throw up."

"Then don't think! Concentrate on what you're good at, namely killing people. Everything else has to sort itself out."

IN HIS smithy, Sic gave the tiara Lady Sephrina had ordered the final polish. It was the last commissioned work he had to do before they went on the campaign in the Dark Forest, and Sic was happy to have finished it in time to send it to Ummana with all the other pieces he had made during the winter. When he put the tiara in a box to get it ready for transport, his gaze fell on the hunting knife he had made for Casto. Sighing, Sic picked up the shimmering weapon. He missed his friend more than he would have ever thought possible. Not knowing where he was and if he was fine was pure torture. That Casto had not tried to contact him only showed how deeply he was hurt.

"My precious! Please, don't look so miserable. I'm sure Casto will be back sometime soon."

Noran had entered the smithy without Sic noticing it, for he was so engrossed in his worries. He snuggled up against Noran's bulky frame.

"How did you know I was worrying about Casto?"

Noran pulled Sic closer and kissed him lightly on the cheek.

"Because these days, you hardly smile, and when you have the look from just now, you're thinking about your friend. Don't worry, I have not acquired the sudden ability to read your thoughts."

Sic rewarded Noran's small joke with a weak smile.

"You know me too well, Master. I really miss Casto. I mean, he's stubborn, irascible, and quite often plain insufferable, but he's also the best friend I ever had. Despite being so disagreeable, he has never shown me anything but kindness. Not being able to help him when he's in need is unbearable for me."

Noran pulled Sic even closer, knowing this was all he could do for his beloved at the moment. As usual, Casto had managed to create a huge mess others had to take care of. Noran knew part of this vicious thought was grounded in the jealousy he felt toward the bond Sic and Casto shared. Nevertheless, he still believed there was a grain of truth in it. Casto never cared about the feelings of others or how his actions affected those who loved him. The only thing he ever protected fiercely was his own precious freedom. How Sic could love the king so deeply remained a mystery to Noran. Then again, Sic loved him as well, and if anything, he was worse than Casto. Desperate to take Sic's mind off his worries, Noran started kissing him, grateful that their relationship was progressing so well.

"COULD YOU please cut it out?"

Laughing, Daran tried to fend off both Kalad's and Aegid's hands.

"We already did three rounds, and I really have to get going, as you well know."

Kalad pouted.

"But we're nowhere near satisfied yet, little thief. You have to take responsibility!"

"You always say that, and yet *you* never take responsibility for your actions."

Sensing an opening, Aegid slung his arms around Daran before he could duck out of reach.

"We're doing it now. We take responsibility for arousing you. Please, just one more round. We know you want it as well."

"Of course I want it. But I do have a whole bunch of tasks to fulfill before we start the campaign, and I'm not sure whether Lord Canubis will be understanding if I tell him that I didn't do his bidding because I was busy fucking around."

Aegid huffed but let go of Daran.

"You're probably right. Promise you'll hurry and be back early."

"You sound like a worried wife, Aegid."

Daran grinned broadly. The image was somewhat alluring.

"That's because he is one."

Kalad stepped next to his desert brother.

"We both are. You must promise you'll be home before nightfall."

The two men made pleading faces, and Daran couldn't help but kiss them, full of love.

"I promise. And once I'm back, I'll let you have your way with me. Aren't I generous?"

"Very much so. Go! Go before we push you down right now."

All three men laughed heartily, reveling in their intimate, perfect happiness.

IN THE pits, Da'Ryen hacked away at the frozen soil. He was almost glad about the hard work, for it kept him from freezing. Like all the desert dwellers in the Valley, he had considerable problems dealing with the cold of winter. All in all, his situation was not as bad as he had feared after the ominous words of the Wolf of War. He was indeed the lowest ranked slave in the Pack, and technically, everybody could do to him as they pleased. Luckily for Da'Ryen, it had been decided that Nya would stay with Frankus, the master of the sauna. He was a highly respected man among the mercenaries as well as the slaves, and when he had made it known he would appreciate it if Da'Ryen was left alone, they all had complied. Nya brought him food three times a day, and it was always rich and delicious. To top it off, he was allowed to sleep at Frankus's place on a real bed instead of in the slave barracks. Da'Ryen knew he owed it all to Nya, or rather, the relationship she had established with Frankus. The two liked each other genuinely, like father and daughter, and because Nya also liked Da'Ryen, Frankus had started to protect him, although he did not like him. The master of the sauna had made that crystal clear to Da'Ryen on more than one occasion. He held him responsible for what had happened to Lord Daran, and if anything, Frankus was fiercely protective of those he loved. Their relationship was highly ambiguous, the only thing connecting them their mutual love for Nya. Despite the tension between him and Frankus, Da'Ryen was content with how things had turned out. He had been given another chance to atone for the sins of his past, something he had not dared to hope for after the barbarians had caught them.

The only real nuisance was two other slaves who were almost as low in rank as he was. Their names were Sindal and Elwan, and they were truly unpleasant. Unlike the other slaves, they did not respect Frankus and used every chance to pick on Da'Ryen and make his life miserable. Even though they were the lowest, they still had the protection of the law, and he could not strike at them as he so wanted to do. He had to bear whatever they did to him, because if he laid his hands on them, he would be executed. The only bright spot was that they had lost their tongues. When Da'Ryen imagined the ridicule they would surely rain on him were they still capable of it, he just knew he would not be able to withstand the temptation to smash their skulls. Most of the time he was able to evade them, since they usually either worked at the pig sheds or had to clean out the privies, while Da'Ryen had to work in the pits and help Frankus in the sauna.

IN HIS chambers, Renaldo stared into nothing. His hands played with the ring he had given Casto as a present while his mind replayed the events of the Spring Ceremony in an endless loop. He tried to discern the point when he could have stopped himself from doing the unthinkable, but there was none. Especially since he knew that it was his right to own Casto. After all, he was his god and master. The contradicting emotions threatened to consume Renaldo completely. To make matters worse, he could feel his control of the fire weakening ever since Casto had broken their connection. It made Renaldo realize how essential the hearts were for him and Canubis and that it was a good thing they had gotten them before they had gained their true power back. All he could do now was hope Casto would come back to him soon, preferably before he lost control and slid back into the difficult times before he had had a heart.

WITH A satisfied sigh, Sic put his seal on the list of items that would go to Ummana. He had also included a letter to Jago and Cassia, as well as the wooden figurine of a horse for Heljia. When he thought about his little sister, Sic felt a wave of warmth wash over him. She was almost two and a lovely little lady. Sic was still amazed that he could meet her in his dreams. The first time it happened, about five weeks ago, he assumed it was wishful thinking on his part, but since that first night, he and Heljia had met almost every night, and he just knew it was real. The dream always started at the villa where Jago and Cassia lived with Heljia. She showed him how her day had been and what had happened. Then they went to play, either in her room or in the garden of the villa. Sic knew all her stuffed toys by name and had become really good at serving tea in the small cups Heljia used for her parties. When they wanted a change of scenery, Heljia took Sic's hand and he pulled her into his memories, where they would run around in the Valley, play with the wolves, and visit Lys down at the stables. And since this was all a dream, Lys carried them around on his broad back without batting an eyelash. Sometimes Sic wasn't sure if the stallion was really only a figment of his imagination or truly there. All the other people and even the wolves had a strange quality to them that suggested they were in the dream but mere projections. Lys, on the other hand, felt larger than life when they played with him. Since the stallion didn't mind carrying Sic and Heljia, Sic had no qualms accepting his kindness. And it was not as if he could ask him anymore. Lys was gone.

A wave of sadness washed over Sic when his thoughts returned once again to Casto. He didn't have to be a genius to understand why his friend had left the Valley, but it still hurt that he couldn't help him. Seeing Renaldo suffer hurt Sic even more. He knew how much the man loved Casto and how he was beating himself up for what had happened at the Spring Ceremony. Noran's barely concealed anger about Casto's behavior added another layer of stress to Sic's tumultuous emotions, and if that wasn't enough, there was the strange connection he shared with Daran and Lukan. The three of them had avoided talking about the issue so far, but the bond between them was getting stronger, and they had to figure out what was going on. They also had to tell Canubis and Renaldo about it. Sic knew all too well the gods would not be pleased when they found out how long he and the other two men had been stalling. Mentally slapping himself for allowing his troubles to disturb the feeling of peace he got from thinking about Heljia, Sic focused on the fun they had together. The memory of Heljia's happy laughter calmed him down, and he was looking forward to meeting her again that night.

"SO THE bastard brothers have signed the contract to get rid of the guerilla forces in the Dark Forest?"

The hooded man looked expectantly at Queen Xe'lien, who tried her hardest not to shudder visibly.

"Yes, they have. They did hesitate at first, but as you predicted, they can't afford not to pursue the rebels for fear what the Good Mother might be plotting up here while they are occupied elsewhere. Everything is going according to your plan."

"The Good Mother will reward you for your loyalty."

Xe'lien bowed her head demurely. Having the gratitude of a goddess was surely a good thing when one wanted to become queen of the East.

"I also gave the bastards the false information about the whereabouts of your men. They're going to start searching in all the wrong places, so it should be easy for you to finish them off."

A cruel smile appeared on the lips of the hooded man. The plan was indeed progressing better than he had dared to hope. Not only would he be able to keep the bastards occupied for at least two or three years to come and thus enable the Good Mother to carry out her plans undetected, he also had the chance to kill one of the Emeris in the process. If he managed to do that, the war would be decided before it had begun. To add to the good news, one of his spies had sent him word this very morning that Casto had left the Valley—and Renaldo—seemingly for good. If the Followers managed to find the heart before the bastards and then kill him…. He shivered with glee. Things were finally looking up.

2. TACTICS

"So THIS is the future king of Ummana. I greet you, Prince Regulon."

Lady Evienna of the Murreano family tickled the newborn under the chin. He had the same expressive blue eyes as his mother and uncle, but his hair was of a deep black, just like his father's and her own. Evienna turned to Queen Anesha, who looked rather pleased with herself, although giving birth had taken its toll. Rumor had it, she had only survived because of the skills of Cassia, the best midwife in all of Ummana.

"Let's not waste our precious time, Evienna. Are you going to back me up, or do I have to look for other allies?"

Evienna shot her bastard brother and father to the future king, Captain Aktan, a short look. He had warned her about the queen's straightforwardness, and after the initial shock, Evienna found it kind of refreshing. She managed a smile that even reached her eyes.

"Of course I'm going to back you up, Your Highness. I had planned to do so even before the happy news. To be frank, none of the possible candidates to replace you has my consent, and I don't like the way Medelina is acting up. We already endured five bad years. I want to see my businesses thriving again."

Says the second-richest woman in Ummana, Anesha thought. Aloud she answered: "I appreciate your take on the situation, Lady Evienna. I, too, think Medelina needs to learn its lesson. Let us work together to reach this honorable goal."

Both women smiled at each other, each thinking a union with the other was not a bad thing indeed.

IN THE guild house of the smiths, Aries listened to the rantings of Desdon, Hellwar, and Irr'es. He already knew what their problem was and wondered when they would finally admit defeat and let the matter go. Given how stubborn and greedy the men were, probably never.

"We really feel you, as the master of the guild, Aries, should intervene in this matter. This concerns us all." Desdon tried his best to sound as if he had the greater good in mind, but Aries had known him for long enough to see through his act. The man was distantly related to the Krapati family, and their ingrained greed was showing.

Aries sighed. "I've already explained it to you, Desdon. More than once, I might add. It is Master Sic's decision with whom he wishes to work, and he has chosen Jago."

"Only because Jago had him in his home. Sic is timid and easily influenced. Of course he will do as Jago says. As his fellow smiths, we have to protect him." This time Hellwar had spoken, and his self-righteousness was almost sincere.

It took Aries a moment before he was able to answer such a blatant statement. When he spoke, he didn't even try to keep the sarcasm from his voice. "First of all, Sic is friends with King Castolus, and I'm pretty sure not even you think the king would allow anybody to get the better of Sic. Second, Jago was the one who took Sic in and fought for him when all of us were determined to refuse his request to become a member of our guild."

Aries still felt shame every time he remembered how vehemently he had opposed Sic undertaking the master exams. "Face it, my brethren. There is no way for you to get a piece of this particular business unless Sic decides so. Now if you would please leave me to my work?"

The three men didn't like how Aries dismissed them, but he was the leader of the guild and they knew better than to anger him.

"This is not over yet, Aries." Desdon tried to sound intimidating and failed miserably. Aries only raised a brow, and the men hurried to get out of his office. With a sigh, Aries sank back in his chair. This situation was getting ugly, and he had no clue how to solve it. When Sic had left Ummana to be with his gods, he had made Heljia, Jago's and Cassia's daughter, his beneficiary and her parents the trustees of the money. Even though he had been in the city only a short time, Sic had made quite a fortune. Combined with the villa he had received from King Castolus, it was enough to give Jago and Cassia the monetary leverage to indulge in the higher politics of Ummana. Only they didn't. Neither of them cared about wealth, and the only reason they were living in the villa was because their original home had become a little cramped with Heljia and Arelo, the young apprentice Cassia had taken on. As head of the royal smithy, Jago already had a great deal of influence on the politics of the guild, one he rarely exerted, but still, it was there. Sic did all of his dealings in Ummana via Jago, and since he stated that he had no use for money in the Valley, the profit remained with Jago. Aries knew Sic had decreed half of his earnings should go to Heljia's trust. The other half went into another trust Jago had set up in Sic's name. And both trusts were growing, which made many people nervous. To top it off, Cassia was now the personal healer of Queen Anesha. Jago's small family had risen to power in the blink of an eye, and their refusal to use said power had more and more people in the city gnashing their teeth. The only reason nobody had taken drastic measures yet was the queen's announcement that anybody who laid a hand on Jago or those close to him would answer to her. Aries shuddered. Anesha may be young, but she was her mother's daughter through and through. It was a lesson the citizens of Ummana had learned almost instantly after King Castolus had left. The queen was as calculating and scheming as the best in Ummana, but she also had no problems reverting to drastic, highly violent measures when she had to. It was a dangerous combination, and so far, nobody had been brazen enough to really test her. Unfortunately, it was only a question of time, and Aries could only hope Jago and his family wouldn't be caught in the crossfire. He genuinely liked the big man, who never talked a lot but let his actions speak for him instead. Perhaps it was time for a long conversation with his friend.

IN THE darkness, the cat of prey yowled angrily. Something oppressing and terrible was forced on it, trapping its mind, binding it with invisible, painful chains. It felt its mind slipping away, drowning under the stream of words of ancient magic, locking it in a place without sun and air, without earth and trees, without freedom and the rapid heartbeat of prey. The cat knew instinctively that fighting this magic was futile, that it had to retreat and wait for a chance to get revenge. The last thoughts before it was lost to the darkness were of bones crushing under the pressure of its powerful jaws and the sweet taste of blood on its tongue.

Ellewinn opened his eyes, disoriented, knowing that something had been taken from him, something so important he couldn't afford to lose it, and yet he couldn't remember what it was. He looked around the small tent he was in, wondering how he got there. A man stepped into his line of view. He had a nasty, overly smug grin on his face, one Ellewinn wanted to wipe out with his claws—why would he have claws? He was human, so he would do it with his hands. The man bent down to the bier Ellewinn was on, the grin stretching wider when he touched his chest. It felt like somebody had burned him with a torch or a glowing red knife. In pain, Ellewinn gazed at the hand and gasped when he saw the dark markings on his chest. Nobody had to tell him they were bad; he could feel the evil dripping off them, seeping into his skin. While he looked, the markings started to fade, the black color vanishing into his body, where whatever it was took root, binding him with chains more powerful than anything he had ever seen. The stranger straightened again. With narrow eyes, he addressed Ellewinn. "You are mine now, slave. You will do as I say."

Ellewinn shuddered. As much as he would have liked to choke the man with his bare hands, a voice inside him, maybe his instincts, told him to wait, not to rush things. If the pain the man had caused him by simply touching his chest was anything to go by, Ellewinn would be in agony if he tried to contradict this man. No, he would play along, at least for the time being.

LOST IN thought, Elua played with a strand of Lukan's mousy-brown hair while she watched him sleeping. Like so many times before, she wondered if she had made a mistake when she had given in to his wooing. It was not that she doubted the depths of Lukan's feelings or that she didn't love him herself—she was crazy for him. Still there was a tiny voice in the back of her mind that questioned the wisdom of having taken a man ten years her junior as a husband. Sometimes she felt like an old hag next to him. Until recently, they had shared a stable relationship with clearly defined roles. She had been the superior one, the better fighter and the more experienced. Then Lord Sic had changed it all.

Right after Lukan had come back from the dead, Elua had felt nothing but relief and gratitude. Things had changed, though. Because she knew him so well, she was aware of all the changes going on inside Lukan, his ability to recover from lethal wounds being the least profound. That was just part of being an Echend'dim. Elua was more worried about the emotional baggage Lukan was carrying these days. He had always been an easygoing character, one who took life in stride and never worried too much about anything. At the moment, he still refused to tell her what had happened when Lord Sic had brought him back, but Elua was sure it was the reason for his strange behavior. Dying was most certainly not easy, and she understood that Lukan was trying to deal with a stressful situation. Unfortunately, the way he distanced himself made Elua uncomfortable. There was something going on between Lukan and Lord Sic—and Lord Daran, come to think of it—that he couldn't tell her about. Elua knew she was acting childish, that her jealousy was immature and stupid, yet she couldn't help herself. Her husband had suddenly become part of something a lot greater than she could grasp, and it irritated her to see him change while she was left behind.

Lukan stirred in his sleep. With a broad smile, he took her hand in his and pressed a reverent kiss to her palm.

"Good morning, my lady."

Elua forced a smile on her lips while she bent down to reciprocate his kiss.

"Good morning to you, too, my lord. I hope your sleep has been refreshing?"

The formal talk was a joke between them, one she usually enjoyed, but not today. Lukan furrowed his brows.

"What's the matter?"

Elua cursed in the privacy of her thoughts. She had forgotten how perceptive Lukan could be.

"It's nothing. Just ignore me. I'm being stupid. Probably a sign of old age."

Lukan slung his arms around Elua, pulled her close, and kissed her sand-colored hair with the first streaks of gray.

"Don't worry about your age, my lady. First of all, it doesn't show yet, and second, once Sic manages to recognize an Echend'dim before they die, you'll be immortal."

Elua froze. There it was again, this huge, unspoken wall between them. Not only did she not share Lukan's optimism regarding her being Echend'dim material, she also wasn't sure if she really wanted it. She loved her life and did her best to enjoy it to the fullest, but somewhere deep inside her soul, she knew she didn't want eternity, and she felt like the worst kind of traitor for not telling Lukan upfront. To distract them both, Elua cupped Lukan's face with her hands, a seductive smile on her lips.

"Let's not ponder things in the future. I'd rather get a taste of your newly acquired stamina. According to Aegid and Kalad, the Echend'dim have unrivaled perseverance."

Chuckling, Lukan sat up, a speculative grin on his lips.

"How about we try to find out, my lady? But don't come complaining to me when I wear you out."

SAR'REFF WAS sprawled on his favorite branch high up the old oak tree and watched the snow melting. It was a highly meditative exercise that kept his mind focused while his thoughts went wandering around. He didn't know what to make of his current situation or what his next move should be. The fiery god had lost his mate. Sar'reff could feel the man's pain like a sword cutting the air. Apparently the demon king was shielding his anchor, thus keeping the fiery god from finding them. Sar'reff could still feel Lysistratos because of their kinship. It was a hazy connection, nothing conscious or even wanted, but it was undeniably there, and he could find Lysistratos and his anchor if he had to. Because the demon king had saved Sar'reff, he would not expose him to the fiery god if he didn't want it. The question was how he should react when the two gods asked him. They hadn't done it yet, though it was surely just a question of time until they would decide to use him. They were not fools, after all. Perhaps it was best to leave the Valley now that his powers and mental state had stabilized. With some luck, he may even find his anchor, or at least the pull. Then again, life was easy in the Valley. After all the hardships Sar'reff had endured, he felt he had earned some peace and quiet. The only question was if the gods would grant him what he wanted.

"DARAN! THIS is the third time you tried to block thin air! If you don't pull yourself together, you'll be killed on a daily basis once we're in the field!"

Daran shook his head in confusion. He could have sworn Aegid was trying to get to him from behind when he was truly coming from his left side. He didn't understand how he could have been so wrong. In less than two weeks the Pack would ride for the Dark Forest, and Aegid and Kalad were determined to teach Daran as many of their fighting tricks as possible before their departure. As first of the Echend'dim, there was no way they could prevent Daran from fighting, so they wanted him to be perfectly prepared. Unfortunately, something seemed to be wrong. Daran lowered his sword.

"I swear you were behind me, Aegid. I don't understand."

Aegid dropped his sword and embraced Daran, trying hard to hide his concern.

"It's okay, little thief. You're probably just tired."

"If he were just tired, he wouldn't see opponents where there are none."

Kalad's voice was a little too sharp. He wasn't very good at hiding his worries—at least not where Daran was concerned. "What is wrong with you, Daran? You've been acting a little strange lately. We are your mates. There shouldn't be any secrets between us."

Daran cringed at the reproach in Kalad's voice. He didn't have to look up to know Aegid wore a frown as well. And they were right. There shouldn't be any secrets between them, but he still didn't know if he was ready to talk to anybody about his connection to Sic and Lukan. Judging from the determination he could feel coming from his mates, he had no choice. Daran took a deep, calming breath and started to confess.

"After Sic brought me back from death, I felt a strange connection to him. Nothing conscious, more like an undercurrent that is stronger the closer I am to him. When Sic called Lukan back, I started feeling him as well. It's unnerving and frightening. I'm sorry I didn't tell you sooner, but I just don't know how to handle this."

Aegid's arms tightened around Daran. He shared a long look with Kalad, who came closer and started caressing Daran's back. Kalad's voice was soothing.

"It's fine, little thief. We're not mad at you. Just a little disappointed."

When Daran cringed, Kalad kissed him on his cheek. "I didn't say this to make you feel bad, but I don't want to lie to you either. Aegid and I understand that there is a lot going on for you. Your life has changed drastically, so it's okay to freak out now and then. We do hope, though, that you know you can always turn to us for help. And we trust that you will do so. We live in dangerous, uncertain times. Given all the miracles happening, even the small things can prove crucial in our fight against the Good Mother. And if it's something concerning the Echend'dim, you have to be open about it. We're all new to this, and the sooner we can figure out what is going on, the better it is for all of us."

Kalad patted Daran's back.

"Now let's get you back to our chambers. I say we clean you up and feed you; then we need to tell Canubis."

Daran stared at his two mates, again wondering how he had gotten so incredibly lucky.

"Thank you. I really needed that."

Aegid kissed Daran on the mouth. "You're welcome."

Together they left the training chamber and headed for the exit, when the door to another chamber opened.

"If you don't get your act together, Lukan, you're in serious trouble. I've never seen you fight so badly. Even when we first met, you were better than today. I don't understand."

Elua's voice was sharp with a worried edge. Kalad squeezed Daran's hand.

"Seems you're not the only one." Then he turned to Elua. "Problems?"

Elua's eyes narrowed. "You could say so. I just wanted to do some light training with Lukan today. Xi'an and Raffal"—she gestured toward the door to the chamber where the two men were standing—"joined us and we did some three-on-one sparring. Normally Lukan is really good at this kind of fight, but today, he kept blocking blows that weren't there. I'm really worried."

Lukan opened his mouth to say something, but Aegid stopped him with a gesture of his hand. He stared from Lukan to Daran and back, a frown on his face. Kalad nudged his desert brother.

"What are you thinking, Aegid?"

The giant closed his eyes, concentrating to get his thoughts in line. Whatever idea had occurred to him, he wasn't entirely sure of it yet.

"Both Daran and Lukan have the same problem when fighting. Daran told us he can feel Lukan and Sic when they are close. Lukan was close. What if they were blocking blows the *other* would have suffered?"

Stunned silence followed these words. Elua turned to her husband, a hint of anger in her eyes. "You can feel Daran?"

Lukan raised his hands in a conciliatory gesture.

"Not always. As Aegid said, only when we are close. And I didn't tell you because Daran and I both think it's creepy."

"We're going to talk about this later." Elua's words didn't bode well. "Now let's test Aegid's theory." She pushed Lukan back into the training chamber. The other men followed. Kalad looked around.

"Now, how do we find out how their connection is working? Oh, I know! Daran, come here."

Kalad took a piece of cloth normally used for cleaning the weapons and blindfolded Daran.

"It stinks!"

Kalad grinned when Daran complained.

"It's not exactly fresh from the laundry, but there are no bloodstains on it either, so we can use it. You could see it as your just punishment for not telling us about this connection thing."

Daran huffed. "That's plain cruel. And this thing is itching like crazy."

"Then stop complaining and get ready to fight." Aegid tried hard to keep from laughing.

Kalad nodded at Lukan.

"You stay here and watch. Xi'an, Raffal, and I will attack Daran."

Understanding dawned on Lukan, and he nodded. The three warriors surrounded Daran, who was still rubbing at the cloth.

"Get ready, Daran," Aegid barked. The young man lifted his sword to show he was good to go.

Kalad made the first attack. He confronted Daran directly with his sword at hip level. At the last moment, he raised his hand and aimed at Daran's head. Daran blocked the blow gracefully, spun sideways to let Kalad's own momentum carry him past Daran, then swung his sword to prevent Raffal from hitting him from behind. Xi'an surged forward, aiming for Daran's leg. The young man jumped, turned, and met Kalad's blade midair.

Kalad, Xi'an, and Raffal attacked three more times, each time unable to break through Daran's defense. Then Kalad stopped the exercise and made Daran and Lukan change places. The same thing happened again. Now Daran was watching the fight, and though blindfolded, Lukan was able to fend off his attackers as if he were seeing. Once Aegid, Kalad, and Elua were satisfied with their experiment, they started questioning Daran and Lukan.

"Do you still think the connection is only on a subconscious level?"

Aegid looked at the two men. Daran and Lukan shared a long look before Daran answered.

"It is not conscious. It's not like I'm thinking 'Oh, Lukan, you have to turn left to duck under Raffal's sword.' It feels more like I have an additional set of eyes. Or senses. I'm not really seeing as Lukan sees the scene, but I feel what is coming. That sounds stupid, doesn't it?"

"No, little thief. Actually, it makes a lot of sense. It's like a hive mind. Or in your case, a pack mind. You act as individuals but are linked like a pack. Once you get the hang of it, this ability will no longer distract you, but make you stronger. The Echend'dim will be able to fight like a pack of wolves. This is great. Canubis will be pleased." Pride shone through Aegid's voice. Daran and Lukan eyed each other warily. Then Lukan suddenly grinned.

"I see a lot of ruthless training coming our way, Daran. Are you ready for that?"

Daran grinned back. "What choice do I have?"

"None and you know it." Lukan grabbed Elua's hand. "I wish you fun telling Lord Canubis about this."

Daran's eyes narrowed.

"Don't think you can get away so easily. You will come with me. We have to tell Lord Sic as well. So get cleaned up and then meet me at my chambers."

Lukan bowed to Daran. "As you wish, Daran." He winked. "I think I liked you better when you were just a little slave."

Daran laughed. "You don't, and you know it!"

3. NEW PATHS

"WHY DID you keep it from me?"

Elua was leaning against the doorframe of their bathroom, watching Lukan wash himself and trying her hardest to keep the anguish from her voice. Lukan finished his quick wash before he went over to her. He opened his mouth to answer, but Elua stopped him.

"Don't give me that crap about you being scared, Lukan. I know you. You are afraid of nothing."

Lukan stared into her eyes, and what Elua saw there made her regret her words. Lukan *was* afraid. He trailed a finger down her cheek. His voice sounded far off, as if he were deep in thought.

"Dying isn't that bad. It's like going to sleep when you're really tired. It's peaceful. A warm blanket of shadows spread over you, making you feel protected and pampered."

Lukan hesitated. There was something in his look that made Elua wrap her arms around him in a protective gesture. When he spoke on, his voice was raw.

"When Sic called me, I didn't think twice about coming back. You were there. My friends were there. I love life. I really do— I just never thought the light could be something to be feared. That it could be so cruel."

He hesitated again, unable to look at Elua.

"Remember when we talked about how we can't understand why Sic would forgive Noran and even accept him as his mate? I can now. If I had to face one of them, I would always choose Noran, because Sic…. Sic is terrifying. And the worst part? He knows it. He knows it and he tries to hide his power, his fear of what he's capable of. He's the sweetest man I've ever met, and I love him as a friend. At the same time, I fear what he is. The connection we're now sharing doesn't make it any easier. I know Daran feels the same. We both want to help Sic. We're rejecting and accepting the bond at the same time, and that is what makes this so complicated."

Elua took Lukan's head in her hands and kissed him long and deep. She understood. She didn't like it, but she understood. Before Sic had called

Daran back, the Echend'dim had been nothing but a dream. Something the mercenaries clung to as a possible reward for their services to the Gods of War. Now that the Eternal Guard was no longer the vision of a seer but reality, it turned out this gift came with a price, just like everything to do with Canubis and Renaldo. The rewards for being with the two gods were sometimes worse than the punishment for opposing them. The powers offered to those loyal to Canubis and Renaldo had to be counterweighted; Elua understood that much. What she didn't understand was why good men like Lukan had to suffer for it.

"It's fine, my lord. I'm afraid I'm just jealous of what you have gained. Or afraid for you. I don't really know. Sometimes I want to pretend nothing of this ever happened. That you are still Lukan, my husband, not Lukan, the Echend'dim."

Lukan pulled her closer, burying his nose in the crook of her neck.

"I wish so, too, my lady. The goddesses help me, but I wish so too."

"YOU REALLY should have told us sooner." Canubis glared at Sic, Daran, and Lukan with barely concealed anger. What the three had just told him meant another liability in the upcoming campaign, one he couldn't afford when Renaldo was still shaken to the core. "We have less than two weeks left to work on this, and I don't think your little problem can be easily solved. I need you at your best during the campaign. A guerilla war is nothing like a siege. This could prove to be a danger for us all."

Daran cringed when he heard the accusation in his god's voice. Disappointing Canubis was a bad thing. He lowered his gaze. "We beg your forgiveness, my lord. We are truly sorry."

Canubis sighed. "I know. Doesn't change the fact that you kept something really important from me. I'm going to inform Hulda. Perhaps she can get to the bottom of this and help you deal with the ramifications. You two can leave. Sic, you stay."

Daran and Lukan bowed and hastened to leave the chambers. They shot Sic a quick sympathetic glance before they closed the door. Once the two Echend'dim were gone, Canubis regarded Sic with an unfathomable look. "I get the feeling you are hiding quite a lot from me, Luksari."

Now it was Sic's time to cringe. He avoided Canubis's gaze. "Please, my lord. I really don't want to talk about it."

"You're hiding, Sic. Ignoring them won't make your problems go away. You know that, don't you?"

"I'm aware. I just don't know what else I can do."

"You could talk to me."

Sic made a sound that was half laugh and half sob. "I don't think you would understand."

"Try me."

Sic shrugged. "I'd rather not."

Canubis's eyes turned to small slits. His voice took on a steely quality. "You feel alone, isolated. There is something inside you the people around you don't have and have no hope to ever understand. You look at them and one moment, they are normal, some of them superior to you, others your friends. The next moment, all you see is servants, people so far beneath you, you're not even sure if they have any significance at all. You hate yourself for the way you look at them, and yet you can't help thinking how fragile and unimportant they seem to be. Everything inside you is pure power, but when you let that power out, there is nobody left to play. Does that sum it up?"

Sic stared at Canubis with wide eyes. "How do you know?" Tears slid down Sic's cheeks, but he did nothing to stop them from falling. "I feel like I'm trapped in my own head, like the world is too tight for me to wear, like the emotions my friends, even Noran, have for me are nothing but a nuisance, like everything I feel is shallow and unreal. I'm walking through a world of shadows, shadows my light creates. And you wonder why I can't talk about it?"

Canubis held out his arms, and after a moment's hesitation, Sic stepped into the embrace of his god. "I know, because this is how Renaldo and I have been feeling since the last Spring Ceremony. This is how Renaldo has felt all his life where his fire is concerned. There were days when we both wished we weren't gods. Days when we thought we couldn't take it a moment longer."

Sic looked up into Canubis's amber eyes that were clouded by unpleasant memories. "How did you survive?"

Canubis smiled sadly. "We are gods. We cannot die." He paused. "Of course, things became easier after I found Noemi."

Sic sighed. "Lord Renaldo is suffering badly, isn't he?"

"With Casto gone, you mean? Yes. It's really bad, and I don't know how to break him from it. I may know how to help you, though. As I said, hiding isn't going to solve your problems. This world fit you once, and it can do so again. For that, you have to face your new reality. Talk to Lukan and Daran. I know you like them both, and Daran is your friend. The three of you have to work this out, because, Sic, there will be more Echend'dim coming. A lot more. As for your other problems—why don't you talk to Noran? He's worried about you."

Sic stepped out of Canubis's embrace. A hint of red tinged his face. "Master Noran and I—it's complicated. Even more complicated than this." Sic gestured at his head. "We're making progress, but not enough for him to be my anchor yet. I'm still alone."

The harsh truth in Sic's words made Canubis flinch. They all needed time to adjust. Unfortunately, time was the one thing they didn't have.

WHEN SIC returned to their chambers, Noran could tell he was agitated. He rose from his chair and embraced Sic, who buried his face in Noran's broad chest. "I assume it didn't go too well?"

Sic made a whimpering sound. Noran stroked his back while he tried to keep his tone as neutral as possible. He didn't want to burden Sic with his feelings of jealousy. Noran had yet to earn that right. There were a lot of things Sic didn't tell him, important things that kept his young lover on edge. It was killing Noran that all he could do was offer his support. So far, Sic had only accepted that offer when it concerned the two of them directly. "What can I do to help you?"

Sic looked up. There was a gleam in his eyes, a fever that made Noran shudder. "Please hold me. I need to calm down. And then—then I'm going to tell you about it, and I'm asking you not to be angry with me."

"I'm not angry with you, my precious. I'm disappointed because you still don't trust me enough to share all your burdens with me, but I also know it is my fault. I will be patient, I promise."

Sic snuggled back into Noran's embrace. "Thank you, Master."

BANTU WAS busy writing in his journal when the door to his room opened. He smiled. There was only one person who would enter his personal space without announcing themselves. "Cornelia. You're back early today."

His sister approached him, dropped a kiss on his head, and slumped into the lounge right next to his desk. She made a huffing sound. "There's so much to do, what with the upcoming campaign and everything, I didn't have a chance to sit down for even a moment. So I decided it was time for an early night. All those chores—they'll still be there tomorrow."

Bantu chuckled. "You're right. Chores never just go away. They're kind of stubborn in that respect."

Cornelia rolled her eyes. Bantu smiled at her fondly before he concentrated on his journal again. "Just let me finish this, and then we can have a nice cup of tea and some of that delicious oatmeal the cook made today."

Cornelia nodded. "Sounds like a good idea. Could have been from me." With that, she closed her eyes and rested her head on the thick cushion. Bantu hurried to finish his writing. When he was done, the siblings went into the main room, called for a slave to bring them their dinner, and then sat down at the small table. They ate in silence for some time. Finally, Cornelia looked up from her empty bowl. Bantu noticed the deep lines around her eyes. The time before a campaign was always stressful, and unfortunately, once the warriors were on their way, the stress didn't lessen. The workload remained the same; there were just fewer people to shoulder it.

"Are you okay, sister? You look tired."

"I am." She smiled reassuringly. "Nothing a good night's sleep can't cure. What about you? You seem restless."

Bantu reached for the teakettle to pour himself another cup. "I am. I've been thinking about something for the last few weeks. It wasn't an easy decision, and I'm pretty sure you won't like it." He took a deep breath. "I will accompany Canubis on this campaign. You know how much the Dark Forest fascinates me. This is my chance to explore it."

Cornelia grabbed her mug so fiercely, her knuckles turned white. "Bantu."

All of her fear for his safety was in that one word, as well as her love for him. Bantu reached out and gently stroked her hands. "I promise, I'll be very careful. I did some training rounds with Aegid, and apparently I haven't lost my touch. I will do additional drills with Kalad until we leave next week. Everything is fine."

Cornelia straightened her back. She stuck her chin out and pinned Bantu with her glare. "Don't you dare get hurt, Bantu. Do you hear me? I have enough to worry about as it is."

It pained Bantu to see Cornelia so shaken, but he really needed to get out of the Valley, and the Dark Forest held a deep fascination for him. It called out to Bantu on a level he couldn't quite explain. "Everything will be fine, Cornelia. We'll be back before you have time to miss me."

4. EMBRACING THE UNKNOWN

WHEN SIC entered one of the smaller rooms of the training hall, Daran and Lukan were already waiting. They looked about as nervous as he felt. None of them knew what to say. In the awkward silence they shuffled around and tried to avoid eye contact. It was Daran who finally broke the spell. "This is plain stupid. I mean, we're friends. And given the bond, even more than that."

He looked straight at Sic. "I'm sorry we got you into trouble, Sic. Whatever there is between us, we should have faced it right after we became aware of it."

Sic smiled and touched Daran's arm lightly. "That was my fault as much as it was yours. We all tried to ignore it, and now we have to own up to our mistakes."

"Was Lord Canubis very angry with you?" Lukan sounded apprehensive.

Sic shook his head. "It wasn't as bad as I thought. Despite his fearsome appearance, Lord Canubis can be very understanding. Nevertheless, I don't plan to incur his wrath again anytime soon, if ever."

"A wise decision." The three men turned around to watch Hulda enter the room. She was dressed in her usual black leather, every hand the intimidating assassin she had once been. "I heard you've kept something important from the gods?"

There was no threat in Hulda's voice, not even a hint of reproach, yet Sic, Daran, and Lukan felt a cold chill crawling down their spines. Hulda might not be Canubis, but she was terrifying in her own way.

It was Sic who found the courage to explain things to her. "Apparently, when I bring somebody back from the dead, I also establish a mind link with them. That mind link is shared among the Echend'dim as well. We can feel each other."

Hulda nodded. Her eyes were small while she pondered Sic's words. "Do you feel each other all the time?"

Lukan furrowed his brow. He hadn't thought about that yet. "Now that you mention it, I think I do. It's not conscious, and most of the time, I'm not aware of it, but there *is* another presence in my mind. I can't distinguish between Sic or Daran, though."

"For me, it's the same." Daran glanced nervously at Hulda. "Something is there."

When Hulda looked at Sic, he simply nodded. She started pacing. "Can you make it conscious? Like concentrate on either Daran or Sic?"

Lukan shrugged. "I could try."

"Go ahead." Hulda made a shooing motion.

Lukan closed his eyes. A frown appeared on his face. Then suddenly he snapped his eyes open. "I can feel Daran. Really feel him, in a conscious act. That's incredible!"

Hulda turned to Daran. "When Lukan concentrates on you, can you feel him as well?"

Daran nodded. "It feels like somebody is pulling my hair from inside my head." He shuddered.

"Can you keep him out?" Hulda was looking almost eager.

Both Daran and Lukan concentrated again. After a few moments, Daran shook his head. "I can't. Every time I try, it feels wrong. As if something inside me would break should I keep on locking Lukan out. It's a weird feeling."

Hulda started pacing again with a thoughtful expression. "This is quite remarkable. Sic, do you just feel Daran's and Lukan's presences, or do you have the impression you could control them as well?"

Sic looked shocked at those words. He trembled slightly when he answered. "I don't think I could control them. I can project images into their minds, though."

"You don't think you can control them, or you know?" Hulda ignored the comment about the projection of images.

Sic cringed. "I think so."

Her eyes narrowed. Sic felt like a mouse, cornered by an entire clowder of athletic cats. Hulda didn't say a word. There was no need, because Sic knew what she wanted. For a brief moment he contemplated turning around and simply running away, but he just knew Hulda would catch him as easily as she killed, so he closed his eyes and reached out to Daran and Lukan. Now that they had admitted to the bond between them, it seemed to be growing stronger every day, and it already felt almost natural to him. *As if the two men were an extension of himself.* The moment this thought appeared in his mind, Sic gasped. The Luksari stirred, looked at him from that place deep inside where it usually slumbered, just like it had done when Sic had met Ana-Isara. It was all logical. Simple, really, now that he saw it from the Luksari's point of view. Daran and Lukan were not only his friends, not only brave souls who had allowed him to bring them back from the dead—they were also vessels for the constantly bubbling well of power that was a Luksari. It was his decision how much of that power he infused in them, but the more he gave them, the stronger their bond grew and the more lethal they became. The Echend'dim were the outlet for the ever-growing power inside of him, the power he was desperately trying to contain at all times so as not to hurt people. Only the Echend'dim didn't get hurt by it. They grew stronger. Sic felt tears sliding down his cheeks. All of a sudden, he understood the dilemma of his kind and why Luksari simply vanished, usually when they were still quite young. At some point all that power became too much, and just letting it go was better than feeling the hull containing it slowly thinning until it ripped. Sic also understood the incredible gift Daran and Lukan were giving him. He had thought it was he who saved them, who brought them back to their loved ones and granted them eternity, but it was the other way around. By allowing him to pull them from the shadows, away from the peace of death, they granted him life. He needed them just as much as they needed him.

Sic didn't hesitate any longer. He opened his mind and let the revelation, as well as his light, pour into his brothers, his saviors. They were one on a level even more primal than the bond between mother and child. Sic could feel Daran and Lukan, all the thoughts and emotions that made them what they were. He opened his eyes.

"There's no need for me to control them. They are me and I am them."

He looked at the two men, the first of his *Zaheerosh*. The word came to him suddenly, provided by the aeon-old mind of the Luksari in a language Sic understood, even though he knew the people who spoke it had been gone before the Mothers created this universe.

"They are my Zaheerosh. My vessels and brothers, my life and my thoughts."

Daran and Lukan nodded. For them, there was no need for Sic to explain. They understood the moment he did. Hulda looked at them with big eyes. Sic knew she was perceptive enough to understand a great deal of what he hadn't said out loud. She was a witch, after all.

With a smile, she reached for the training swords on the wall. "Let's find out what you can do."

"HOW WAS it?"

Aegid and Kalad came over to Daran the moment he entered their chambers. He had forbidden them to come with him to the training with Hulda, because of the distraction they posed. Now they were dying of curiosity, and their eager tone had Daran smiling despite how tired he felt. Even with the new understanding about the connection between Sic, Lukan, and him and the hefty dose of raw power Sic had channeled into them during the fight against Hulda, the killer was still a formidable opponent and almost impossible to beat. The way they had been able to stand their ground against her, though, gave Daran considerable hope for future fights with less gifted enemies. He could see how the Echend'dim would become an unstoppable force once there were more of them. It still felt a bit weird to be connected to somebody other than his husbands in such an intimate way, but what he shared with Lukan and Sic wasn't sexual in the least, something for which all three of them were grateful.

"It went really well. As it turned out, our connection with Sic is even deeper than we thought. The three of us almost managed to beat Hulda, even though she started stepping behind time." Daran couldn't keep the pride out of his voice. When it came to fighting, Hulda came close to Renaldo and Canubis. She even outdid Kalad and Aegid, so forcing her to revert to stepping behind time during a training fight was an accomplishment he and his brothers could be proud of.

Kalad whistled. "Wow. I don't know when that last happened. I gather the whole problem is more or less solved now?"

Daran's shoulders slumped. "To be honest, I don't know. We understand now what's happening, which is good. And we liked each other before, so it's not as invasive as I feared it would be—or, no, that's not right. It *is* invasive, very much so, but I can deal with it. But—it's a lot to take in."

Aegid opened his arms, and Daran gladly stepped into his embrace. When the warmth of his huge husband surrounded him, Daran felt himself calming down. Kalad's hands landed between his shoulder blades and on his lower back, rubbing him in soothing circles.

"Do you want to explain?" Kalad's voice was soft, low, offering comfort and understanding. Daran inhaled deeply on Aegid's massive chest, knowing he had the best husbands in the world.

"Apparently, it's not Sic doing us a favor by calling us back from the dead but the other way around. By bringing us back, he establishes a connection with us that allows him to channel his power into us and keep it on a manageable level for himself."

Over Daran's head, the desert brothers exchanged a long look. They knew by now how important Casto and Noemi were for Renaldo and Canubis. Hearing that their own husband, their precious little thief, had a similar meaning to Sic left them with a mixture of different emotions. Jealousy over a bond they had no part in. Worry about Daran being forced into something he didn't want. Anger that Sic was using Daran. Joy that Daran would most probably be strong enough to be perfectly fine on his own should they get separated. It was difficult to understand what they were feeling, especially since Daran seemed to be so torn himself. Aegid kissed him on the top of his head.

"Do you want to take a bath? Maybe talk about it some more?"

Daran's arms around Aegid's waist tightened. "Yes. To be honest, I still don't know how to feel about this. It's terrifying and wonderful at the same time."

Kalad slung Daran's braid around his wrist and bent his head back for a kiss. When he let Daran up for air again, he had a smug look on his face.

"You will sort it out, little thief. And we're there to help you."

Daran sighed with a contented smile. "I know. Thank you."

"We love you, little thief. You are our world." The desert brothers took Daran to the bathroom, determined to ease his mind.

ON THE ROAD

1. LOSING IT

CASTO STARED at the ragged men surrounding him with their battered swords and desperate looks on this road that was perfect for an ambush. There was little traffic here, for it was only a side road connecting a few small villages, and the forest flanking it provided the cover a band of highwaymen needed. And, of course, Casto was a perfect target. Alone, obviously wealthy, and still looking too young to be able to defend himself. The sword he carried surely complicated things for the men, but not enough to back down. They needed his money badly enough to risk their lives getting it. He felt Lys staring at him from where he was standing between two trees, waiting for him to take action. He had dismounted to check if there was a place suitable to make their camp for the night, and the highwaymen had taken that chance. Casto looked at them. It would be so easy, calling the fire and killing them all. Casto remembered all too clearly what it was like to control the blaze, to direct it the way he wanted to. The rush of power, the ability to decide life and death—it was all there, on the tips of his fingers. Only it wasn't a joyous thing at all. It made him cringe in fury because it meant his subconscious had given in and accepted Renaldo as his master. Casto hated himself for it. Unable to let the Barbarian triumph, he had kept it a secret, both out of spite and for tactical reasons, something that was so ingrained in his very nature, he didn't even think consciously about it anymore.

He knew he had to use the fire now to save himself. Yet another perverted part of him refused to draw from something that was linked to the Barbarian. If given the choice, Casto was still angry enough that he would rather die than utilize Renaldo's power. With a grim smile, he picked up his sword, ready to defend himself with his own strength.

It was then that the arrow hit him in the back.

In disbelief, Lys watched as Casto neglected to eliminate the attackers with his fire. The Emperor of the Storms had always known his rider was stubborn beyond sanity, but even he would have never anticipated such a downright stupid move. When the arrow hit Casto from behind, Lys could feel him die. He roared in anger and pain and then dissolved into the shadows. It was already afternoon, and among the trees, darkness had started to gather. It was more than enough for Lys to act.

Those thugs who were lurking in the shadows were simply sucked up as if they had never existed. Some of them tried to fight back when Lys bore down on them, seemingly out of nowhere, teeth bared and deadly hooves ready to strike. The Emperor of the Storms enjoyed the crunching sound when bones broke and skulls smashed. He fought his way to the place Casto had gone down. Three of the men were bent over Casto's lifeless body, fumbling with the knots securing the pouch with the gold to his belt. Lys came over them like a force of nature. His teeth sunk into the nape of the first, jerking him away from Casto. Lys tossed the unlucky man high into the air and then hit his body full force when it came down again. The man smashed into a tree, and Lys savored the satisfying crunch when his spine broke in several places. The other two men had risen to their feet in panic. Both stared in horror at Lys's blood-smeared coat and his burning eyes. One of them had the presence of mind to turn around and run for it; the other was frozen in terror. Lys killed him with a single blow of his front hooves, almost ripping his head off with the sheer force of his movement. Then he galloped after the fleeing man and simply ran him over, stomping his body into the wet, muddy ground.

Satisfied with the destruction he had caused, the Emperor of the Storms returned to his fallen rider. With his teeth, he pulled the arrow out of Casto's back and then waited while his brother's body started to heal. Coughing, Casto rose to a sitting position, patting off the dust from his clothes.

"Damn, what just hit me?"

Lys didn't answer. Instead, he bit Casto's shoulder hard enough to draw blood. Casto winced.

"What was that for?"

Just to bring his point across, Lys pushed Casto to the ground, looming over him like a particularly bad nightmare. His anger flooded Casto until the king held up his hands in defense.

"I get it. I get it. I'm sorry. What I did was stupid. I really don't know what came over me."

Lys snorted and kept Casto from getting on his feet again. Their gazes locked. It was Casto who broke first. His eyes lost the hint of an impending thunderstorm as the color returned to its usual stunning blue and something akin to contrition tinged his features.

"Really, I'm sorry, Lys. I promise I'll stop with the self-destructive behavior from now on. I just don't know what to think. I can feel my anger gradually dissipating, because I really understand why the Barbarian acted the way he did. Also, I miss him like crazy. And whenever I start thinking about forgiving him, about going back, I get angry with myself. I just want to hurt, and I don't care whom. Oh, Lys, what should I do? I can't go back like this. Nothing will ever change if I do."

Tears streamed down Casto's face like a river. Lys knew he was the only one Casto allowed to see his weakness, his vulnerability, and so he nudged him gently and blew his warm breath on Casto's face. As much as he resented it, the connection between Casto and Renaldo was already too deep to be easily severed, as he had dared to hope when they left the Valley. If he wanted his rider to be happy, he had to help him gain perspective. Lys cursed in the privacy of his thoughts. He could understand Casto's dilemma a lot better now that he faced something similar. Helping Casto find peace also meant helping Renaldo, and Lys hated the Barbarian for everything he had done to Casto. Unfortunately, Casto was bound to Renaldo as much as Lys was bound to him. The Emperor of the Storms had no choice, and he abhorred it.

TWO WEEKS had passed since the Pack had left the Valley for the Dark Forest, and Cornelia was already wishing it would be fall soon. In addition to the increased workload the absence of the mercenaries and so many slaves meant, she also worried about her brother. She couldn't remember when Bantu had last gone on a campaign with Canubis and Renaldo, but she did remember the feeling of dread that accompanied her like a shadow. She sighed. It was a good thing she had so much to do; otherwise she would probably worry herself to death. A knock on the door to her office tore her thoughts away from all the bad things that could happen to her brother.

"Come in!"

The door opened and Sira entered. When Sic had brought the young woman to the Valley, Cornelia hadn't known what to make of her. She felt a connection to her, based on their similarly bad experiences with men, but as an Emeris, she had also resented her for being such a stubborn slave and causing Sic so much trouble. After the big fallout with Renaldo, Sic had come up with an interesting solution to his whole slave-keeping problem, namely giving them all their freedom and paying them for their services. It worked remarkably well, and Cornelia had to admit Sira was a great help. Since she didn't accompany Sic to the Dark Forest, she had offered her services to Cornelia, and with each passing day, she found herself relying more and more on the young woman.

"Good morning, Cornelia."

"Good morning, Sira. How did you sleep?"

It was more than just politeness that had Cornelia asking this particular question. Sira looked tired. She had dark circles under her eyes and her skin was pale. She combed her hand through the wild strands of hair sticking out from her head in all directions. She had come to the Valley with a shaved head and was now growing her hair out.

"Not so well. I had several nightmares, and not even drinking some tea helped. I feel like I've been run over by a bunch of horses." She tried a smile and failed quite spectacularly. "But there's work to be done, and with some luck, I'll be so tired tonight, I won't dream at all."

Cornelia furrowed her brows. She had heard several people complain about nightmares and not sleeping well but had chalked it up to the recent departure of the Pack. Now she wondered how many people were affected and if she should inquire.

"Is this the first time you had those dreams?"

Sira looked thoughtful for a moment. "No. I've been having them for a few days now. And they're always the same." She shrugged. "Probably all the stress. I never thought I'd ever say this, but I wish the masters were back."

Cornelia smiled. She knew well what Sira thought about masters and men. For her to wish them back, she had to be really stressed. "I'm sorry to break the bad news to you, but they won't be back for another ten weeks, at least. Probably more. And our list of things to be done is steadily growing. Are you ready?"

Sira winked and smiled back at Cornelia, which made her look like a little girl without a care in the world. "Since I'm being paid, I'm more than ready."

Cornelia got up, with two sheets of paper in her hand. She gave one to Sira. "This would be your itinerary for today. Do you think you can manage?"

Sira quickly read over the impressive list before she nodded. "Consider it done. Can we meet for lunch? Just in case I run into trouble."

"Of course. My chambers. At noon." Cornelia grazed Sira's arm with her fingertips and felt the young woman shudder through the thin cloth of her simple dress. There was something between them, something growing from the connection they had through mutual experiences in life. Cornelia wasn't sure if she wanted to explore it or to run.

Sira touched her arm as well, mumbling her goodbye, and from the way little jolts of energy erupted under her skin, Cornelia knew she would have to make a decision soon.

"MAY I come in?" Canubis tapped his fingers on the closed flap of Renaldo's tent. They had set up camp the day before, and his younger brother hadn't come out since then. Canubis could feel Renaldo's despair, the big black hole threatening to swallow him with every heartbeat his immortal body gave. For what had to be the thousandth time, Canubis cursed Casto for leaving them and creating such a mess.

The campaign against the rebels in the Dark Forest had already run into the first problems, and they hadn't even really started yet. The spies he had sent out to check the places Xe'lien had told them about were all deserted. Worse, they looked as if nobody had ever been there. Which meant either Xe'lien's own people were just plain inept or the queen was trying to play Canubis. He did feel the urge to break up camp and march directly to her palace to have an intimate chat, but for the time being, he decided to give her the benefit of the doubt.

The Dark Forest was vast, after all, and laced with magic. Canubis could feel it deep in his bones, and he didn't like it. What he liked even less was that Noemi wasn't sure what kind of magic it was. Whether a remnant of the wild, chaotic power that had destroyed so much of Ana-Darasa before the Mothers had found ways to bind it or if it was put there by man, most probably followers of the Good Mother. While the first was already bad news, the latter would be catastrophic. Canubis had no intention whatsoever to fight against an enemy on territory said enemy had rigged with magic. As with Xe'lien, he couldn't be sure. Not with magic so basic. And while he didn't care much about what people thought about the trustworthiness of the Pack now that the end was in sight, his pride forbade him to simply turn his back on a contract.

Since he hadn't gotten an answer from inside the tent, he pulled the flap away and entered. It was gloomy inside, the only light coming from the opening through which he had come. Renaldo was sitting in a chair, a cup of wine in his hand. His usually expressive gray eyes stared into nothing, and his features, while still breathtaking in their beauty, lacked any kind of life. The only thing indicating Renaldo wasn't just a lifeless hull was his inner fire shining through. Given how empty Renaldo seemed, it was a disturbing thing. Like watching a statue burn, knowing the fire could spread any minute and there was nothing to stop it.

"How are you today, brother?" Canubis tried to sound soothing and encouraging at the same time, not an easy feat for somebody who was used to giving orders that were instantly obeyed. This wouldn't work with his brother, though, and Canubis didn't want it either. Renaldo slowly raised his head. The pure agony in his gaze made Canubis flinch.

"I'm worse than yesterday. Every day is worse than the one before." He exhaled and slung his arms around his torso as if he wanted to protect himself from whatever pain was ailing him. "I feel like my soul is dying, even though I know that's impossible. And I'm losing control, brother. Every day a bit more. The less I move around, the better I can keep it contained, which is why I stay inside the tent."

Canubis wasn't surprised his brother was voicing his exact thoughts. They were siblings and gods. There were no secrets between them.

"Do you think you can fight?" Canubis wanted Renaldo to get his mind off his loss, though not at the price of losing some of his own fighters when Renaldo lost control.

"I'm not sure. To be honest, I wouldn't risk it. You know what it was like after Mother took our hearts. This here—this is a hundred times worse. There is so much power, so much more than before. I'm not sure I can contain it under stress. I will try, of course, but I don't want to be a liability. If I let loose, I'm probably going to burn the entire Dark Forest."

Canubis allowed himself a grim smile. "It might come to that, brother. I'm almost sure we're running into a trap here, and I don't like the way this place is laced with magic. Your fire might be exactly what we need."

Renaldo let out a short, humorless laugh. "Don't even joke about that. This has to be our last resort, as you well know. We cannot repeat Quell'renar."

Canubis shook his head. No, Quell'renar had been a mistake. A grave one, even though it had been necessary and inevitable. He put a hand on Renaldo's shoulder. "We won't let that happen. We're gods now, true gods, and we're more mature than we were back then. There is a way. We will find it, and we will grind our enemies into the dust."

Renaldo nodded. "We will. And I will be ready to fight at your side as I have always done, brother."

Satisfied with his answer, Canubis patted Renaldo's shoulder and left him alone again.

2. STARTING THE JOURNEY

IN SILENT awe, Casto stared at the seemingly endless fields of Quell'renar. They stretched out in front of him like a promise of paradise, all lush green fields, beautiful meadows, and sparkling brooks. On their way here, Lys and Casto had passed through the countless shires that made up the crop chamber of the continent. The fields in the southeast of the Eastern Kingdoms were the most fertile on Ana-Darasa, and the food growing here was one of the reasons why Ummana had become so unbelievably rich. Yet compared to the fields of Quell'renar, the shires appeared almost dry. There was an invisible barrier at which the rectangular shapes of soil cultivated by man turned into wilderness. No paths led into the space behind that border, and the farmers living close to it made sure to never cross over. Beautiful as they were, the fields of Quell'renar were cursed.

Casto patted Lys's neck.

"Do you really think this is a good idea?"

Lys shook his head. They both could feel it, the patches of raw magic burned into the earth, the heavy atmosphere of a loaded history. Quell'renar was a place that had seen it all, the birth of different species as well as their downfall, the love and wrath of the goddesses and the despair and fury of their offspring. It was too much for one place to bear. Going there seemed like madness.

Determined, Lys stepped over the border into the wilderness. They passed through a small wood that opened into a field where different fruit-bearing trees were loosely scattered. Casto recognized apple trees, pear trees, and the small, sad assemblages of dried-out twigs that were red-berry bushes. Those bushes always looked as if they had died a long time ago, until they suddenly started to bloom like crazy and sprouted the most delicious fruit Casto knew. Red-berries were hard to cultivate, which made the sheer mass of them on the fields of Quell'renar even more astonishing. *At least we're not going to starve here*, Casto thought as they ventured on toward the distant outline of Quell'renar itself.

The closer they got to the ancient city, the more Casto felt as if he was being watched. More than once did he spot the quick movement of hares and small birds at the corner of his vision, none of which seemed to take more than a casual interest in him and Lys. When they fought their way through a patch of wheat that had grown high enough to obscure them completely, they heard the sound of footsteps running over the soft grass. Lys made haste to leave the wheat, only to be rooted on the spot when he reached the fringe. A group of ten naked people was passing them by in a hurry, their gazes fixed on the quickly moving body of a deer. The female in the lead suddenly reared her head back. Her body started to shimmer, and then she turned into a wolf. Casto gaped as the other people in the group did the same. The pack dashed after the deer, driving it into the forest to Casto's left. Before they reached it, the pack vanished as if it had never been there.

A screech made Casto and Lys turn around. From the sky, a bird of prey the size of one of the wolves dropped down on the ground, killing a hare with its razor-sharp talons. The bird shimmered like the woman from before, and then a young man sat on the ground, his face and fingers smeared with blood. Without minding his audience, he started tearing the hare apart with his hands.

Casto watched in fascination, knowing this had to be a scene from the past, for the clans of the *remusi* and *elusi* had died out long ago. Quell'renar was showing him and Lys glimpses of times long gone, and he started to understand why people thought the fields were cursed. Lys snorted, indicating things would become even weirder from here on out. He didn't seem to be fazed by the thought of running into ghosts, which made Casto wonder which of them was the crazier one. Lys chose to ignore that question, explaining to Casto that the people they had seen were not ghosts but memories, and for him, they were there all the time. He allowed his rider a glimpse of how he perceived their surroundings and quickly severed the connection when he felt Casto's discomfort.

"I had no idea, Lys! Is it always like this for you? How can you bear it?"

In an attempt to soothe Casto, Lys snuffled reassuringly. Since he was a creature of chaos, not time, he perceived things differently. For him, all the things that had happened and were happening were the same. There was no linear succession of events, just a mind-numbing clash of everything. Since he was chaos personified, it was rather soothing. Casto buried his face in Lys's thick mane.

"So that's how you were able to wait for me. Somehow, I was already there. You never cease to amaze me, my brother."

Satisfied, Lys quickened his pace. Revealing his secrets to Casto bit by bit was a terrifying process for him. He trusted his brother implicitly not to misuse the power he was giving him. Lys was more afraid that Casto could be spooked by their bond, once he realized how irrefutable it was. Given how much Casto resented his connection to Renaldo, Lys's fear was not unsubstantiated. Once Casto understood all of Lys's talents, he would also come to comprehend the burden it meant—yet another shackle to his precious freedom.

THE BOY ran across the field, chasing after a butterfly. This was his favorite dream, where the sun was always warm on his skin without burning it, where he didn't have to do any chores and got to play as long as he liked. He never felt hungry or thirsty, and if he was really lucky, the little girl with the white hair would toss a small sparkling ball with him. At six years, he knew he was—strictly speaking—too old to still be playing with a little girl of maybe four, but she was really fun and knew the best tricks. She had also told him not to mention their meetings to anybody, which made the whole endeavor even more adventurous.

The butterfly took a turn to the right, and the boy suddenly realized he was no longer on the field under the warm sun. Instead, he found himself in a thick forest he couldn't remember entering, the butterfly gone, the light nothing but a shadow, only slightly brighter than the darkness pouring out of the gnarly, leafless trees whose bark looked as if people were trapped inside. The boy started to shiver. This was no longer his beautiful dream. This was a scary place, and he wanted out. He turned around, ready to run, but the path was gone, leaving only trees standing so close, it looked as if their roots were forming a prison cell, like in the dungeons in the Valley. He spun around, looking desperately for a way out, but with every turn, the trees seemed to be coming closer, boxing him in.

For a moment, he caught a glimpse of something bright, of white hair and a shining smile through the black thorny branches. His little friend was standing there, looking at him with huge eyes full of tears. "I can't get through. I'm sorry. I'm too weak."

Her light started to fade, burrowed under the darkness of the nightmare he was now caught in. The boy wanted to scream, to thrash around, to plow through the branches no matter how badly they would scratch him, but it was too late. The forest closed around him, swallowed his screams and his struggles as if he had never existed.

"WHAT A day." Daran tossed his tunic into a corner of the tent he shared with his husbands. They'd been in the Dark Forest for two weeks now, chasing an invisible enemy who always seemed to be one step ahead of them. One of their patrols had been ambushed, all ten warriors not just killed but slaughtered in the bloodiest way possible. Only three of them had come back as Echend'dim, and what they had told about the attack didn't bode well for their campaign. The men who had killed them had come out of nowhere, and one of them had been a fighter almost as skilled as Hulda, moving with the grace of a cat of prey, killing without mercy. Daran sighed. Canubis was furious, and with Renaldo seriously hampered by the loss of Casto, they couldn't strike back the way they would want.

At the moment, all of the Emeris were on patrols of their own, in addition to the ones Canubis formed with his warriors, and even though they did cover a lot of ground, they never seemed to find the right places, not even with the wolves. The powerful predators were jumpy and restless, clearly affected by the magic drenching the forest. Daran took off his boots. He could feel it as well, through his connection with Sic. The magic was strange, diluted and distorted, always shifting, and it was impossible to tell where it was coming from or how old it was. Because of that, Canubis had forbidden Hulda to step behind time, since Noemi wasn't sure how ancient magic would affect Hulda's power. The assassin was less than pleased, and Daran tried his best to stay out of her way. A scraping sound at his back had him turning around to greet his husbands. Aegid and Kalad looked as beat as he felt, and Daran didn't hesitate to fall into their arms, even though their armor scratched the skin on his naked torso. He couldn't care less, especially since he could feel the wounds—if they even deserved that name—closing almost immediately. With every Echend'dim Sic brought back, he seemed to be pouring more of his magic into them, making them faster, stronger, and more resilient. About that part of his bond to the Luksari, Daran would never complain.

"Little thief, how was your day?"

"About as bad as yours, I guess. I helped retrieve the bodies from the patrol, and I was there when Sic brought three of them back."

Aegid pressed a kiss to his forehead, and Kalad stroked his back. His husbands knew how disturbing it sometimes was for Daran to be so closely connected with Sic. The stronger the bond between them became, the more glimpses Daran got of how Sic's powers worked. When his friend had brought him back from the dead, Daran had thought it was a simple process. Just deciding between sleep and waking up again. But it was so much more, with deeper, darker implications not even Sic could really grasp.

The web the Luksari was weaving among the Echend'dim was growing with every new member, and even though they were all loyal to Canubis and Renaldo, ultimately, they were bound to Sic. Sic, who could withdraw his light at any time; Sic who knew this, but who wasn't sure if that meant the death of the Echend'dim or if they would simply stay with the level of power he had last infused them with; Sic, who was shaken to the core by his gift, if that was what it was.

Daran shuddered. He knew what it was like to be off-balance, to search for inner peace and not find it. He had had to come to terms with the fact that the men he loved with all his heart were also cruel predators who didn't know the meaning of mercy. Worse even, he had been forced to acknowledge his own inner predator. Embracing that side of his being was probably the hardest thing Daran had ever done, and he was still sometimes struggling with the demanding, arrogant side of himself, the side that had no problem punishing an insolent slave, even though he had been one himself not too long ago.

Shuddering, Daran lifted his head, offering his mouth, his body to his mates, his lovers and, today, his masters. He needed their strength, their dominance to silence the voices in his mind, to erase the memory of Sic's light burning through the peace of the shadows, bringing men back who then became his charges, his responsibility as the First of the Eternal Guard. At moments like this, Daran was eternally grateful to Aegid and Kalad for taking him as their slave all those years ago. In many respects, that had been the best time of his life, when he was spoiled and pampered, without a care in the world except making his masters happy. Daran didn't regret becoming a warrior, not if it meant he could protect his precious mates, but after a trying day, he craved nothing more than being their slave again. And

Aegid and Kalad, the best lovers a man could wish for, had no problem acquiescing to his silent demands.

The desert warriors shared a look over Daran's bowed head. Their precious thief had come such a long way, had become such a fine, capable man. That he still needed their strength and love, that he relied on it to carry him through difficult times, humbled Aegid and Kalad to the core. Taking care of their warrior, their lover, their mate, and ultimately, their slave, became their sole focus. And if it meant they could also enjoy Daran's gentle ministrations while he washed their bodies, then that was a nice bonus they wouldn't complain about.

CORNELIA LOOKED down at the little boy, who was twitching in what seemed to be a nightmare he couldn't wake up from. "I wish Noemi were here," she sighed. Sira touched her hand, only shortly, but the gesture soothed Cornelia more than even her brother's presence had done in the past. She turned her attention toward the mother.

"I think it would be best to take him to the healing ward until the healers find out what is wrong with him. I assure you we will do all in our power to help him."

The mother just shrugged, her gaze riveted on the small body of her unresponsive child. Cornelia sent a silent prayer to the goddesses, asking them to guide the hands of the healers.

"I have to inform Frankus of this." She looked at Sira, who simply nodded. "Can you please see to it that the boy is brought to the ward and then continue with your duties? We will meet again in the evening."

Sira made something that vaguely resembled a bow before she hurried off after one last worried look in her direction. For what felt like the hundredth time, Cornelia thanked Sic for having brought this remarkable woman into the Valley.

3. DIVING INTO TIME

STEPPING LIGHTLY on soft grass, Lys approached the entrance of Quell'renar. Even though the city was ancient, it still looked surprisingly well-preserved. Not one of the slim pillars supporting the elegant stone arches showed so much as a chink, and the road they were traveling on was as smooth as if it had been laid only days ago. While Casto marveled at this unbelievable fact, Lys made a sound between a snort and a whinny.

It was as if somebody had taken a bucket of water and splashed it on a picture. The colors started to fade and drip away, leaving broken pillars, smashed arches, and a road overgrown with weeds. Casto sighed when he realized he had fallen prey to yet another memory. He stared at the broken city gate and watched as it rebuilt itself in front of his eyes. Lys snorted derisively, ready to break the illusion again, but Casto stopped him. Deep down, he understood. Quell'renar was not trying to drive him crazy—it was welcoming him. As soon as he realized this, Casto felt himself relax a little bit. On some deep, unconscious level, he knew he had returned to the place where it all had started, even though he had never been here before. Somehow this place, so full of memories and ancient magic, was his home, even more than the Valley. The thought was both disturbing and comforting. It stirred Casto up and made him even more susceptible to his unreliable surroundings.

Lys's ears played nervously. Although it had been his idea to come here, he didn't like how easily Casto adapted to this place that was strange even for a creature as old and powerful as himself. If Casto got in too deep, he may get lost in the violent current of memories that permeated the crumbling stones and rotting timber. In order to give Casto some peace of mind, he had to understand the past, though Lys would have preferred to be the one in control of the memories. Apparently Quell'renar itself had different plans, probably because it recognized Casto as Renaldo's heart. For the city, a god had returned home.

They entered the city through the once-impressive stone arch, walking along the main road that led directly toward the temple of Ana-Isara and

Ana-Aruna. It was the oldest building in Quell'renar and probably the oldest building on Ana-Darasa as well. For centuries, it had been the heart not only of the city, but also of the La'ides. Here, the witch clans had learned to tame magic and use their talents in order to make Ana-Darasa inhabitable. Here, the story of them all had begun.

Lys stopped in front of the temple, where two statues depicting Ana-Isara and Ana-Aruna guarded the entrance. They were roughly three ells high, made from white-and-black marble, and looked out over the city with an unfathomable expression on their stone faces. Casto had never met Ana-Aruna and had always assumed she would look similar to her pale sister. He was surprised when he saw her rather plump figure, with the full breasts and broad hips. Ana-Isara emanated a sharp, edgy feeling, as befitted the Empress of the Dead. Ana-Aruna, on the other hand, seemed softer and more lenient. Only when he looked closer into the faces of both women did Casto realize that death and life could be equally cruel. The sisters were the same, just on different sides of the coin.

Slowly, Casto slid off Lys's back and started to walk into the temple. It was rectangular, about fifteen paces long and ten paces broad, with statues of wolves, cats of prey, and birds of prey lining both sides. The shapeshifter clans had played an important role as guards and messengers for the Mothers, so it was only natural they would have a place inside the temple. Casto knew many of those statues had broken, that the pillars supporting the roof were full of cracks, and that the roof itself had partially caved in. What he saw, though, was a temple in all its glory, with the sanctuary awaiting him behind a golden gate at the far end of the hall. He stepped through and gaped at the fountain taking up most of the space. It was perfectly round, about three paces in diameter, and hewn from the most exquisite blue marble Casto had ever seen. In the middle of the fountain was a golden tree that stood one and a half ell tall, with two branches ending in a white and a black diamond, each the size of a child's head. From these two diamonds, water flowed in steady streams into the pool. The floor was tiled with white marble, as were the walls. There was a vague outline of a ceiling, but since it was so weak, Casto assumed the fountain had originally been in the open and the roof had been added at a later time.

Casto turned to Lys.

"I guess it's okay to stay here for the time being. Let's find a place where we can set up camp, and then you can explain to me why you dragged me here."

Still worried, Lys followed his rider out into the open again.

"DAMN IT all!" Renaldo threw his cup full of wine against the tent flap, watched with no satisfaction at all as the red liquid dripped down into the carpet the slaves had changed just a few hours ago. It looked a lot like blood, and Renaldo couldn't shake the ominous feeling he got. Their campaign was not going well. The rebels they were supposed to flush out were running circles around them, seemingly always one step ahead. They had already lost more fighters than usual at such a relatively early stage, even though Sic had called more than a third of them back. Which posed the next problem. The more Echend'dim Sic woke, the more difficult it seemed to become for them to adapt to being part of a low-level hive mind. Thankfully Daran and Lukan remained stable and were able to help the new guards get used to the power influx from Sic and their heightened abilities. According to Canubis it was a strain for the two young men, but they were warriors, and especially Daran took a lot of strength from his husbands, which helped him to meet this challenge head-on.

Renaldo sighed. He was sitting here, in his tent, almost as useless as a freshly hatched chick, with his powers flaring uncontrollably, turning him more and more into a liability where he should have been an asset, the rock his brother could stand on. It took all of his willpower to control the beast within him that wanted nothing more than to burn the entire Dark Forest down and turn their enemies into a pile of ash.

Back when he and Canubis had just come to Ana-Darasa and Ana-Isara had taken their hearts, his control had been equally shaky. The difference was then he didn't have his full power, and even though he had been a terrible, deadly weapon, he had not been absolute destruction. Now he was, and what would become of his brother, his friends should he let go completely had him hiding in his tent.

He couldn't even be angry with Casto anymore. No, thinking about his elusive husband only made the beast hungrier and more difficult to tame. Sleep was the worst, because with sleep came the dreams, flashes of single pictures he suspected were seeping through the blocked bond with

Casto. On one hand it gave him hope, knowing that apparently not even Lys's power could completely separate them, that their connection was too deep to ever break. On the other hand, he hated what he was seeing: Casto on the ground with an arrow in his back, dead, the faces of ragged men bent over him, clearly wanting to harm him, endless planes Renaldo wasn't sure were really on Ana-Darasa, a wolf howling at the full moons. Renaldo didn't know what to make of those glimpses, didn't know if they showed him reality or things his own subconscious was cooking up through the connection with Casto's. It was maddening, and the beast was rearing its head, wanting to break free, to find their mate, their heart, and never let him out of their clutches again.

Renaldo rubbed his temples with his fingertips and picked up the empty cup. Perhaps it would do him some good to get out of the tent. Later, when it got dark and there weren't as many distractions around so he could concentrate on not burning everything down.

"LUKAN, TALK to me! You've never been this silent before. What is it you can't tell me?" Elua knew she sounded like a nagging old hag, the very thing she never wanted to become, but she couldn't help it. Her sweet Lukan was troubled, and he refused to let her in on it, claiming it had nothing to do with her and was his problem to sort out. Elua had enough of that. Ever since Lukan had told her about his connection with Sic and Daran, and now with all the other mercenaries who had become Echend'dim, she felt oddly left out whenever he went to spend time with them. Which was necessary for the warriors to bond and get a handle on their new powers, which made her feel even worse for pressing the issue. Lukan looked at her with his huge puppy eyes, full of love and a sadness that clawed at Elua's heart.

"To be honest, I'm not sure what I should tell you, my lady." He looked so lost, Elua had to suppress the urge to take him in her arms. Now was not the time to be lenient. Now it was time to be stern. She furrowed her brows.

"How about you start with why you always tense up when Lord Sic wakes more Echend'dim. Shouldn't you be glad your numbers are growing?"

Lukan winced, and Elua realized her mistake a little too late. *Your numbers, not ours. Stupid old bat. What a way to deepen the rift between you.* "I'm sorry, Lukan. I didn't mean it the way it sounded. I'm just so worried."

Lukan's shoulders slumped. "I understand, my lady. And if there was a way to explain myself properly, to help you understand, I wouldn't hesitate. I simply have trouble adjusting to all the changes. And every time new Echend'dim join us, I feel the weight of my new responsibilities weighing down on my shoulders."

"I understand, my lord. I really do. I know what responsibility means. So why don't you share it with me? Why do you keep me out when I could help you?"

The sadness was back in Lukan's eyes, together with that wall Elua was learning to hate. "I don't know, Elua, I honestly don't know. Please, be patient with me. Don't give up on me. I—I just have to work this out for myself."

Elua closed her eyes. She knew, if she didn't want to lose Lukan, she had to give him space, something she wasn't used to. The changes in their relationship, in their dynamic as a couple terrified her, as well as the mere thought of Lukan breaking off from her. So she smiled and placed a gentle kiss on his forehead. "I love you, Lukan. You know that. I will be patient, my lord."

"Thank you." Lukan pulled her into his arms, his warm breath ghosting over her hair. "Thank you, my love."

"DA'RYEN, DA'RYEN, look, I've gotten a new dress for my child!" Nya's cheerful voice and happy smile were like a ray of sunshine on an otherwise dreary day. Da'Ryen looked up from where he was hacking at the hard ground, trying to prepare it for an infusion with the rich soil from the pits. The sun was slowly setting behind the mountains, which meant the end of his workday was close. He straightened and put his tool on the ground to take the little doll from Nya's hands. Even though Frankus had given her a new doll, Nya was loyal to the little bundle of rags Da'Ryen had made for her so long ago.

It was a humbling thought, that something apparently so small and insignificant could have such deep meaning.

"It's beautiful, Nya. She looks good in it." Da'Ryen smiled warmly at her.

"I love the colors!" Nya exclaimed happily. Then she took her baby back from Da'Ryen before she grabbed his hand. "Let's go. Dinner is ready."

Her brows furrowed. "Frankus is very stressed. We have to see to it that he eats enough. He works too much, if you ask me."

As funny as it was hearing the little girl talking like a grown-up, the truth behind her words worried Da'Ryen. He and Frankus weren't friendly with each other, not by any stretch of the word. The only reason Frankus looked out for him and allowed him in his home was Nya's love for Da'Ryen. But even though Frankus still resented him for what had happened to Lord Daran, Da'Ryen was intent on helping the man wherever he could.

Frankus had taken Nya in and treated her like a beloved daughter. For that alone Da'Ryen owed the man a lifelong debt. That he also found Frankus rather attractive made serving him easier, despite the man's gruff attitude. Da'Ryen was under no illusion concerning him and Frankus in a romantic setting; it was clear such a thing was never going to happen, but a man could dream. Even when he technically had lost the right to have something as precious as dreams or hope.

He followed Nya back to the sauna, where Frankus had his home. It wasn't as big as one would expect from somebody with Frankus's standing in the Pack, but then nothing about Frankus was as expected. In the small, comfy dining room, Frankus was already sitting at the head of the wooden table, looking so tired Da'Ryen felt his heart clench.

"Good evening, Master." He bowed low to assure Frankus of his submission. That he didn't get a dismissive answer, clothed in polite words as not to upset Nya, worried Da'Ryen even more. Before he could stop himself, he spoke. "Is everything all right, Master? You look tired."

Frankus blinked at him. "Things are a bit tense at the moment. With so many people gone, everything is more stressful, as you have surely realized."

Da'Ryen winced when he thought about all the work he still had to do. It seemed as if the day never had enough hours.

"And then there's the matter of the little boy who still hasn't woken up." Frankus put his fork down to take the cup of wine next to his plate. Da'Ryen stared intently at his own food. The whole Valley knew by now that a little boy was with the healers, and he seemed to be caught in a nightmare, unable to wake up, no matter what the healers tried. Whatever illness he had didn't seem to be contagious, which was a small relief.

"Is there anything I can do to help, Frankus?" Nya looked up from her own plate, her big eyes shining with the determination to help. Frankus's loving smile was enough to bring Da'Ryen to his knees, at least in his mind.

"You're already doing it, sweeting, by being your delightful self. Now eat up. It's time for bed."

A shadow crossed Nya's features at these words, something neither Frankus nor Da'Ryen missed.

"What is it, Nya?" Frankus reached out to stroke her hand.

"I'm just not tired, Frankus. Can I stay with you and Da'Ryen a little longer? Or can Da'Ryen sleep in my room tonight? I miss him."

Da'Ryen furrowed his brows. He did spend his nights at Frankus's house, since Nya had almost cried her eyes out when Frankus had tried to explain to her why Da'Ryen had to sleep in the barracks, but she hadn't asked for him to sleep in her room since before the Pack had left for the current campaign.

"Is there something you want to tell us, little one?" Da'Ryen used the soothing tone that had always calmed Nya when they had still been with Ma'Duk. Nya evaded his gaze, which alarmed Da'Ryen. "What is it, Nya? You know you can tell us everything." He put a little more strength in his tone and was grateful to see Frankus taking Nya's small hands in his. The girl shivered.

"It's just, the bad dreams won't go away. Not even when the shining girl is there."

Da'Ryen and Frankus shared a look over Nya's bowed head. With a slight nod, Da'Ryen told Frankus he would follow his lead. This seemed to be serious, and nothing Nya had ever expressed before. There had been nightmares, of course, but the little girl had always managed to cope with them, especially when she was with Da'Ryen. He wondered what had her spooked so terribly.

"You have bad dreams, Nya?" Frankus's voice was low, soothing.

"Yes. I'm trapped in a cave and the walls are closing in. I can't get out, because it's so dark and I trip over stones and other things."

"How often do you have this dream, sweeting?" Frankus was kneading Nya's hands, while Da'Ryen was stroking her back.

"Every night. I have it every night."

The two men shared another glance. This sounded bad.

"And this shining girl, she helps you?"

Nya nodded. "Yes, she's really nice, with pure white hair, and the darkness is afraid of her. But she's still so small, she can't stop them. She lets her light shine as bright as possible, and when I follow it, I find my way out of the cave. It gets more and more difficult, though."

"Mmm." Frankus was still holding Nya's hand while he stared at the wall over her head. "This girl, does she talk to you?"

"I guess. Not like we're talking right now. She's still small, perhaps two or three years? I don't know. And the words she uses sound foreign to me. Very musical. But I always know what she wants to say. Like it's in my head?" Nya sounded unsure.

Frankus mumbled something under his breath before he focused on Nya again. "I know this is hard for you, sweeting, but do you think you could ask the girl what is going on?"

Nya shuddered. "I'd have to sleep." It sounded as if she wanted to avoid that at all costs.

"Yes, you would have to sleep, sweeting. Would it help if Da'Ryen and I stayed with you?"

"Until I'm asleep or the entire night?"

Frankus looked at Da'Ryen. "The entire night. Promise."

Nya nodded hesitantly. "I could try."

"That's so brave of you, sweeting. Now go get ready for bed while Da'Ryen and I have a little talk."

Nya obediently left the room. When she was through the door, Da'Ryen looked at Frankus. "Do you know something, Master?"

Frankus heaved a sigh. "It's just a hunch. It was something Nya said about the girl. I think I know who she is, though I honestly don't know what she's doing in Nya's dreams or how she's doing it."

"Who is she?" Da'Ryen knew he probably shouldn't push Frankus, but his desire to protect Nya overrode all his self-preserving instincts.

For once, Frankus didn't seem to mind, which was alarming. "Her name is Heljia. She's Sic's niece, and she anchored him after he received Ana-Isara's kiss. I wasn't there when it happened, but it was intense, and Heljia has been marked by Sic's magic. Sic told me her hair is pure white, and according to her parents, the light seems to follow her, keeping her from casting a shadow. I have no clue how she can appear in dreams, since she's roughly two years old, but if it's really her, we might be able to gain some insight into Nya's bad dreams."

"I hope so too. And if she's not? Heljia, I mean." Da'Ryen didn't know what he should wish for.

"Then we have to pray to the Mothers that this is all just something in Nya's head without further consequences. Though I doubt it. I have a bad feeling about the whole situation."

Da'Ryen couldn't hold back any longer. He was standing so close to Frankus, he could feel the man's breath on his face. He reached out and touched Frankus's arm. "Everything is going to be fine, Master."

Frankus didn't shy away from the touch as Da'Ryen had expected. Instead, he leaned into it, if only slightly and just for a heartbeat.

"I hope so. Let's go find Nya. We all need some sleep."

Deeply worried, Da'Ryen followed Frankus to Nya's sleeping chamber.

4. PATHWAY INTO THE PAST

"So you brought me to this place hoping I would forgive the Barbarian? I thought you hated him even more than I do!"

Casto stared at Lys, who was almost invisible in the flickering shadows the campfire threw on the stone walls of the small house they had chosen as their base. One of the walls was completely gone, but the roof was still stable, which was more than Casto could say about the other houses in Quell'renar. It was also adjacent to the temple, a fact that made it an attractive option. For reasons he didn't understand, Casto wanted to stay close to the heart of the city.

Lys huffed. Explaining his incentive to Casto proved even more complicated than he had anticipated. He held Casto's gaze while he tried to explain his motives without revealing the bits he felt Casto was not ready to understand yet. As always, Casto listened intently to Lys's thoughts.

"Basically, you're unhappy about my connection to Renaldo, but since it's already too strong to be severed and you don't want me to suffer, you're trying to help me gain perspective. I really don't know whether I should punch you or hug you. And I'm truly sorry about dragging you into this whole mess. This should be solely between the Barbarian and me, and yet here you are, acting as guard for the stupid idiot who's not able to control his emotions. You deserve better than that."

Lys nudged Casto's shoulder to reassure him of their bond. There was no need for Casto to feel bad about the current situation.

It's not as if you had a choice.

Casto leaned his forehead against Lys's blaze. It was a very welcome gesture, so familiar after all those years they'd spent together, Lys no longer perceived it as any movement on their part. It was part of their unique way of communication, although he had now switched to actual words, which he rarely did. Usually their understanding of each other was absolute, something words could not contain, let alone transmit. By using them, it felt as if he was creating a barrier between them, something that kept deeper meaning outside—which was exactly what Lys was doing. For the discussion to come, the task he had set himself, he needed to create some distance between him and his anchor, superficial as it may be and only to protect Casto. The human mind was not made to withstand chaos, and even though Casto was special in many ways, Lys was sure he wouldn't be able to survive the full impact of what Quell'renar was throwing at them, combined with the knowledge Lys wanted his anchor to gain. He had to take this one step at a time, getting Casto slowly used to whatever madness Quell'renar would unleash on them. And because of their bond, Casto understood all this on a subconscious level, thus not arguing over Lys suddenly reducing their communication to something akin to baby talk. Instead, Casto focused on the problem at hand, namely his obviously temporary estrangement from the Angel of Death, may his name be cursed forever. Or at least until Lys decided to forgive him.

"I know. And I hate it. I never have a choice. Even you—even our connection is beyond my control." Casto hesitated a moment before he spoke on. "Though I have to admit, ours is also the only connection I wouldn't want to miss. I don't regret being your brother, Lys, so don't worry about it so much."

Lys closed his eyes. Because he was with Casto all the time, he sometimes forgot how perceptive he could be.

So you're not spooked by the things I may show you? Or by the responsibilities it brings?

"No. Not really. To be honest, I'm hoping to find something that will give me the edge over the Barbarian."

I may have just what you want. I also gather from your words that you will return to him?

Lys already knew. Had known from the moment they had left the Valley. It didn't mean he couldn't nudge his anchor a bit, perhaps stir the flames of his rage so they could be free for a little longer. Angrily, Casto tossed another dry stick into the fire. There was a glint in his eyes that reminded Lys of a dagger.

"Not that I want to, but we both know I can't escape him anymore, don't we? No matter how well you shield me or how angry I am, Renaldo is burned into my very being. I'm going to defy him as long as possible, and the more he hurts in the process, the better, but there's no way I can escape him. It makes me furious just thinking about it."

Cling to that fury, my brother. You're going to need it once we start our journey into the past.

"You're worried."

Lys huffed. If he wanted this mission to be successful, he had to play with open cards. Or at least as open as he dared at any given moment.

This place is not as I remember it. I'm afraid it's reacting to you. My control is not as absolute as it should be, and to be frank, I also don't like the way you're reacting. You're way too calm, even though the boundaries between illusion and reality, between now and then, are completely annihilated. Any other human would have already gone crazy from the flows of errant magic alone. You, on the other hand, don't seem to feel them at all. It makes me nervous.

Sighing, Casto patted Lys's neck, reveling in the warmth coming from his brother's body. When he spoke, he couldn't keep the bitterness out of his voice.

"I don't feel anything except a weird sense of being welcomed home, but you know as well as I do that I'm not human, Lys. Not anymore. I probably never was. I can feel Quell'renar deep in my bones, as if it is—or was—a part of me. It's strange and a little frightening and wildly exciting. I don't think you have to worry about my sanity. At least not yet. And if things get out of hand, you can always drag me out of here, can't you?"

Lys chose not to answer this last question and made himself comfortable behind Casto, trying very hard not to think about all the things that could go wrong.

DARAN LED his men through the forest, Lukan's presence at his back soothing the anxiety that was trying to sneak up on him. They had been in the Dark Forest for almost three months now and there was no progress at all. Whoever those rebels were, whatever magic they possessed, it was powerful enough to cause serious problems for the Pack. Canubis still wouldn't allow Hulda to step behind time because Lady Noemi was deeply worried about what could happen. The Angel of Death was holed up in his tent, barely coming out, and when he did, he was tense like a bowstring at breaking point in his effort to control his fire. Even Aegid and Kalad were more serious than usual, though it didn't keep them from making his nights interesting, which in turn helped them all to relax at least a bit.

There had been another ambush just two days ago, wiping out a patrol of six men, of which Sic had been able to call back only two. Canubis was seething, which was one of the reasons this mission had to be successful. If the Wolf of War didn't get any positive results soon, he might decide to let Renaldo have free rein, and Daran, who knew firsthand how terrifying the Angel of Death could be when he didn't have his full powers, had no desire to find out what would happen if he truly let go when he was at the height of his abilities.

They had been sent to find and capture some rebels, not that they hadn't been trying this for weeks now, but Daran had decided on a new approach. So instead of sneaking through the forest while the wolves chased after trails that always seemed to vanish like smoke in the wind, they were being as obvious as possible in the hope of provoking another attack. A subtle nudge from Lukan had Daran hoping. Somebody was closing in on them, hopefully some rebels. Daran didn't like playing bait, so when the underbrush around them started to rustle, he was glad the nerve-wracking wait was over. All of a sudden they were surrounded by at least twenty warriors armed to the teeth with the long, slim blades typical for the Eastern Kingdoms at the ready.

Daran shuddered. One look told him there were just too many for his eight men to stand a chance. Perhaps taking more fighters with him wouldn't have been such a bad idea, though then the chance of them being attacked would have gotten slimmer. No matter how he looked at it, they were screwed, though they wouldn't go down without giving these assholes a fight. He just wished he could avoid dying again. It was a painful and unpleasant business, and his husbands always freaked out afterward.

The enemy attacked and Daran drew his sword, perfectly in sync with Lukan, who was standing back-to-back with him, waiting for the first wave. He had to give it to the rebels, they were excellent fighters who already had two of his men down, though Daran couldn't see if they were dead or just wounded. He raised his sword, ducked under a blade that was coming at him, and used the momentum to hack off the feet of a woman who had been trying to get him from the side. Her shrill screams almost prevented Daran from hearing the whooshing sound of another blade coming at him from the left side, but he was able to twist out of harm's way. The fighting got more heated, with most of the enemy's efforts pointed at him and Lukan. *So they know*, Daran thought. He parried another blow and felt a burning pain in his side. Somebody had managed to break through his defenses. Daran winced. He could feel blood trickling down his hip, and the cut must have been deeper than he first thought, because even his accelerated healing didn't prevent his leg from getting soaked. Another blow came far too close for his liking. Through their bond, he could feel Lukan not faring much better; he, too, was already wounded. A quick glance told Daran that four of their men were down, as well as half of the attackers. Unfortunately, those attackers still standing were all unscathed, while none of his men were without an injury. Things were not looking good.

Still, he owed it to his men to fight until his last breath.

Lukan felt Daran's resolve reverberate in his own bones. The man he had gotten to know when he was still a slave was one of the fiercest warriors Lukan knew. He was aware they were probably going to die—again—because there were just too many enemies for another outcome, but he agreed with Daran; they would give those damn rebels a fight many of them wouldn't survive. Lukan gritted his teeth and allowed his connection to Daran to open even more. Despite their rigid training with Hulda, neither of them felt completely comfortable erasing all barriers between them. There were some things Lukan just didn't want to know about Daran, or at least didn't want to have confirmed. Suspecting something and knowing it were two very different things indeed.

In this case, though, letting the connection grow stronger was in their best interest. Lukan felt invigorated and instantly calmer the moment he consciously let Daran in. Clinging to Daran's mind, making use of his broader field of vision and felling their enemies, Lukan didn't realize when he let the last of his barriers drop. It felt as if somebody had hit him from the inside of his skull, and the moment of disorientation almost cost him an arm. He barely managed to evade the blade coming down on his shoulder, a cold draft against his cheek emphasizing how mighty that blow had been. Lukan raised his sword for a counterattack, when he suddenly felt it. It came quick, like a storm in fall, washed through his body with a force that would have brought him to his knees if it hadn't also kept him upright.

It was Sic, or more precisely, the Luksari coursing through his system, filling him with its limitless power. All of a sudden the attacking warriors seemed small and insignificant, their movements too slow to be of any consequence to him or Daran. Without having to concentrate on it, Lukan knew Daran had just killed two men with one single blow of his sword, slicing through their bodies as easily as the sun's rays through dark clouds. Lukan focused on the remaining enemies. After two quick strides, Lukan propelled himself into the air, much higher than he would have ever thought possible, and crashed with his heavy boots into the chest of a man while his blade found a home in the gut of a woman. Before the man under him could so much as think of defending himself, Lukan rammed his dagger into the man's left eye. There were still five enemies standing. They seemed to realize, however, that their ambush had not gone as planned. Two were already heading for the security of the underbrush from which they had come.

"Lukan, get them! I'll take care of these morons here." Daran's order came out gruff; Lukan felt it more than he heard it. Without hesitation he gave chase, following the fleeing men between the trees. He reached the first one with ease, slicing his throat in passing. The other one was faster and nimbler, navigating through the forest like a deer. Lukan gritted his teeth and pulled on the power inside of him to reach the man. For a moment he felt a strange tug, as if a twig had gotten caught in his sleeve; then he stumbled. The light inside him flared, righting him before he could crash to the ground. The fleeing man was now too far ahead, which left Lukan with only one option. He took one of his daggers and threw it. The weapon glinted as if the sun was reflecting off its blade, which was impossible under the dense canopy of the trees. For a moment Lukan thought the dagger was slowing down, as if some invisible force was holding it back, before it accelerated again. With a sickening crunch that could be heard even across the distance, the weapon sunk into the back of the fleeing man, who fell hard. Lukan approached him carefully, though it turned out he needn't worry. Glassy eyes stared into nothing after Lukan had removed his dagger and shoved the body around. He cleaned the blade on the man's clothes and took some time to look through his belongings, searching for clues to the whereabouts of the rebel camp. Finding nothing, Lukan returned to the place where the ambush had started. Daran was bent over one of their men, applying pressure to a wound on the shoulder. A quick glance around told him all their men were still alive, though the two who had gone down first didn't look too good.

"Help is on the way." Daran sounded absentminded, answering a question Lukan had only just started forming in his head. Before he could ask how Daran knew, it became obvious. They were connected to Sic, and Sic had to know what had happened here. Lukan started to help one of the men on the ground. Out of the corner of his eye, he saw Daran had managed to catch one of their attackers. The woman was unconscious and bound. Lukan smiled. Canubis was going to be pleased.

A WAIL tore through the house and had Jago up and running to Heljia's room before his brain was fully awake. He muttered a few choice curse words while opening the door to where his daughter was sleeping. These damn nightmares were starting to wear him out. With a by now practiced movement, he lit the small candle next to Heljia's bed, even though it wasn't strictly necessary. His little girl glowed like a beacon, her white hair almost blinding.

She was sitting in her bed, her hands already stretched out for him. Jago sat down and pulled her into his arms, making soothing noises at the back of his throat.

"It's fine, little one, it's fine. Don't be afraid. I'm here. I'll take care of you."

"I-I-I'm not a-a-afraid." Heljia buried her head in Jago's shoulder. She didn't sound afraid. She sounded upset and a little bit angry, just like her mother when she found a situation she couldn't change but wanted to—a dangerous mixture that needed instant interference before it got out of hand.

"Do you want to tell me what the problem is?" Jago used his best reasonable adult voice. For a two-year-old, his daughter was quite well-spoken and sometimes frighteningly insightful, two things Jago didn't know who to blame for—his wife or Sic. But she was still a little girl, and the past weeks, she had stubbornly refused to tell him or Cassia why she woke almost every night crying—she definitely got her stubbornness from her mother, no doubts there. Silence followed his words, only interrupted by occasional hiccupping sounds while Heljia seemed to be making up her mind. Jago knew better than to push her.

When she finally leaned back in his arms, the look on her little face was too serious for somebody whose biggest concern should be getting enough sweets per day.

"I don't wanna. Is' com—compli—comple—"

"Complicated," Jago provided, which got him another *look*. Heljia hated being corrected when she was trying to figure things out for herself. That she didn't dive into a tantrum right away only made Jago worry more.

"Perhaps I would understand," he suggested. Another long look reminded him so much of Cassia it was creepy. Then Heljia sighed, the sound telling him she didn't like what she was about to do but would do it anyway because—because the women in his life often had reasons he would never understand.

"Is about Uncie Sic's home."

"Uncle Sic?" Jago furrowed his brows. They had two paintings of Sic in their home, and not a day went by on which they didn't mention him to Heljia, but why would she say anything about the Valley? She'd never been there.

"Uncie Sic is gone." Heljia furrowed her brows. "Away?" She sounded insecure, and Jago was starting to sweat. He wasn't sure he had the mental capacity at this time of night to discuss an absent uncle with his little daughter.

"Yes, he's in the Valley, sweeting. He lives there. You know that."

Heljia made a frustrated little sound. "Not now. Now, he's... away. Others are there. They nice. We play a lot." Her face darkened. "Shadows there too. They 'fraid of me, 'cause of Uncie Sic. They not 'fraid of the others. They...." She was clearly searching for the right word. When she found it, a triumphant smile flickered over her face. "They *trap* them. Meanies." Her lower lip started to tremble again. "I can't help." Heljia sounded both frustrated and angry. Since sleep wasn't going to happen now that his daughter had frightened him with a few sentences, he decided to get to the bottom of whatever was happening.

"Come on, little lady, let's go to your mother. I'm sure she knows what to do." *And if she doesn't,* Jago thought, *it's at least no longer my problem.*

When they entered the sleeping chamber, Cassia was sitting upright in bed, her beautiful eyes narrowed, though when Heljia stretched her arms, a warm smile appeared on Cassia's face. She took her daughter from Jago, and after they were snuggled together under the light linen blanket, Jago told Cassia what Heljia had told him. Cassia thought about it while she gently stroked their daughter's white hair. When she finally spoke, it was in that all-knowing mother tone Jago loved so much.

"Heljia, sweeting, all those times when you told us you had seen your Uncle Sic—you really did, didn't you?"

Heljia nodded. "Yes, Mommy, Uncie Sic and often Lyth too."

60

That got Jago's attention. Slight lisp notwithstanding, there was no way Heljia would know about Lys, King Castolus's horse, who always seemed to be shrouded in shadows and who was way too intelligent to be a normal horse.

"What did you do with Uncle Sic and Lys?" Cassia's voice was still firm, though with a small ripple he was only able to detect because of their many years of marriage.

"We play. Lyth carries us around. He's sooo big." Heljia lifted one of her arms over her head, hitting Jago in the chin in the process. "He's strong too."

"I see. And Lys, is he gone as well?"

Heljia nodded. "Most of them are. They go to huge forest."

Cassia looked at Jago. "I guess the Pack went on a campaign, probably to the Dark Forest. For some reason, Heljia can no longer find Sic in her dreams, but she keeps going back to the Valley because she has friends there. Is that right, sweeting?"

Heljia nodded, her eyes big. "They not like Uncie Sic or Lyth. They... they... they *thin*. But we talk and play. Until shadows come."

"When the shadows come, do they threaten you? Are you in danger, sweeting?" That was what Jago wanted to know as well. Heljia shook her head wildly. "No. Shadows afraid of light. Uncie Sic's light." Her grin was almost evil now. "They can't touch light."

"That's good, Heljia. I think your friends in the Valley have a problem, and I also think maybe you shouldn't go there until your Uncle Sic is back." Cassia's tone was just steely enough to make clear this wasn't negotiable.

Heljia pouted. "But my friends...."

"Your uncle will help them as soon as he finds out. Try reaching him if you must, but please don't go back there."

The gleam in Heljia's eyes told them this argument wasn't over yet. Jago sighed.

"Why don't we try to get some sleep before the sun rises? We can talk tomorrow." He slung his arms around both females and pressed a kiss to Heljia's forehead in a silent plea to close her eyes. It must have been his lucky night, because after another pout, his daughter's lids fluttered and closed. Cassia snuggled closer to her, stroking her cheek absentmindedly.

"Yes, let's talk tomorrow. Good night, Jago."

"Do you know something?" Jago knew the question was stupid. Cassia always knew something. She was a very wise woman.

"I think I do. You probably won't like it too much, though."

"Do I ever?" Jago huffed.

Cassia just grinned. "No, my love. Not when it comes to your daughter." She blew him a kiss and closed her eyes as well. Jago buried his nose in Heljia's sweet-smelling hair. It was going to be a long night, followed by a long day. He just knew it.

"THIS IS bad. This is really bad."

Frankus couldn't stop himself from muttering those words when he looked at the little boy who was lying in a bed in the infirmary. He was only five years old, and his slim body looked so very small in the big bed. What was even worse was the pale complexion of his face, the beads of cold sweat on his upper lip, which formed anew every time somebody wiped them away. The boy was very still. Too still. Cornelia pressed her hands together.

"He has been like this for days, just like the others. His mother put him to bed four days ago, and then he had a nightmare, again. When she tried to wake him, he started fighting her and suddenly went limp. He hasn't moved a muscle ever since."

Frankus stared at the little boy and knew this was only the beginning. More and more children and even some adults had started having nightmares. Nightmares bad enough to have them screaming night after night. Nya, too, was now affected every time she went to sleep. After her talk with Heljia, Frankus and Da'Ryen had started taking turns sleeping in her room because this seemed to help her a bit, but there was no mistaking that the dreams were getting more intense. Something was happening, something dangerous. Frankus shot a sidelong glance at Cornelia. She was the only Emeris in the Valley. Normally her brother would be here as well, but Bantu had decided to join Canubis on this campaign. Cornelia was a capable woman, one Frankus gladly followed, but he could sense that she was nervous.

"Thanks to Heljia, we at least know this isn't some kind of disease." Frankus wasn't sure if this was really a blessing. If it had been some kind of disease, the healers could have started looking for a cure. Frankus doubted there was a cure for something that had to be magically induced.

"I wish she could have told us more." Cornelia sighed. It was obvious how much the situation stressed her.

"Well, Heljia is two. To be honest, I'm surprised she and Nya had a meaningful conversation at all." One that had freaked his adoptive daughter out and made her even more afraid to go to sleep.

"At least I figured out why Heljia isn't able to contact Lord Sic." Frankus furrowed his brows. That had been their greatest hope, that Heljia could get through to the Luksari, who would then deal with whatever was invading the children's dreams. It had puzzled them why she couldn't do it when she could so easily walk the dreams of the people in the Valley, and now that he had figured it out, Frankus felt incredibly stupid. He saw the questioning look from Cornelia and shrugged. "Time zones, my lady. It's not a concept widely known because it has little effect on people's daily lives, but it basically means it's not the same time everywhere on Ana-Darasa."

Cornelia's eyes lit up in understanding. Of course the sister of the keeper of all books in the Valley would be familiar with the concept. "Bantu explained this to me once, and I thought it odd, but it makes sense. With Ummana and the Dark Forest being basically on two different sides of the continent, it's highly likely Heljia goes to sleep when Sic gets up. Since the Valley and Ummana are closer, there is some overlapping."

Frankus nodded. "Which unfortunately throws us back to square one. Should we try and reach out to Lord Canubis in the Dark Forest?"

Cornelia shook her head. "I'm tempted. Sic or Noemi could probably deal with this easily. The problem is, we don't know for sure where the Pack is now, and we have absolutely no clue what the situation there is. Our messenger could run directly into the arms of the enemy, and one thing we don't want to get out is word of our weakened state."

Frankus nodded. No, that would be bad. They did have the manpower to defend the Valley when push came to shove. Against a small number of attackers. If the enemies of the divine brothers got wind of a possible weakness… it would mean their death. "What do we do, then?"

Cornelia looked at the boy on the bed. "I'm not sure yet, Frankus. I need to think this through. There are—possibilities. I will tell you once I've come to a conclusion."

With that, Cornelia exited the room, leaving Frankus with more questions than answers, a knot of worry in his gut, and the gnawing suspicion that Cornelia knew more than she let on.

5. GOING BACK

WHEN DARAN and Lukan returned to the camp with their prisoner, Canubis was already waiting for them with Sic by his side. The look on Sic's face told Daran that the Luksari had already told Canubis everything and that he was as shaken as they were. On their way back, Daran had had time to think everything over, and some of his suspicions made him shiver. He only hoped the woman they had caught would shed some light on what was going on in the Dark Forest. But first, he had to talk to his god.

Two of their men brought the struggling prisoner to one of the tents, while Canubis gestured for Daran and Lukan to follow him. Sic walked next to Daran, put his hand on Daran's shoulder in a silent gesture of comfort. Neither of them spoke until they reached Renaldo's tent. Daran felt hesitant to enter since he knew firsthand what happened when the Angel of Death lost his control. The god was terrifying on a good day, but since he lost his heart, Daran had seen the deadly beast inside of him gain more and more power. Renaldo was still in control, but barely, and it was only a question of time until that control would snap. Daran was not too proud to admit he wanted to be as far away from the Angel of Death as possible when that happened.

The inside of the tent was lit by several candles, which cast a soft light on Renaldo's angelic features. At first glance, he seemed almost normal, though Daran had learned a long time ago to look behind the mask of perfection.

The Angel of Death was in agony. Daran felt bad for disturbing his god when he was so obviously in pain, but his other god didn't seem to have the same reservations.

"Renaldo, there has been a development."

Renaldo gestured to the lounges on both sides of his small desk. "Sit. What happened?"

The exchange seemed oddly cold for the two brothers, and it took Daran a moment to understand that this was Renaldo's way of coping—by pretending everything was about the fight.

"Daran and Lukan have managed to catch an enemy. We're going to interrogate her as soon as we've talked about *how* they caught her."

Canubis looked first at Sic, then at Daran and Lukan. Sic sighed and lifted his hands in the air. "I told you, I didn't know this was possible. It's as new to me as it is to you."

"But you felt it?" Daran knew this was more of a rhetorical question. Of course Sic had felt it. Otherwise they would have had the pleasure of coming back from the dead—again.

Sic nodded. "I did. I even saw it… kind of. It's how I knew you needed more power, though I have to admit you have to thank the Luksari for that. I wouldn't have known what to do."

"Could somebody please fill me in on what you're talking about?" Renaldo sounded impatient, and there was just enough of a growl in his voice to make Daran wary. He looked at Canubis to see if he would tell his brother what happened, and when he nodded at Daran with a strange glint in his eyes, Daran groaned inwardly. It seemed as if it was up to him.

"As you already know, Lord Renaldo, Lukan and I took some men into the Dark Forest to provoke an attack and hopefully take a few prisoners. We walked into an ambush, and for a few moments it seemed as if the rebels had once again gotten the better of us." He looked at Lukan. "We were both tired of always being played, and somehow the barriers we usually keep between our minds went down. Perhaps it was the determination to survive and show those assholes what we're made of, or perhaps it was just that we were tired of always losing. Anyway, all of a sudden, our minds were wide open, not only connected to each other, but also to Sic in a way we haven't experienced before. I mean, we knew Lord Sic is able to transfer power to us, but so far it was more like we were just taking in the leakage whenever it is too much for his human form to contain. It all happened on a subconscious level, though somehow there was a sense of purpose behind it…." Daran hesitated. "I guess there's still a lot of experimenting going on. Anyway, this time it felt a lot more deliberate, as if he somehow felt what we needed and was giving it to us actively, reacting to the situation. He was infusing us with additional power—" Daran looked to Sic for confirmation, and he nodded. "Power that made us faster, stronger, and… I'm not sure how to describe it. Better able to see, perhaps. As if everything was clearer. As if the forest was somehow translucent?" Daran trailed off, gazed at Lukan, who furrowed his brows.

"I don't know anything about translucent, but then again Lord Daran is the first Echend'dim. It's only logical he has a different connection to Lord Sic than I do. Though I can second everything else. My mind worked sharper. I saw things I would normally not notice, like dewdrops on a leaf or a spiderweb between two branches. We already talked about how the forest seems to be infused with magic and that we're not sure what, if anything, it does. Now I'm convinced the magic helps the rebels. It's nothing obvious, more like a tipping of the scales in their favor. Our men tripping over roots, arrows getting off track on a breeze, daggers slowing down...." Lukan shrugged. "To be honest, I'm not even sure what I'm talking about. It's as if the realization suddenly appears inside my mind."

"It's the Luksari." Sic's voice sounded thin. "Everything Daran and Lukan have told you is true, Lord Renaldo, Lord Canubis. That dagger Lukan was talking about, when he threw it, it got caught in a magical web, and only the Luksari's magic pushed it through."

Lukan grinned. "That was so strange and sooo great."

"Can you control it? The amount of magic you give to the Echend'dim, I mean." Canubis had a speculative gleam in his eyes.

Sic thought about it for a few minutes.

"I haven't really tried yet. To be honest, I'm too afraid to actively experiment with my Zaheerosh. I don't want to hurt them, and the Luksari's magic is—vast. So far, I only do a steady trickle with some flares now and then when my emotions are—unstable, but as today has shown, I can apparently give them a lot more. Though I don't know where their breaking point is." Sic didn't have to add that there was no breaking point for him. A Luksari's power was almost limitless, like a well connected directly to the sea, only that Luksari didn't need a source, they just were.

Renaldo nodded. "This could finally be an edge over our opponents. Obviously your magic is able to overpower whatever is lurking in the Dark Forest, which is good." He turned to his brother. "Maybe we should rethink Noemi's ban on Hulda stepping behind time. If the magic is only strong enough to tip the odds in the rebels' favor, she shouldn't have any problems."

"You're right. Though I'd still prefer to know what we're dealing with. Noemi isn't entirely sure, and neither is Sic. Or do you have any new insights?"

Sic shook his head. "No, Lord Canubis. Judging from what happened today, I'd say the followers of the Good Mother have somehow managed to manipulate the residual magic from when Ana-Darasa was created to work for them. I'm almost positive this is all there is to it, though I wouldn't bet Lady Hulda's life on it. We don't know if the Good Mother herself has tampered with it, and by now, I think this woman is capable of anything as long as it suits her goals."

"Why are you not afraid? What happened in the forest seems like a big interference to me." Renaldo lifted a brow. Sic only shrugged.

"First of all, I only counteracted the magic with my own. I didn't interact with it directly, which Lady Hulda would do when she steps behind time and starts coming across runes. Second, I'm a Luksari. It doesn't matter how strong the magic is, it poses no threat to me because I *am* magic."

At that Renaldo actually laughed. "Well spoken, Sic. You can't just erase it all, can you?"

"Like you could do with your fire, my Lord? I'm afraid not. It's technically possible, but my powers are not—I don't know which word describes it best. I'm sorry. Let's say, inclined to destroy other magic. That would be like cutting off my own limbs. Even though the magic in the forest is not mine, it's still magic, and as I said before, that's what *I* am, when all is said and done."

Canubis nodded. "Fair enough. Since we seem to have a better grasp on what is going on, why don't we talk to our visitor? Perhaps she can shed some more light on this puzzle. Do you want to join me, brother?"

They all looked at Renaldo, who rubbed his hand over his face. "I'm not sure if that's a good idea, but I want to. I have to start finding a way back to normalcy again. Or as normal as life without my heart can be."

The unspeakable sadness in the eyes of the Angel of Death made Daran avert his gaze. He already knew he was nothing without Aegid and Kalad, and the mere idea of losing them had his heart shattering in his chest. He couldn't even begin to imagine what the Angel of Death was enduring at the moment, and it only heightened his respect for the god.

"You know he will come back, don't you?" Sic's voice was soft, carried its own pain over losing his best friend. "He just needs to cool that hot head of his, and then he'll be back in your arms. It just takes time."

Renaldo actually managed a smile for Sic. "I know, Sic. Doesn't make the waiting easier."

Canubis clapped his hands. "Fine. Now that the heart-to-heart is over, let's go and torture the enemy!" His cheer was only slightly forced and got his brother going.

Renaldo rose from his chair and gave a slight nod in the direction of his brother. "As you wish, Lord Canubis."

They left the tent, with the divine brothers taking the lead.

WHEN CASTO woke, the sun had already heated Quell'renar to the point where the air became thick and heavy like a living monster, although it was still early. Casto couldn't help but smile blissfully. This was a lot better than the stinging cold and nasty blizzards in the Valley. There was nothing more refreshing than being soaked in sweat just from sleeping. For the first time in weeks, he felt something akin to contentment.

Lys had already gotten up and greeted him with a snort. Casto smiled. He enjoyed the tranquility of the moment. After a breakfast of dried meat and a handful of red-berries, Casto felt ready to face the past. Together with Lys, he returned to the fountain, where he splashed the cool water on his face and body to refresh himself. Then he turned to Lys.

"So, what's happening now?"

Lys looked around, and his ears played nervously.

It's already started. Just relax and try to stay close to me. Quell'renar is eager to show itself.

Casto edged a little closer toward Lys. He could feel it too. A certain pressure in the air, as if a storm was drawing closer. His thoughts slowed down to a lazy trickle, while his senses bombarded him with impressions of scents, sounds, and even textures. It all washed over him like a tidal wave, almost burying him underneath. Thanks to Lys's presence, Casto was able to withstand the assault, although only by a hair's breadth. If he wanted to persevere in Quell'renar, he had to build up a stronger resistance.

Once his senses were back to normal, Casto looked around suspiciously. Quell'renar was gone. He and Lys were standing on an open plain covered in grass that grew up to his waist. In the distance, he thought he could hear Ana-Raina, the great ocean, even though they were at least three leagues away from it. There was a soft wind rustling the grass. All of a sudden, the culms bowed down, and two women appeared right in front of Casto. He recognized Ana-Isara immediately; her white hair was like a banner in the breeze. The other woman could only be Ana-Aruna. Her hair had the color of the most fertile soil, with streaks of green so dark it almost seemed black. She was smaller than her sister, if only by one hand, and her body was plumper. Where Ana-Isara was thin enough to be bony, her sister had the full, lascivious curves of a woman in her best years. Her eyes were as dark as Ana-Isara's and her lips had the same deep red, but the healthy bronze tone of her skin made her look a lot more approachable. Ana-Aruna was crying. Her tears flowed down her cheeks in a rich stream, building a puddle at her feet. Casto felt inclined to reach out to her, to soothe her, until he realized that the women could not see him, that what he was witnessing was a mere memory. Ana-Isara pulled her sister into a tight embrace. Her voice was a low, reassuring drone.

"Don't be sad, my beloved Ana-Aruna. Everything will be fine."

"How can you say such a thing when we just lost our great, beautiful forest to a streak of untamed magic? It's all gone! Only sand and death where we built a powerhouse of life."

"I know, my sweet sister, I know. We underestimated the power of magic and chaos. But you should know best that life will always prevail. Otherwise the balance would be disturbed."

Ana-Aruna freed herself from her sister's embrace. A determined expression appeared on her face.

"Of course you're right, my beloved sister. We need to find a way to use up all that raw magic so it cannot harm our creation anymore. A creature, modeled in our image and strong enough to harness the power of magic and chaos."

Ana-Isara smiled broadly. She lifted her outstretched hands to her chest, her palms directed at Ana-Aruna, who had done the same. Between the two goddesses, the air started to flicker. Dust rose from the ground, forming the crude outline of a human being.

"What a splendid idea, Ana-Aruna. Let us create something superior. Something able to tame not only the raw forces of magic, but also our creation."

The outline of the human being was taking on more and more substance, while Ana-Isara and Ana-Aruna kept on talking, their hands still outstretched to channel the magic. It was Ana-Aruna who spoke next.

"It shall rule on this world and recognize us as the mothers of everything."

"It shall bow to our will alone and express in its living and dying the eternal rhythm we stand for."

"It shall procreate and bear more of its kind in order to inhabit Ana-Darasa."

The sisters locked gazes. The creature hovering between them was by now solid, yet still strangely blurry, as if the edges had no focus. Ana-Isara and Ana-Aruna spoke in unison now, their voices echoing over the green plains with irresistible force.

"There shall be male and female to carry on the race, and love to bind them all. They shall honor life and death as they fear living and dying. This is our will, and it shall be carried out now."

There was a sound like thunder rumbling on distant skies while the two goddesses poured their magic into the creature between them. At one point, the writhing thing doubled so that there were two of them accepting Ana-Aruna's gift of life and Ana-Isara's gift of death.

When the magic finally subsided, a man and a woman were standing in front of the goddesses, staring at them with wonder and incomprehension in their eyes. Ana-Aruna hugged both of them while Ana-Isara kissed them on the forehead.

"Welcome to Ana-Darasa, our children."

Casto watched in fascination as the goddesses led their creations away in order to teach them the ways of the world. Where Ana-Aruna had cried so desperately, a small pool had appeared. Thin ripples originating at the center indicated that a spring had formed. Slowly, Casto approached the new source of water, knowing it would become a fountain with marble basins in a future that, to him, was also the past. Lys stood next to Casto as he bent down to touch the water with his fingertips. The tears of a goddess. Quell'renar was the source of more wonders than Casto cared to think about, while he tried to understand the deeper meaning of what he had just seen.

The birth of the La'ides, of humankind, was due to the goddesses' need to stabilize the world they had created. Casto wondered whether this made the La'ides more or less precious. They were, originally, a means to an end, and they had been created to fulfill a certain task. Once their mission was completed, namely taming the stream of magic, there was no longer a need for them. Casto knew the legends about the creation of the world, but this was the first time he truly understood that there was a lot more to them than just their entertainment value.

Suddenly tired, Casto closed his eyes. He'd had enough of the past for one day. Lys snorted next to him, and when Casto opened his eyes again, they were back in front of the fountain, under the glaring midday sun.

How did you like your first expedition into the past?

Casto leaned against Lys, still confused.

"I don't know. It wasn't as bad as I had feared. Still, it has shaken me. Only two years ago, I still denied the fact that the Mothers truly existed. And here I am, watching them create humankind. It's so crazy, I would laugh if I didn't feel like crying. When I think that you endure the past like this all the time, I'm grateful you have refrained from letting me see your true self until now."

Lys nuzzled Casto's hair with his soft nose. His anchor hadn't seen more than a glimpse yet.

You are strong, my brother. A lot stronger than you give yourself credit for. I'm proud to have you as my anchor. I understand that you have a lot to think about. How about we take a little stroll outside, maybe try and catch a deer? You should eat fresh meat to keep your strength.

Chuckling, Casto leaped onto Lys's back.

"You're right, brother. I need food, and I would love to have a juicy sirloin for dinner. Even though it's very nutritious, eating dried meat becomes boring after a while. And while we're at it, let's pick more redberries. I know you like them as well."

CORNELIA LOOKED around the Valley in the dim half-light of the dream. Ever since the day she was almost raped to death, she had tried to avoid this kind of lucid dream, where she was fully conscious and yet unable to control what was happening. Over the years, she had gotten so good at not entering this strange dreamland, she had been sure the ability was gone for good. Given how easily she had slipped into it tonight on the first try, her ability to suppress what was really there was the only thing that had gotten stronger. Even after all these years   it had to be more than a century since she had last been trapped like this—the feeling of cold fear running down her spine was terribly familiar. Cornelia shook her head. She had no time for this nonsense. She had to act. In the last weeks, more and more children, as well as the first adults, had fallen into the same catatonic state, which was definitely caused by nightmares. People were afraid to fall asleep, and according to Nya, Heljia rarely came back these nights because her parents had forbidden it. Cornelia was glad that the little girl from half a continent away who had helped them understand what was going on would be safe. She didn't want to imagine what Sic would do should anything happen to her. Though this also left the burden of doing something against this threat on her shoulders.

Cornelia knew the key was here, in the land of dreams, and she only had to find it. She sighed. The sleeping potions the healers were handing out weren't even half as effective as she and Frankus had hoped, and time was running out. If only this place wasn't so laced with darkness and bad memories. At least she wasn't back in her old village, reliving the nightmare of the attack.

At the corner of her eye, something slithered, something long and huge, staying just out of sight. Cornelia shuddered. This was getting bad fast, and she was all alone. Determined not to let her own fears keep her from finding a solution, she started walking around the houses of the Valley, looking for something, anything that would help her save her people. When she reached the forest, she detected a spot of pure blackness in the underbrush. When she got closer, she recognized the first child who had fallen into the catatonic state. The boy's small body was tangled in the twigs and branches, darkness enveloping him like the mockery of a blanket. Another flash of movement behind her had Cornelia spinning around, but there was nothing but the path she had come down and the houses in the distance. She turned back to the boy and was shocked to see that the darkness was getting thicker, extending smoke-like tendrils toward her, clearly wanting to suck her in, keep her here where she would be of no use to anybody, caught forever in this land where nothing was real and yet everything had more substance and meaning than in the real world.

She made a few hasty steps backward, the darkness following her, the tendrils growing thicker with every moment. Cornelia wanted to scream, wanted to do something to escape, to free herself, yet no sound found its way out of her mouth, and she could feel her limbs growing heavy with her impending defeat. The first tip of darkness was just about to reach her, tangling in the seam of her dress, when suddenly a blinding light flared up. Cornelia was almost sure she heard a pained screech before the tentacles of blackness retreated back to the boy, quivering as if they were afraid.

"You should leave while you still can." The voice was of a young girl, and even before turning around, Cornelia knew who it was. Heljia looked like Nya had described her. White hair, huge eyes, a sweet button nose and slightly rounded mouth, as was typical for young children under the age of three. The only thing not matching was the mature statement.

"It's the dreamworld. Things are different here." Heljia's voice sounded in Cornelia's head, even though the lips of the girl hadn't moved. She was surrounded by a halo of light, reminding Cornelia of Sic.

"I thought your parents forbade you to come here? I agree with them, by the way. This is too dangerous."

Heljia cocked her head. "Not as dangerous as for you." Before Cornelia could find an answer to this very correct observation, Heljia went on. "I won't be coming back after tonight. I just wanted to tell Nya goodbye and explain to her why I can't protect her anymore. There's too many dark things here now, and even though they fear my light, without Uncle Sic, I can't chase them away. I'm sorry."

Cornelia crouched in front of the little girl and dared to stroke her cheek. "It's fine, Heljia. You did what you could. It's not your fault the darkness is so strong. We will find a way, and before you know it, you can come back here to play with your uncle."

"Is Lys coming back as well? He's so much fun."

Cornelia did her best to hide her surprise. Heljia knew Lys? "I'm sure he will. He and Casto are gone at the moment, but they will come back."

Heljia shrugged. "Casto is no fun. He's always sheathed in fire, like the other one. They're never aware I'm even here." She pouted.

Cornelia couldn't help but smile. "These two are a unit. For them, nothing else exists, I guess."

"Anyway, you should leave now. There's more darkness out there, and it's looking for you. I have to go home now." With that, Heljia vanished like she had never been there. Cornelia looked at the spot where the little girl had been. A rustling sound had her close her eyes and concentrate.

As easily as she had slipped into the dreamland, she left it again, not closer to a solution but a lot more frightened of what would happen. Perhaps it was time to use the other potion, the one the healers had advised was too dangerous.

THE GOOD Mother screamed in rage. Almost. She had almost trapped one of the Emeris in darkness. And this annoying light had thwarted her plans once more. Stupid Luksari and their stupid brand of protection. The Good Mother knew better than to try to harm the little light. The magic protecting it was pure and would erase anything that attempted to hurt the girl. She wasn't even sure if she would be able to overcome that magic. And if there was one thing she couldn't afford, it was wasting her precious resources and energy on something not worth the trouble. She only hoped the little girl would make good on her words and not come back. She still had time to trap the Emeris, though it was getting closer than she liked. The bastards were already putting together the puzzle pieces in the Dark Forest, and with the Luksari's powers extending faster into his Zaheerosh than she had ever thought possible, she needed to raise her army and destroy the home of her enemies. If only her followers could find the heart of the Angel of Death. The Good Mother would love nothing more than to extinguish him from the face of Ana-Darasa, but not even with the additional power she had poured into her seers had they been able to find him. Victory was still within her reach, though. She only had to be patient.

LEARNING

1. DREAMS AND THE PAST

RENALDO WAS the first to enter the tent where the prisoner was held. On their way over, Sic had left them, which didn't surprise the Angel of Death. Sic was too soft-hearted to witness torture if it wasn't absolutely necessary.

Daran and Lukan had stayed with them, as was their right since it was their catch. Renaldo could feel his brother's gaze on him, trying to gauge what was going on inside of him. As twins and gods, they were almost as close as if they were one person, so keeping secrets from his brother was near impossible. The first weeks after Casto had left, Renaldo hadn't even tried to mask his feelings. They had been too raw, too obvious anyway. But when Canubis's worry had become too much to bear, he had started putting up walls to avoid his brother's scrutiny. Renaldo still didn't trust himself around people, not to mention in a fight, but until Casto returned—and he had to believe his capricious heart would sometime soon because the alternative didn't bear thinking about—he had to manage without him. It wouldn't do any good if their enemies thought them weakened. Questioning a prisoner might be just the thing to focus him on something besides the emptiness inside his chest.

The woman Daran and Lukan had caught was bound to a pole, her arms raised above her head to make her body easily accessible to any kind of pain Renaldo and Canubis wanted to subject her to. She had a defiant look on her face, though her underlying fear permeated the air in the tent with its sweet perfume. Her gaze darted between Renaldo and Canubis, never once stopping on Daran or Lukan, which only showed how stupid she was. Dismissing the two Echend'dim was beyond foolish, especially when they were as pissed at the moment. Lukan in particular was an expert in dealing pain, a talent nobody believed him capable of when meeting him for the first time. Renaldo smiled coldly. Lukan wouldn't get to have much fun today.

"I see you are awake, scum."

The woman scowled at his words, clearly trying to gauge his mood and how to best respond. It was like what playing with a weakened mouse had to be for a cat, and Renaldo felt his senses come alive like they hadn't since Casto had left him. This was what he was good at; this was what he was, a predator without mercy and conscience. He approached her with his most blinding smile, while the beast inside him started to stir. Almost lovingly, he stroked her swollen cheek, enjoyed the fearful tension in her body, the way her breath caught and her eyes went wide. Whatever she saw in his gaze made her heart pound so hard, he could hear it from where he was standing.

"I have to give you my thanks, scum. You're just the distraction I need on this gloomy day. I'm not going to tell you things will be easier for you if you cooperate, since we both know that's a lie. And truth be told, I would love for you to resist. Makes the game more interesting."

Renaldo watched as the woman processed his words. That was always the best part, at least to him. Seeing how a prisoner realized the severity of their situation and that it was all nothing but a game to Renaldo. He could tell the exact moment the woman gave in to her fate. It was in the subtle hitch of her breath, the utter defeat in her eyes. She was trapped and as good as dead, and she knew it.

"I can't tell you anything." There was a hint of defiance in her voice. And triumph, which neither Renaldo nor his beast liked. He felt heat rising in his mind, ready to burn this insolent worm who dared to contradict him. She obviously had no idea what she was dealing with, who she had angered. It would be his joy to teach her the error of her ways, to show her the meaning of terror.

For a moment he allowed himself to revel in the fierceness of his fire, in the utter power building inside him. It felt so good, so perfect. He could—

"Brother!" Canubis's voice brought him abruptly back, and with a feeling of regret, he reined the fire in, much to the beast's dismay. Sighing, he concentrated on their prisoner again.

"And why would that be? To me it seems as if you're more than eager for at least a chance to cut your pain short."

The woman shuddered. "We both know I want that. But as you said already, that won't happen. I still can't tell you what you want to hear. I'm just a mere foot soldier who does what I'm told. My mission was to kill as many of you as possible during ambushes that were orchestrated by our leaders. For some reason, we were extremely lucky until today."

Now she did look at Daran and Lukan, who both grinned maliciously. Renaldo marveled, not for the first time, at how far Daran had come. From filthy thief to pampered love slave to fierce warrior. It just showed how many different sides there were to humans, often wrapped in the same package. He shook his head slightly. Now was not the time to ponder Daran's life journey.

"Then what can you tell us, scum? Because so far, the only good thing about your capture seems to be the opportunity for me to let off some steam." Renaldo felt the beast stir at these words and saw the woman shudder.

"Even if I did know anything of importance, I wouldn't be able to tell. The priests have put a spell on each of us to prevent us from talking. No matter what you do to me, I can't give you what you want."

Renaldo furrowed his brows. He concentrated for a moment, focusing on the aura surrounding the woman. She had not lied. The magic branding her was similar to what they could sense everywhere in the Dark Forest. Slippery, twisting coils of darkness that didn't allow a closer look to determine the origin of the magic. Renaldo was sorely tempted to try to burn the coils binding the woman, though in his current state, he would likely turn her to ashes instead of getting the answers they wanted. Then again, it seemed as if they wouldn't be getting any answers either way. He didn't have to look at his brother to know what Canubis was about to say.

"Use her to trace the magic in the camp and destroy it. Then we decide what happens next."

Renaldo nodded, not once taking his eyes off the woman, who was trembling violently. He smiled at her coldly. "Time to pay for your sins."

The beast roared, eager to come out and play. With his inner eye, Renaldo followed the lines of magic from her body down into the ground, where it seemed to be woven into the soil. Since he now had a line he could follow, Renaldo could finally understand the enormity of what they were facing. Somehow the priests of the Good Mother had managed to latch their own magic onto the remnants of the ancient, pure magic residing under the Dark Forest. Powers that had been reduced to a fading background hum by the laws Ana-Isara and Ana-Aruna had introduced were now feeding whatever twisted spells their enemies were using. No wonder they had such a hard time gaining ground against them. The magic wasn't prominent enough to really be felt, but just so potent it could tip the scales of chance in favor of the enemy. It was clever and devious and would end today.

Renaldo sent his fire along the black tendrils, reveling in the pained screams of their captive, even though they died much too fast. Much to the beast's joy, there was plenty of magic that could be burned, and so Renaldo let his fire burst forward to destroy the spider's web they had found themselves in. The hotter the flames became, the more powerful Renaldo felt. This world was meant to bow before him and his brother, to provide them with whatever they required. That anybody even thought about defying them was an insult he would not let go unpunished. He would burn them all, everybody who was against the Angel of Death and the Wolf of War. When he was done with this world, there would be only ashes left, pure and perfect, on a world who knew what opposing its gods meant.

Renaldo felt his power surge, reminding him of another time when he had done the same. The outcome had been devastating, and not only for their enemies. It was the memory of that day that made Renaldo call his fire back. It wasn't easy. The beast was now fully awake, and without Casto, it was almost impossible to tame. But he had to, for the sake of those who were loyal to him and Canubis, for the sake of destroying the Good Mother and not playing into her hands by eliminating his own people. The beast fought him with all its might, and only the self-control Renaldo had learned over the centuries made it possible for him to finally stop the fire. He was panting from the great effort, and when he opened his eyes to the real world again, the first thing he saw was the worried face of his brother. Daran and Lukan were standing close to the opening of the tent, as if that would have helped any if he'd really lost control.

Suddenly tired, Renaldo wiped his face with his left hand. "I'm fine," he answered the unspoken question in his brother's eyes. "The camp is now free of any magic that isn't our own. I can't use my fire again, though. Not without Casto." Admitting it had bile rising in his throat, but it was the truth. "I'm too close to losing control."

Canubis acknowledged his words by putting his hand on Renaldo's shoulder. "Thank you, brother. We can work with what we have. Now that we know what we're up against, we can react accordingly."

What Canubis didn't say out loud was that they didn't have a choice. He, too, remembered all too clearly what Renaldo's fire could do if it got out of control. Renaldo nodded at Daran and Lukan, who both bowed slightly, showing their respect to their god. Then he left the tent without sparing the pile of ashes that was all that remained of the captive a second glance. He was eager to get back into his tent, where he could muse about just how close he'd come to destroying them all.

SIC FELT Renaldo's fire burning the magic in the soil. It wasn't pleasant, and the Luksari stirred, ready to defend himself. Only when he realized the fire wasn't directed at him did the ancient creature return to its slumber. Sic still couldn't bring himself to think of this entity as him. He knew all too well that they weren't simply two sides of one half, or even two separate beings who happened to share the same body. No, they were one, but because Sic's mind needed to create a distance between him and the powers he controlled in order to not go insane, he allocated them to the Luksari, thus making all the crazy things he was capable of not his own deeds but those of something outside his control. Sic knew this tactic would only work for so long, especially now that he had given Daran and Lukan such a huge dose of his power. But he still needed time to get to know himself. To get acquainted with the idea of being more powerful than the creator goddesses themselves. He could easily understand why so many Luksari preferred to leave the physical realm as soon as possible. The responsibilities that came with his power weighed on him, and if it weren't for the oath he had sworn to Renaldo, Sic would have been tempted to follow their example. Of course, there were also Heljia and Noran, and all the other people he had come to love, but Sic was honest with himself. The one thing binding him more securely than any connection born out of love was his bond with Casto, the only person who probably didn't know what love really was. When he thought about it, Sic had to snigger at the unfairness of it all. Casto, who had never learned to love or trust, who didn't know a thing about healthy relationships, and who was the complete opposite of everything Sic represented was the best friend he'd ever had. A friend who hid his affection behind growls and coldness because he didn't know how to deal with it. A friend who thought nothing of leaving Sic behind to indulge in his rage about the Angel of Death because, and this was what had Sic almost in hysterics, he would completely accept it if Sic did the same when he needed to. The things he and Casto expected from a relationship and were willing to invest in it were as different as the sun and the moons. And yet it worked, because in the end, they both wanted the same. Somebody to rely on. Somebody who at least had an inkling about what was tearing them up inside. Somebody who wasn't their mate.

Sic stilled. His relationship with Noran was still balancing on a knife's edge. Knowing that the man was the darkness to counter his light didn't help Sic at all. Not when his understanding of his own nature was still so shaky. The part of him that represented everything he had been before the Luksari woke craved Noran's affection and at the same time fought against the bad memories of what his master had done to him. The part of him that was the Luksari demanded to finally claim Noran and make light and darkness one. It chilled Sic to the bone to add another aspect of power to this mix that was already threatening to overwhelm him completely. He had a responsibility toward Daran and Lukan and all his other Zaheerosh, as well as to his gods. Letting Noran in meant endangering everything he had already accomplished. Not letting Noran in meant endangering his own sanity and Noran's mental stability. Sic was no fool. He could see how his master and lover was struggling with himself to give Sic the space he needed. It was sweet—or would have been if Sic wouldn't have been able sense the despair underneath. Noran felt the need to connect with Sic probably even stronger than Sic himself, and it was only a question of time until the fragile peace they were currently navigating would shatter under the weight of both their expectations and fears.

As if his thoughts about him had conjured the master smith, Noran approached Sic from the direction of the smithy. He furrowed his brows when he came close enough to Sic, no doubt picking up on Sic's strange mood, which in turn made Sic even more restless.

"Sic, is everything all right?" The worry in Noran's voice made Sic feel even more guilt.

"Yes, Noran. Or it will be. I'm just shaken by what has happened today."

Noran nodded with sympathy in his eyes. "I understand. Seeing Renaldo like this is never easy."

For a moment Sic was tempted to let Noran believe that was all it was, a lingering fear of Renaldo's terrible fire. It would have been easy and the reprieve he needed. It was also wrong. As much as Sic wanted to run and hide from everything, he knew it was time to start facing reality. If he did it in small steps, perhaps it wouldn't be so bad. Sic inhaled deeply.

"It's not just Lord Renaldo's fire. I'm… I don't know how to explain it, Master. I'm getting stronger, more like the Luksari every time I wake an Echend'dim or pour my strength into my Zaheerosh. And it's strange thinking about them as mine when they are Lord Canubis's and Lord Renaldo's Echend'dim as well. Or in the first place. I can't even tell for sure."

Noran put his hand on Sic's shoulder in a gesture that was meant to be soothing but only managed to rile Sic up even more. A strange mixture of pure lust and desperate want coursed through him, and he had to step away abruptly to avoid jumping Noran like a bitch in heat.

"I'm sorry, Master. The need to claim you is riding me so hard. I can't stand being touched by you at the moment."

Sic saw the pain in Noran's eyes, as well as an answering flare of heat as the darkness responded to the call of the light. "It's fine, my precious. Well, not really, we both know that. But we're doing this at your pace. I can wait."

Sic looked at the man who was both his sweetest dream and worst nightmare. "I wish I could already give in. I feel it deep in my bones, how right it is to finally become one. It's not just my wish, but that of the Luksari as well. I'm just afraid my fear could somehow ruin it. Sully our union. When we make the final step, I want to be free of doubts or regrets. I want it to be perfect."

Noran smiled sadly. "Oh, Sic, it will be perfect, no matter what. Because you and I, we belong together, just like light and darkness. I'm ready to be yours forever as soon as you'll have me."

Sic stared at Noran, not only with his eyes but also with his other sight, and he could find no deceit. Only openness and a longing on the precipice of obsession. Noran's sureness was steady as a rock, promising Sic a future of acceptance and love, if only he found the strength to finally let it happen. Sic took Noran's hands in his own and kissed them reverently. He may not be ready just yet, but he could feel the decision firming in his mind.

"Soon, Master. Soon."

2. ENEMY AT THE GATES

FRANKUS STARTLED in his bed when he heard a long, drawn-out wail. Knowing it could only be Nya, he rushed to her room and stopped dead in his tracks when he opened the door. Da'Ryen cradled Nya close to his chest. She was fighting him like mad, her fingernails digging into the skin on the man's arms, and there were bloody scratches on her own face. During all that, she never stopped screaming at the top of her lungs. Frankus hurried to help Da'Ryen secure Nya so she could no longer hurt herself. Da'Ryen was close to tears.

"She was fine. She slept deep, and I thought this would be a good night. Then she suddenly started to squirm. Before I knew it, she was covered in sweat and trying to claw her skin off her face. When I held her down, she started to scream. We can't let her go. She's going to hurt herself."

Frankus tried to give Da'Ryen a reassuring look and failed miserably. The animosity he had once felt for the man had vanished in the past weeks. He now saw him as a reliable help and one of the few people in the Valley who kept a cool head in this terrible mess. The one weakness Da'Ryen had was Nya, a weakness he shared with Frankus. Keeping the girl safe was getting more and more difficult.

"How much of the sleeping potion did we give her?"

Da'Ryen shook his head in reaction to Frankus's unspoken suggestion.

"Too much to give her another dose now. We need to get her awake. Cold water perhaps?"

Frankus hesitated. Nya hadn't slept more than four hours in one go for the entire week. It was already affecting her health, which was the reason they had given her the sleeping potion. Waking her would worsen her condition. Letting her remain in the nightmare could make her catatonic, like the other people in the Valley. Frankus got up to fetch some cold water. When he came back, Nya had stopped struggling. She hung limp in Da'Ryen's arms, and one look at the man's face told Frankus they had lost her. He dropped the bowl with the water. Da'Ryen had tears in his eyes.

"What do we do now?"

The despair in the other man's voice pried Frankus from his own misery. He had people to take care of and a daughter to save. Cold determination grew inside him. Whoever was messing with them was in for a nasty surprise.

"Take her to the others. I'm going to see Cornelia."

IT TOOK Casto almost four days to muster the courage for his next visit of the past. He had gotten used to all the illusions Quell'renar was constantly showing him, but they were merely glimpses, nothing that could stir him up. The things Lys exposed to him were of a different caliber. For one, they were a lot more intense and made Casto doubt his ability to distinguish between memory and reality. After witnessing the creation of the La'ides, Casto had felt lost and alone and insecure, none of which he enjoyed. Because of this, he anticipated the next confrontation with the history of Quell'renar with mixed feelings. Lys nudged him on the shoulder to give some reassurance. For a moment, Casto leaned against his brother's broad frame, glad that he wasn't alone in this. His lips thinned in determination.

"Let's get this over with."

As you wish.

There it was again, the feeling that Casto's thoughts were slowing down while his senses were on high alert. This time, though, he was prepared and withstood the torrent more easily. The past unfolded. Again, Casto and Lys were standing close to the spring. The high grass was gone, and the spring was adorned with a crude woodcarving of Ana-Isara and Ana-Aruna. Around this center stood primitive huts where people went in and out, carrying pieces of raw meat and baskets full of fruit and nuts. In front of one of the huts, Ana-Aruna sat in a circle of people, teaching them how to use a simple bone flute.

The picture wavered, as if somebody had thrown a stone into a puddle. When it came back into focus, the huts were gone, as were the two wooden carvings. Instead there was already a stone basin containing the spring. Even more people than in the previous scene were busy building a stone wall in front of the spring under the stern glare of a middle-aged woman. Casto thought he could already discern the layout of the temple. The ground was paved with roughhewn lanes, one of which led in the direction of Ana-Raina. The houses were built from bricks and already had two levels. Casto found Ana-Isara a little way outside, watching as a young man turned into a bird in front of her. She looked very pleased.

Once more the picture wavered, and this time, the temple and houses matched the layout Casto knew from the current Quell'renar. There were hundreds of people now, dressed in fine silk and soft linen with intricate embroidery. Wolves as big as the ones from the Valley sauntered through the streets, as if it was the most natural thing to do for a predator. Casto stepped into the temple, where he found Ana-Isara and Ana-Aruna in a lively discussion with three men and two women. Casto's Ancient was good enough to understand the topic. Apparently the different witch clans were thinking about building towers to house the members of each clan. The goddesses liked the idea and helped with their suggestions. The entire scene was so sickeningly perfect, Casto felt bile rise in his mouth.

While he was watching, the goddesses vanished and the faces of the La'ides changed into different people, as did the expressions on their faces. The discussion was no longer about buildings but focused on something graver: the gradual loss of their magical powers.

"My grandmother was able to translocate more than a hundred sheep at a time. I can count myself lucky if I manage thirty."

"It's getting harder to step behind time. I feel resistance whenever I try to do it."

"The birds are already gone. I haven't seen one in over three years. And the cats—well, they are fickle by nature. Nevertheless, it worries me that there are fewer of them every year. The only ones who seem remotely stable are the wolves."

"When I try to see into the future, it's all hazy. I have trouble discerning the different strands of possibility."

"There is no doubt, we're losing our powers. It's as the Mothers have told us. We were created to tame magic, not to use it for eternity."

The group looked uncomfortable. Fear of the unknown, of a future less predictable and stable harassed their features. An older man sighed.

"The Mothers aren't visiting as often as they used to. I'm afraid we're not only losing our magic but also our gods. And what use are we without someone to worship?"

Casto shuddered. This was indeed a valid question. What use was a people who had lost their gods? A woman stepped forward. Her eyes shone wild and bright in her broad face.

"The Mothers never promised to stay with us. It is not in their nature. Perhaps it's up to us to get ourselves worthy gods. Let's beg them the next time they come here to give us somebody made from this world, who can lead us into the future. Gods we can trust because they will stay with us. I'm sure the Mothers will understand."

The other members of the group nodded in agreement. Casto could almost taste their insecurity, as well as their determination. He understood how desperate the La'ides were and how difficult it was to love mothers who abandoned their children once they had fulfilled their task. Then again, those cruel goddesses were all the La'ides had. The seed of revolution, the will to turn their back on the Mothers was born during the time *before* the Good Mother first set foot on Ana-Darasa. She had simply found an opening and latched on to it, without having a hand in the creation of its origin. *That* was all on the Mothers.

The insight jolted Casto out of the memory and back into the present. Panting, he stared at Lys, who watched him with an unfathomable look in his eyes. And Casto understood how crucial a moment he had just witnessed. All that had happened until now, everything had been set in motion at that very instant when the La'ides failed to accept the true nature of Ana-Aruna and Ana-Isara, of life and death, and when the Mothers underestimated the determination and despair of their creation. Seen with some distance, it had only been a misunderstanding, but one with consequences that could destroy creation itself.

Casto glared at Lys.

"Bring me back. Do it right now! I have to know what happens next."

As you wish.

The same instant, Casto was back in the temple, watching as the leaders of the La'ides pleaded their case to Ana-Isara, who seemed rather detached. Her voice was as smooth as Casto remembered it from his wedding night, only this time there was a hint of bafflement in it.

"This is what you were made for. Aren't you satisfied with fulfilling your destined role?"

"How can that be?" The man who spoke was shaking with fury yet tried his hardest not to offend the goddess. "We're losing our powers and our gods at the same time. If this is the gratitude of the Mothers, then you are indeed beyond cruel. You taught us to use magic. You made us dependent on it. And now you're telling us we should just forget about it all? If that wasn't enough, you're also planning to turn your back on us? What did we do to justify such treatment?"

Ana-Isara's black gaze wandered through the temple while she thought about the man's words. When she focused on the group again, there was a smile on her lips.

"It seems I have to apologize. My sister and I never thought about showing gratitude to something we created ourselves, and for a special purpose as well. But your words carry weight, and they do have meaning to me, even if I did not see things from your perspective until now. Life and death are the rhythm to which this planet will dance for all eternity, even though Ana-Aruna and I won't be here for much longer. If I gave you two new gods, gods who are bound to stay because they are a part of Ana-Darasa, will that suffice as gratitude?"

The leaders looked at each other, unsure what to make of this offer. Again the tall man spoke.

"We had hoped you and your sister would stay here, Ana-Isara."

With a sad smile, Ana-Isara touched the man's cheek.

"This is a wish we cannot grant. There is only one place we can stay for a prolonged time, and that is the Green Lands."

The man inhaled deeply.

"So be it. We humbly and gratefully accept the gods you will send to us."

Ana-Isara bowed her head slightly.

"I shall go, then, and collect the essence of Ana-Darasa."

The group watched her leave the temple. After a long silence, the tall man spoke again.

"At least we won't be a people without gods."

One of the women made a hissing sound.

"To be frank, I'd rather be without a god than without my magic."

"That can't be helped. You know it. The stream of magic is tamed, and it won't be long until we can no longer use it at all. You better get used to the idea."

Again the woman made a derogatory sound but couldn't find any other response. She was the first who left, closely followed by a young man and another female. The tall man watched them go and sighed.

"I only hope Ana-Isara can bring the new gods soon."

Upon those words, Casto heard a trickling noise from the back of the temple. Unconsciously, he followed the sound to the fountain. The water was overflowing and seeped into the cracks between the tiles. In the gloom it looked dark, like blood. Casto shuddered. As an Ummanian, he wasn't prone to superstition or beliefs in Mothers and magic, though he had had to adjust his system of belief several times since he'd met the Barbarian. The ominous color of the water, though, combined with what he had just witnessed, was enough to make the hair on the nape of his neck stand up.

"Lys! Get me out!"

There was a sharp whinny, and the next moment, the illusion was gone. Casto stood under the glaring sunlight between the remnants of the roof that had once covered the fountain. Lys was right next to him with a worried expression. Casto patted the muscular neck of his brother.

"It's fine, Lys. I was just overwhelmed. I don't think the water really changed into blood. I guess this image was there to stress the impact of the memory. Like a vision about a future that has already happened."

Casto made a face.

"And, yes, I do realize how utterly ridiculous that sounds."

Gently, Lys guided Casto back toward their little camp. What they both needed now was some rest, something to eat, and time to sort through their thoughts.

CORNELIA WASN'T surprised when Frankus came barging into her room. One look at the stormy expression in his eyes told her that he had a bone to pick with her. Frankus was so agitated, he ignored all protocols by slamming his fists on the table where Cornelia was sitting.

"It has Nya. Whatever *it* is. This has gone on long enough, Cornelia. I know you're keeping something from me, and I didn't want to pressure you, but things are getting out of hand. If this goes on, Canubis will return to a Valley full of corpses. If there is anything you know, anything that can be done, then tell me now!"

Cornelia actually flinched at the unrelenting tone. She had always suspected Frankus was more of a leader than he wanted to let on. In this moment, it showed. He wasn't the polite, forthcoming master of the sauna anymore, but a fierce, dominant male protecting his own. If she hadn't known him for so long, Cornelia would have been afraid. She gestured toward one of the chairs.

"Please, sit."

Frankus glared at her a little longer before he took a seat. Cornelia pushed a strand of hair from her face. She was uncomfortable, and it showed.

"You are right. I do know more than I have let on. I think we're being attacked by the Good Mother. Somebody is messing with the realm of dreams. Unfortunately, there isn't much we can do. I researched it in my brother's library, but all I could find was that only somebody with strong magic or a god can control the realm of dreams."

Frankus stared at her as if he didn't believe his own ears. "You mean there is nothing we can do about it?"

"With Heljia gone and no way to contact Sic—not until Canubis and Renaldo return. I found the recipe for another potion, one that prevents people from dreaming. Fortunately, we have all the ingredients. I'm afraid this is our only option at the moment."

"What's the catch?"

Cornelia raised a brow. "Catch?"

Frankus rose and started pacing the room.

"A potion as potent as that always has a catch. The one we've been giving out so far can cause serious health issues, and the healers said it was comparatively harmless. Which makes me wonder what the side-effects of this one are, especially since you hesitated so long to suggest using it."

Cornelia pinched her nose. Frankus had put his finger right in the wound. Things were getting seriously messed up. Her own nightmares had increased since she had spoken with Heljia, and only her iron will had kept her from falling prey to the darkness that wanted to consume her. Cornelia shuddered when she thought about the sounds of scales swishing over the ground and the barely there whispers of large paws treading on what sounded like fine sand. She knew if those creatures ever caught up with her, she would be lost forever. The potion she had mentioned would only be a temporary reprieve.

"If taken in too large quantities, it is poisonous. We have to be very careful with the dosage. Only people who already have nightmares should take it, and only when they think they can't bear it anymore or are close to becoming catatonic. It is a thin line, Frankus, and we have to tread with care."

Frankus hid his face in his hands.

"Do you think we can make it until the gods return?"

Cornelia shrugged. It was a question she had pondered with growing dread herself.

"I don't know. I honestly don't know. I thought about sending them a message, but we both know the Dark Forest is far and guerilla warfare is tough. They won't be able to send help, not with Renaldo's powers getting out of control."

"We're on our own." Frankus squared his shoulders. He now looked every hand the fierce warrior he never wanted to become. "Let's make this potion and inform the people. We have a lot of work to do."

"No MATTER how long you're going to crawl on your knees and whine to those statues, they won't be coming back. Face the facts, Ulerion. Your precious Mothers have abandoned us."

Casto watched with pity as the once tall Ulerion with the impressive appearance, the man who had dared to confront Ana-Isara and convinced her to give the La'ides their own gods, slowly got to his feet. He had grown old, his hair had become thin and white, his face was full of wrinkles, and there was a desperate look in his eyes. When he answered, his voice trembled with age.

"I refuse to listen to your rantings, Sanbia, especially here, at this sacred place. The Mothers have not forsaken us, but they are testing our loyalty. If you keep your current stance, they won't have reason to be merciful."

Sanbia spat on the floor with a disgusted look on her face. She, too, had become older, but unlike Ulerion, she had not developed a softer view on things. Quite the contrary in fact. Sanbia had become cruel.

"Well, you're lucky, Ulerion. You won't have to listen to my ramblings any longer. Word has reached me that there is a new goddess on Ana-Darasa, and she promises to restore our power. I'm going to leave tomorrow to see what she has to offer."

Ulerion's eyes bulged.

"You can't be serious! Whoever that goddess is, she has no right to be here! If the Mothers find out…."

"They won't. They have left us. They don't care what we do. So why shouldn't I seek out a new god on my own since the ones who created me are gone?"

Ulerion shivered. He looked tired and worn, as if he was carrying the weight of the world. Which, in a sense, he was doing.

"If you have so little trust in the Mothers, then perhaps it's really better if you leave. I'm just asking you to reconsider. If Ana-Isara and Ana-

Aruna find out about this, they will be furious. And they won't accept any apologies along the line of 'I felt neglected, that's why I turned to another god.' The whole point of worshipping a god is to accept even the willfulness and cruel sides in exchange for the rewards."

A derisive smile contorted Sanbia's features.

"That's definitely not what I expect from my god. I only worship those who are worthy of my belief. The Mothers have turned their backs on us, and I won't crawl on my knees just to gain their love again. If they don't want me, don't want the La'ides, they have to accept that our people will look for somebody else."

With those spiteful words, Sanbia turned around and stormed out of the temple. Ulerion stood there alone, staring at the place she had just left for a long time. Casto could read all kinds of emotions flickering over the old, worn features before Ulerion finally resumed a mixture of defiance and desperate hope. He turned back to the statues of Ana-Aruna and Ana-Isara, knelt down once more, and started praying again.

Like watercolors on a sheet of paper, the figure of Ulerion changed into that of a woman, who quickly aged and was replaced by another man and then yet another woman, and on and on it went, a rapid succession of desperate faithful who clung to an impossible hope. Casto felt pity for them, as well as contempt for the Mothers, who had abandoned their own creation so cruelly. He could understand why Sanbia and the likes of her had accepted the Good Mother as their new goddess. What good did it do to place your hopes on someone who wasn't there anymore?

The changing pictures slowed down and came to a halt. A young woman with generous curves and thick black hair falling down to her waist was kneeling in front of the statues. She didn't have the same desperate aura as the ones before her. On the contrary, she was full of happy anticipation. From the entrance, footsteps resounded. Casto turned his head to see who was approaching. It was a man who looked about the same age as the kneeling female, perhaps two or three years older. He had the same plump body, and his hair was as thick and black as hers. Even if they had not looked so alike, Casto would have known they were siblings. There was a certain atmosphere around them, similar to that of Bantu and Cornelia, that spoke louder than words about their ties. The man placed a hand on his sister's shoulder. His voice was gentle.

"Dria, please, take a little break. Ever since we had that vision, you haven't left the temple even once. You need to rest or you'll be too weak to greet our new gods once they arrive."

Dria turned to her brother, a feverish light in her sparkling green eyes.

"I don't need rest, dear brother. I can feel it. They're already on their way. I'm so excited! Finally, the Mothers return to us and bring us our new gods!"

"They won't be pleased, though." The man, who Casto assumed had to be Dweian, as he had read in the prophecies about the Emeris and the hearts, sounded nervous. "The Good Mother has grown strong, and many of our kind have turned to her. It's only because the Mothers' power is still strong here that they haven't tried to conquer Quell'renar. I don't want to imagine what Ana-Aruna and Ana-Isara have to say about the treason of their children."

"What treason?"

The voice sounded like honey but had an edge that made Casto shiver. Ana-Isara had appeared in front of her own statue, and behind her, Casto saw two young men whom he recognized as Canubis and Renaldo, although they had almost nothing in common with the two fearsome warrior gods he had come to call husband and brother-in-law. Their looks were identical; neither of them had changed much over the course of the centuries. What had changed was their aura. The two men in the temple reminded Casto of wolf yearlings who already looked like their fierce, lethal parents but still emanated playfulness. Even Canubis, who Casto had always thought had been born with unwavering dominance, had the air of a young boy. The brothers looked insecure and nervous behind their mother and even flinched slightly when she repeated her question.

"What treason?"

Dweian and Dria were back on their knees, both of them trembling with fear and awe. It was Dria who managed to tame her quivering voice enough to answer.

"Please, forgive us, O Ana-Isara. Some of your children doubted that you would return to us, and in their despair, they started worshipping a new goddess who came to Ana-Darasa shortly after you had left."

Ana-Isara stared down at the kneeling siblings, her eyes so dark they seemed to swallow all light. She looked up slowly, and in that moment, Casto realized she had known all along. He felt his stomach turn and his heart constrict. She had known. It was all just a game for the Empress of the Dead. A game in which she tested the loyalty and perseverance of her creation. A game she had set up on purpose. A game in which her sons were nothing but pawns to help achieve her hidden goals. Dimly, Casto remembered that his own mother had been the same. That there had always been a meaning to everything she did and where those around her were reduced to the status of pawns. What made things worse was the knowledge about the love Ana-Isara felt for her two sons. There was no doubt she truly cared for them, which made it harder to hate her. Just like his own mother. And even though Ana-Isara as well as Queen Isiris had loved their sons, they still used them because they deemed something else more important. Or worse, didn't even realize what they were doing to their children. *Because mothers don't make mistakes*, Casto thought, full of bitterness.

He felt pity for Renaldo and Canubis. They were so young, so inexperienced. So completely at the mercy of their Mothers' whims.

"You're telling me my and my sister's creation have abandoned us because they grew tired of waiting?"

Dweian and Dria flinched. The question was accurate and painful. Dweian managed to whisper, "Yes, Ana-Isara."

The goddess stared at the kneeling siblings. There was a cruel light in her eyes, one that Casto knew only too well. It was the almost childish joy of having someone completely at your mercy. Apparently not even the Empress of the Dead was above such petty notions. Casto didn't know if that made her more likable or less. Definitely relatable, though. Perhaps the La'ides had influenced the Mothers more than Ana-Isara and Ana-Aruna had realized. Or the goddesses had always been like that and merely infused their creation with not only their magic but also their shortcomings.

"A people who would betray its Mothers so easily does not deserve to be led by gods. Seems like I made a mistake when I carried my sons to give them to you. A mistake I can correct at any time."

With those words, she turned around to Canubis and Renaldo, who stared at their mother in utter surprise. They obviously had no idea what to make of her behavior or the situation. Casto had to grit his teeth. He knew he could do nothing, that all of this had already happened, yet he felt the overwhelming urge to slap Ana-Isara in the face. Treating her own children so cruelly was beyond despicable. It did not fail to impress Dweian and Dria, though. The siblings raised their hands in a pleading gesture, begging Ana-Isara to change her will.

"Please, Empress of the Dead! Please reconsider! There are still many who stayed loyal to you and your sister. Many who waited patiently for this day to arrive! Please do not punish them for the wrongdoing of a few who could not muster the courage to face the changes your absence brought."

"Then tell me, who stayed loyal to me? Where are my children? Why isn't the temple bustling with life as it used to? Where is my guard?"

Dweian didn't dare to face his goddess when he answered.

"The cats and birds are long gone. The last bird died about three hundred years ago, and the cats vanished shortly after into the wild. We don't know if there are any left. Only the wolves are still here, and it's getting harder and harder for them to change. Some of them are caught in one shape, unable to shift anymore, yet still they protect the temple for you and stand guard in front of the doors."

"Their loyalty will be rewarded. What about my other children? The witch clans and the common people?"

This time it was Dria who answered.

"The common people are doing well. They are building cities along the Umman and out in the plains. They still worship you and your sister, although some of them have also turned to the Good Mother. The witch clans are almost gone, just like the wolves. Our powers are waning. It has been fifty years since the last time-bender was born, and the other clans aren't faring much better. My brother and I were a pleasant surprise. Seers as strong as we are have last walked Ana-Darasa more than two hundred years ago. The only ones who are still doing quite well are the healers, and even their numbers are decreasing. Without our gods, we will perish soon enough."

Ana-Isara had listened intently to Dweian's and Dria's pleas. Her voice was a lot softer now, with most of the edges gone.

"I see. And you are right. I cannot punish those who stayed loyal to me and my sister. On the other hand, I also cannot allow those who turned their backs on us get away unscathed."

She looked up at the ceiling of the temple.

"The wolves shall come now."

Ana-Isara had not raised her voice, yet still an answering howl pierced the air. The temple's gates burst open, and about thirty wolves and humans entered. Ana-Isara regarded them with warmth in her eyes.

"You stayed loyal and kept on trusting in my sister and me. For that, you shall be rewarded. I cannot give you back the power of change, not anymore. But I can give you a promise. If you decide to stay loyal to my sons and serve them as the new masters of Ana-Darasa, then, on the day they take over this world in all their glory, what was lost will be returned."

The pack stared at the goddess for a long time. Casto found it unnerving to see the same predatory gaze in beasts and humans alike, but Ana-Isara didn't mind. She held the gazes to show her sincerity. Finally, a tall, lean woman spoke.

"It would be our pleasure, Ana-Isara."

Like one, the wolves and humans lowered their heads to show their devotion. Ana-Isara beamed at them. She was obviously pleased about the decision.

"So let it be!"

There was a growl, and then the remaining humans turned into wolves as well. Casto knew they would never change back to their biped shape, not in a long time. It also explained the bond between the wolves and Canubis and Renaldo. It had been forged by Ana-Isara herself. The pack looked expectantly at its new gods, but before anything could happen, Ana-Isara spoke on, now with vengefulness tinging her voice.

"That still leaves the matter of punishment. I will not take your gods from you, but the La'ides have to prove that they are worthy to follow their gods."

She turned around to her sons once more. Her hands snaked out quickly and vanished inside Renaldo's and Canubis's chests. The two boys—because in this moment, that was all they were—grabbed their mother's wrists in a helpless attempt to stop her. Ana-Isara kept on talking as if nothing were amiss.

"I take your hearts and entrust them to chance. Only when you find them among the La'ides will you be able to regain your full power. From today on, you will rule as demigods until the La'ides are once again united under one reign. My sister and I won't walk Ana-Darasa anymore except in the dreams of those loyal to us."

Ana-Isara pulled back her hands with a rigid motion. Something glittered in her palms like a dying star and then winked out. The goddess kissed her sons' foreheads and then faded from vision like mist in the morning sun.

The silence following Ana-Isara's leave was beyond awkward. The wolves cowered, whimpering on the ground, and Dweian and Dria only stared at the spot where the goddess had vanished, while her sons stood like statues, with their hands pressed to their chests. It was Dweian who finally managed to shake off the spell and slowly approached the two young men who were his leaders and gods.

"Welcome to Ana-Darasa, Masters. How do you wish to be addressed by us?"

As if the words had jolted him from a dream, Canubis focused his amber eyes on Dweian, who flinched at the fierceness.

"My name is Canubis, the Wolf of War, and this is my brother, Renaldo, the Angel of Death. You may call us master or lord. We don't care either way."

Dweian cleared his throat. If Canubis's behavior offended him in any way, he didn't show it.

"As you wish, Master. Would you like me to show you around?"

"You may do so. And tell us everything about this other god. We don't like competition, so you better prepare yourselves for war."

Dweian shuddered but didn't comment. Together with Dria, he led Canubis and Renaldo outside the temple to introduce them to their people and show them Quell'renar.

Casto didn't know what to make of the scene he had just witnessed. He felt pity for Renaldo and Canubis, who had been so cruelly used and abandoned by their own mother. It also made him more understanding of their behavior, which in turn fueled his anger about himself. Then there was the contempt he felt for Ana-Isara and her sister. It was a resentment he had been nourishing from the moment he realized that his fate was already decided, that he was irrefutably linked to Renaldo. Seeing how Sic had suffered and now reexperiencing what Renaldo and Canubis—and the La'ides—had gone through did not soften his attitude toward the Mothers.

The things he had seen also made him understand another part of the bond he shared with the Barbarian. They both suffered from strong, merciless mothers, even though he had not really known Isiris, for she had died when he was too young to see her as anything but the woman who had given birth to him. What he had known was the despair of a child realizing the person it adored most did not reciprocate the feeling of love offered and, at the same time, knew it would, and had to, do the mother's bidding.

Casto grinned grimly. As twisted relationships went, he and the Barbarian always seemed to win the first prize. He turned to Lys, who had been standing next to him all the time.

"Get us out of here. I'm done for today."

Lys snorted, and the illusion crumbled like dried-out earth.

3. FINDING TRUTH

WHEN LUKAN entered the tent he shared with Elua, he looked as if he had taken a bath in the blood of his enemies. His eyes shone unnaturally white in his dirty face, and where his armor wasn't red, it was smeared with other things one could only hope were just mud.

"I assume you were successful?" Elua approached her husband, wondering where she could touch him without staining her clean clothes. With a sigh, Lukan started fumbling with the clasps of his belt.

"Yes. We took out a group of twenty. Now that Lord Sic is pumping us full with his power, all those little magical traps that cost us so many of our people don't have an impact anymore. At least not on the Echend'dim. I lost five warriors today. Four of them are now part of the Eternal Guard."

"Your numbers are growing." Both Lukan and Elua flinched a little when she said that, again putting up walls between them by her choice of words. They tried their best not to talk about the implications of Lukan's status as not only Echend'dim but also second-in-command after Lord Daran. The changes in their relationship dynamic were weird enough without Elua adding to it all by confessing to her husband how unwilling she was to become immortal. Sometimes she had the feeling that Lukan viewed it all as a great adventure, and it hurt her feelings because it made her wonder how her young husband saw their marriage. Was that, too, just another adventure? One Lukan was now replacing with another? Deep inside, Elua knew her thoughts were not only unkind but also unsubstantiated, though it didn't keep her from pondering them. She watched as Lukan slipped out of his tunic, dropping it next to his belt and his boots.

"Yes, we are growing in numbers. Though I'm not sure Lord Sic is as happy as Lord Canubis and Lord Renaldo."

"Does he still have problems with the bond?" Now Elua was worried. She had known Sic since he came to the Valley as a boy. The changes he had seen in his life were more than most people had to suffer, and if Sic was insecure, it meant danger for her husband, whom she loved deeply, no matter the strains their relationship was currently experiencing.

"I'm not sure if it's the bond. There's a lot going on with Lord Sic, and most of it has to do with his Luksari nature. Nobody says it out loud, but with Lord Renaldo being so unstable at the moment, Lord Sic is the one whose powers are most important, after the Wolf of War." Lukan made a face. "And Lord Sic doesn't do well under pressure."

Elua nodded. From slave to traitor to free man to Luksari and Emeris within a year, and yet until now, Lord Sic had managed to not fall apart, even though there had been some close calls as rumor in the Pack had it. If she were a cynic, she'd say it was about time. Lukan was now completely naked and on his way to the back of the tent, where they had a bathtub waiting. The water was cold, which wasn't too pleasant because the temperatures in the Dark Forest were, while not exactly cold, not hot enough to make a cold bath desirable. At least the blood went off easier that way.

"Do you think he will crack?"

Lukan shrugged and then winced when he started rubbing off the grime of battle with a sponge. "To be honest, I don't know. He's a lot stronger than he looks and gives himself credit for. And there's Lord Noran, who seems to have become his pillar of strength, surprising as that may seem. We can only hope Lord Sic will find a balance which allows him to serve the gods well."

Elua stepped closer to the bathtub, took the sponge from Lukan, and started washing his back. Only a few months ago, her husband wouldn't have found such diplomatic words. His new status had not only changed their relationship but also him, and Elua still wasn't sure if she liked it. Sighing, she traced the now clean skin with her fingertips. Her husband was a very fine man, one she didn't regret taking into her bed.

The question was, would he one day regret following her?

THE MAN in the camp cursed loudly and swept the three cups on the small table in his tent to the ground. Things were not going as planned, and the displeasure of the Good Mother was like a weight around his neck. The red wine spreading on the woven carpet at his feet reminded him of all the unpleasant ways a person who disappointed the Good Mother could die. He was not at a happy place at the moment, caught between the Gods of War and the wrath of the Good Mother. While he had expected for things to get rough, he hadn't anticipated for it to happen so fast. With the Angel of Death crippled because of his missing heart, they should have been able to do a lot more damage to the Pack. Instead, more than half of the men they had managed to kill had come back as Echend'dim, a lot stronger and potentially immortal. To make matters worse, they still hadn't been able to find King Castolus, who would make a fine hostage if they ever managed to get their hands on him. Normally, the king and the snake witch were like beacons, drawing the inner eye of the seers with their brightness. While the witch was still emitting said light, the king was now wreathed in shadows, not even glimpses of him permeating the darkness hiding him from the world. The only consolation the man had was that not only their own seers but nobody else, not even the Angel of Death, was able to track the king.

The man went over to the huge wooden chest he had standing next to his bed. At the bottom, buried under layers of clothing and furs, there was another chest, much smaller and flat. The wood had turned black because of what it contained. If it weren't for the runes keeping the thing inside quiet, the wood would have already burned to ashes. This was the ace up his sleeve, the one thing that could turn the tide in their favor before the real battle even started. But he had to be careful. If he showed his hand too early, if the bastard brothers found out about this little tool that could destroy them, they would be able to act. No, he had to bide his time, had to find the perfect moment to literally stab the bastards and their Emeris in the back.

TIRED TO his bones, Jago approached the house of Aries, the guild master of the smiths. After a long day in the smithy, all he wanted was to be home with his daughter and wife and her apprentice, who was quickly becoming a part of their household. Arelo reminded him a bit of Sic, not in his looks, for the boy was tall and lanky, moved still with the awkwardness of youth, where Sic was small and compact, his movements steeled by a life full of hardships, but in his gentle nature and his willingness to see the good in people, even if they constantly proved him wrong. The cynical part of Jago, the one that had been living in Ummana for too long, wondered when the young man would finally get corrupted by the city's general wretchedness. He hoped it wouldn't happen too soon, because Heljia needed positive influences in her life. After the shock about finding out she was visiting Sic and the Valley in her dreams, Jago and Cassia had kept a close eye on her. Apparently their daughter had stopped going to the Valley, but not necessarily because he had forbidden it. Jago was under no illusion that

Heljia would do whatever she thought was best, regardless of what he or Cassia told her. And she was only two. He didn't dare think about the conflicts in his future once she grew older.

With a sigh, Jago entered the house after a servant had opened the door. Aries's message had been cryptic, stating he needed to talk to him immediately. Since refusing a summons from the guild master was considered rude to the extreme, and because Jago liked Aries better than most of the other smiths in the guild, he had agreed to visit him right after he was done with his daily duties. Every last piece of Sic's work was already sold, and the list of new orders was growing steadily. In an attempt to shield Sic from the demands of the Ummanians, far away as they may be from the Valley, he had started to schedule some of those orders for the winter after the coming one so Sic wouldn't feel pressured to work himself to the bone during the winter when he should technically recover from the strains of the summer campaign. Jago wasn't sure how much recovery time a Luksari needed, but he knew for a fact that Sic was prone to overworking himself because he didn't want to disappoint people.

With his thoughts still half focused on Sic, Jago entered Aries's study, a room as pompous as one would expect from the guild master of one of the most influential guilds in the city—which was exactly what Aries wanted to accomplish. Jago had known the other man long enough to be aware of his strategies. By giving people what they expected, Aries lulled them into a very false and dangerous sense of security. After all, an enemy you knew was an enemy you didn't have to fear. Unfortunately for all those seeking to take advantage of the seemingly luxury-loving and slow-thinking Aries, there was a reason the man was guild master, and it wasn't because of the pretty color of his eyes.

Jago would never be so foolish as to think he knew how Aries thought, which was the reason he approached this whole meeting with caution. "Master Aries." He inclined his head toward the man, who had been sitting behind his desk and was now getting up with more grace than one would have given a man of his stature credit for.

"Master Jago." Aries extended a hand and they shook, keeping up the pretense of a formal meeting. Aries led Jago to a low couch at the wall on the right side of his huge desk. On a small table next to it stood a jug and two cups made of silver with an intricate pattern etched into the rims, which Jago recognized as Aries's signature form. The guild master poured some wine into each of the cups and held one out to Jago. He took it with a small nod, thanking Aries for the gesture of hospitality.

"What can I do for you, Master Aries?" Jago was too tired to wait for Aries to do the typical Ummanian dancing around the subject until it passed out from vertigo. And yes, he was willing to admit he had taken a page out of King Castolus's book in that regard. If Aries was taken aback by his bluntness, he didn't show it. Instead, a small smile flitted across his usually stern features.

"I think the question should rather be what can I do for you, Jago." By leaving out his official title, Aries made clear this meeting had just turned into something informal, though not less important. Jago took a sip from his wine, a very good one, he noted, light and fruity, just like he preferred them. He had an inkling where this conversation was headed and chose his words carefully.

"Is there something I need the backing of the guild master for?"

Aries sighed. "You know there is, Jago. Let's cut to the chase here." When he caught Jago's raised eyebrows, Aries flashed him a smile that even reached his eyes before turning serious again. "It may not always seem like it, but I'm perfectly capable of being as blunt as King Castolus himself, and since I know you've come to appreciate this approach to things, I can adapt. As to why I've asked you to come here, I recently had the great joy to be visited by Desdon, Hellwar, and Irr'es and listened to their ranting about how unfair it is that you get to hog all the business Lord Sic generates here in Ummana. It was the fourth time I had to endure their laments, and while their predictability helped me tune out for most of it, the growing hostility yanked me right back. These men are becoming more and more impatient, and it's only a matter of time until my power as guild master ceases to hold sway over them."

Jago groaned. "Are you telling me you fear they're going to go against you or me or both of us? Or is this your way of subtly informing me that you won't be protecting me anymore?"

Aries hesitated for a moment, took his time to have another sip of wine. "You may not believe me, but I do consider myself your ally, if not your friend. I have every intention of making you my successor, even though you're still opposed to it." Aries held up a hand to stop Jago from telling him exactly what he thought of this idea. "I know every point you have to make about the topic, so don't waste your breath. I also know you will come around to see things from my perspective in time, and I'm a patient man. This also means the two of us have a mutual problem, one we have to address soon, before it gets out of hand. The time to feign ignorance is over."

Jago stared at Aries, not sure how to react now. He knew the man was right. He was grateful Aries was willing to back him up. He was furious because he didn't want what Aries was offering—more power—and knew deep down he would give in just like the guild master had said. Sometimes Jago wished King Castolus and the Gods of War had never come to Ummana. He always felt guilty for it, because then he wouldn't have met Sic, and he probably would have lost Cassia when she gave birth to Heljia. It was a good thing the gods had come to Ummana. If he didn't like part of the aftermath, it was entirely on him.

"What do you suggest?"

For a moment, Aries had a look of disbelief on his face. Clearly, he had anticipated more resistance from Jago. "I'm not a fool, Aries. I may wish things were different and I may have hesitated to act until now because all this scheming makes me want to throw up, and I had hoped by clearly showing my disinterest in participating, I could avoid getting involved, but this strategy has obviously failed if you feel the need to confront me so directly. So again, what do you suggest?"

Aries grinned. "And this, my friend, is the reason I want you to be my successor. You have no ambition for power, yet you do what's necessary when the time comes. The hallmarks of a good guild master." When Jago opened his mouth to comment on this, Aries hurried to keep talking. "There are several things you can do. The first and easiest would be to give in to their demands and talk Lord Sic into letting them have a share in the profits. We all know he listens to you. Unfortunately, others will follow in our trio's footsteps, which is not what we want. Plus, we both know how greedy those three bastards are. If you give in, they're going to demand more and more to the point where you have to put a stop to it. Which brings us to possibility number two, ending this whole mess once and for all. Since you have the queen's ear, you could go to Anesha, ask her for help. Some would see this as a sign of weakness, others would perceive it as a demonstration of power. Depending on how elaborate our queen's reaction would be, it would very publicly cement the status you're still trying to pretend you don't possess."

"What makes you think Queen Anesha would help me? I may be the master of the royal smithy, but I can be easily replaced." Jago was aware how stubborn he sounded. Like Heljia when it was time to go to bed.

All Aries had for him was a pitying look. "Please, Jago. Cassia saved Anesha's life when she gave birth to our prince. Everybody knows that, and even in Ummana, there is such a thing as a life debt. And I know Cassia would never invoke it, which is one of the reasons Anesha protects your family so fiercely. The other three reasons are King Castolus, Lord Sic, and Heljia."

"Heljia?" Jago had a sinking feeling in his stomach. He knew Anesha would side with him because of Sic and Casto. He had hoped to keep his daughter out of it.

From the compassion in Aries's eyes, Jago knew Heljia's secret wasn't so secret anymore.

"There are rumors about your daughter, how she doesn't cast a shadow and carries her own light, blessed by the Luksari. So far, it's nothing more, but you can bet Anesha knows, and the older Heljia gets, the more obvious things will become."

Jago felt his shoulders slumping. "She's only two."

"And well protected, never doubt that. I dare say nobody in Ummana is foolish enough to go against the girl who calls an Emeris uncle. At the moment all it means is added protection from Anesha. Which is why you should entertain the thought of involving her."

"Is that what you would do?"

Aries shrugged. "I'd probably choose a more direct approach, but I know you don't like bloodshed."

The coldness in those words made Jago shudder. Yes, Desdon, Hellwar, and Irr'es were insufferable assholes of the highest order, but still, Jago couldn't bring himself to even think about removing them permanently from his long list of problems. "Would this be the third possibility? Getting rid of them?"

"It's a point to be considered."

"What about talking to them?"

Aries laughed without any humor in his voice. "Good luck with that. All they would see is an attempt to keep them from profits they think they have a right to."

Unfortunately, Aries was right. In their heads, the three master smiths were doubtlessly thinking they had a right to get a share of any profit Jago made through Sic. How they came to this conclusion was not important. Nobody could hope to understand the mix of sheer arrogance, denial of reality, and entitlement it took to reason that way. It wasn't a uniquely Ummanian trait either, though definitely better developed in the Twin Cities than elsewhere.

"Anesha it is. I'm trying to get an audience with her within the week. Do I have a week?"

"Definitely." Aries touched Jago's arm. "You're doing the right thing."

"Then why do I feel like an apprentice on his first day in the smithy?"

Aries raised his cup. "Welcome to the higher politics of Ummana."

Jago made a face. He couldn't wait to get home to Cassia and Heljia.

CAPTAIN AKTAN rocked his son in his arms while he watched the boy's mother, the Queen of Ummana and his lover, mull over the reports from her spies. The way her brows were furrowed told him what she was reading wasn't entirely to her liking, though not bad enough to have her mumbling under her breath. Only once had Aktan been close enough to hear what she was saying in those moments, and it made him grateful his beautiful queen didn't have access to the same powers as King Castolus. Anesha wasn't made of stone; she was hewn from a diamond, all sparkling and pretty and just as cold and unfeeling. Aktan had no illusions about the place he held in Anesha's system of values. Even though he knew there was no real love between them, knowing his place so exactly made things easier. And he had certainly risen in his sister's esteem. While his relationship with Lady Evienna had never been bad—she did appreciate his position as Captain of the Royal Guard and knew better than to endanger it with petty schemes when there was a bigger goal on the horizon—it hadn't been one of familial love either. If such a thing was even possible in any of the great families in Ummana. Sometimes Aktan envied Jago the simple and deep love he shared with his wife, Cassia.

Seeing the distress on the master smith's face during the audience with Anesha earlier this day, where Jago had asked the queen to help him with some overly greedy fellow smiths, had reminded Aktan how dangerous emotions could be. Because of the very thing Aktan envied him for, Jago had to rely on others to help him protect his family in the predator-infested waters of Ummanian politics. If pressed to choose, Aktan was almost sure he would go for the life he had now—colder on the emotional side, though safer, because when you didn't have anything of value to lose, life was less complicated.

He looked down into the face of his now peacefully sleeping son. He had something of value to lose now. Not the future king of Ummana, not a valuable piece on the huge gameboard that was the Twin Cities, but a tiny person he loved more than anything else in the world. It was a strange feeling, this warmth in his chest whenever he thought about his son. Aktan wondered what he was willing to sacrifice for this little person who was part him and part a woman he may not love but had a deep respect and admiration for. The answer was too startling to consciously grasp it.

The soft rustling of silk on the intricately woven carpet made him look up. Anesha had almost reached him, her usual indifferent mask of queenly arrogance replaced by a soft smile that was as close to affection as she could get. Aktan didn't hold it against her. The way Anesha had been raised, he was surprised she was as stable as she appeared to be. Then again, King Castolus had endured even worse, and he had turned out… not normal, not sane, not well-adjusted, but balanced enough to function effectively in a world that had always let him down. Aktan shuddered, thinking about the power Castolus had at the tips of fingers. If he wanted to, he could destroy everything, either with his own means or by batting his lashes until the Angel of Death did the work for him.

Anesha sat down next to him on the lounge, briefly touching Regulon's peaceful face. Their son was developing perfectly, a fat, happy baby with the disturbingly blue eyes of his mother. "Erac is starting to get on my nerves."

It was a simple statement. Aktan knew Anesha did not seek his council, at least not in words. What she needed was somebody to listen to her while she thought out loud, playing different scenarios in her head, weighing the outcome of every path she could take. Sometimes he would offer some words of encouragement or—very rarely—his take on a particular situation, but so far this had only happened with problems relating directly to Anesha's safety. Politics concerning the Alliance were too complicated for Aktan's taste.

"The other cities are starting to question my leadership, not out loud, but Erac's constant nagging is getting to them." Anesha tapped her right index finger against her cheek. "I guess it's time to show them all how dangerous angering me is for their health." The cold glint in her eyes told Aktan Erac's days were numbered and he wouldn't need all his fingers to count them down. The stupid man had never gotten over the fact he'd first been led around by the nose by King Castolus, who he had refused to acknowledge as his king, and then thwarted in his desperate attempts at finding a way back into power by Anesha, whom he saw as no more than a child. Well, Anesha was no child, and anybody who thought her being a woman made her in any way weak was in for a nasty and deadly surprise— as Erac would find out soon enough.

"What do you make of Jago's request?"

It took Aktan a moment to realize his queen was addressing him directly. He thought about it for a moment.

"I think he's woefully unprepared for Ummanian politics and now finds himself in the middle of it. I have no idea how a man as honest as him has made it to master smith of the royal guild, because normally men like him are destroyed quickly in this city. He needs you to keep his family safe."

Anesha started undoing the braids that made up her elaborate hairdo. "Not to mention Castolus would be standing at my doorstep the minute he thinks I can't protect his best friend's family. And where Casto goes, the Angel of Death isn't far away." Anesha shuddered, no doubt remembering the disturbing show of force she and Aktan had witnessed when the Gods of War had visited Ummana. It was another thread binding him and the queen with a strange kinship—knowing the terror the Angel of Death and the Wolf of War could unleash at any given moment.

"Not to mention Lord Sic. His ties with Heljia are more than just between uncle and niece." It was an open secret that Jago and Cassia's daughter was magically gifted. Anybody who saw the child could immediately tell there was more to her than just the white hair or the fact she never cast a shadow.

Anesha had her hair loose now, carding through the wheat-blond strands with her fingers, sometimes twisting parts around themselves before letting them go again. "Even if it wasn't for the very real threat of my brother and the Angel of Death coming back to Ummana, Heljia must be protected at all costs. I'm not sure what she's capable of, but I want whatever power she wields to be on my side." She got up to get a brush from her vanity. "It's decided, then. I'm going to crush those three master smiths in a very clear show of strength, letting everybody know Jago and his family are under my protection. Anybody who goes against him, goes against me." Anesha started brushing her hair. "Let's just hope there are no suicidal fools around who decide to act against Jago out of spite."

That was a possibility, though an unlikely one, always depending on how hard Anesha came down on those smiths. Given her situation, he had no doubts people would think twice and then again before doing anything foolish.

CORNELIA STOOD in the plaza of the village where she had grown up, the by now all too familiar stench of burning wood and other, more unpleasant things, assaulting her nose. She didn't move, didn't dare to, for she knew what kind of horrors she was going to face, the same she had been facing for the past seven nights. Although the events of that day had taken place hundreds of years ago, they had decided to come back and haunt her, now of all times, when she needed all her wits to face the dangers threatening the people in the Valley.

Sound joined the stench, the high-pitched screams of children in utter panic, the wails and curses of the old folks as they were slaughtered like pigs. Out of the corner of her eye, Cornelia glimpsed movement and spun around. Nothing but smoke illuminated by the ghastly flames eating away the small, pitiful huts she and the other villagers called home.

Gravel crunched under heavy footsteps, footsteps she dreaded every time the nightmare set in. She turned again, this time slowly, hoping against better judgment that things would be different this time.

Her heart sank. He was there, about her size, small, cruel eyes made savage by all the killing they had witnessed, thin, cracked lips contorted into the parody of a smile, a sturdy yet somehow worn body splattered with the blood of his victims. He parted his lips, letting out a voice she would never forget, no matter how long her existence may drag on.

"You're not much, but you will do."

Cornelia tensed, then straightened her back. This man had almost killed and broken her once, had been haunting her for more than one lifetime. It was time to face him. She watched as he extended his hands toward her, those callused, unrelenting hands that had taken all joy about the Mothers' gift from her. Again she heard that rustling sound behind her, but she didn't dare turn her back on the human monster in front of her. If she had to relive the most terrifying moments of her life, the moments that had shaped her very being, she would do it with her head held high. She was a survivor, and even though the monster in front of her seemed all too real, part of her knew she had outlived him by centuries. This knowledge was a small consolation for what he had done—and would do again, if the nightmare played out the same as every single night during the last week.

One last time before he could reach her, Cornelia tried to leave the dream like she had practiced so often, and just like the other nights, something held her back, kept her from fleeing into safety. Her instincts were warring, some of them screaming at her to try to flee while others insisted she had to stay, had to see what would be happening, had to take control, even though she didn't know how to. Before she could decide either way, she felt something moving at her back. It was the same presence she'd always felt when her dreams were especially vivid, the very reason she had trained so hard to be able to escape the dreamworld. Only there was no escaping now.

The rapist's eyes suddenly grew wide, almost popping out of their sockets, and the genuine terror on his face would warm Cornelia on all the cold winter days to come. The movements and rustling behind her back raised the hair on her nape, but before she could decide how to react, which threat to address first, a nightmarish shadow pounced forward. She could feel a whiff of air as the creature brushed past her to grab the immobilized marauder in front of her. Three snake heads, each as big as a pony's and armored with fangs as long as the span between her elbow and the tip of her middle finger, shot out and tore into the body of the shrieking man. The torso of the creature was that of a bear, with a coat the color of dried leaves. It was about three times bigger than a horse, with sturdy muscles coiling underneath the thick pelt. Each of the heads had gained a steady hold on their victim, trying to get the biggest chunk out of him. When the body finally tore, a rain of blood and innards splattered on the ground and smeared the sleek, brilliantly yellow scales on the heads with different hues of red.

Strangely detached, Cornelia watched as the heads tossed their prey high in the air, caught it skillfully, and devoured the pieces greedily. It was the most fitting punishment for that lowlife she could have thought of, and a surge of gratitude swamped Cornelia's heart, that had been turned into stone so long ago. The creature turned to her. Its middle head stretched slowly, as if to assure her that it meant no harm. Or perhaps it was just lulling her into a false sense of peace to be able to devour her more easily. This close, Cornelia could see the creature possessed an innate beauty, despite the red and greenish smears on the gorgeous scales. There was an elegance to the movements of the head, how the muscles bunched under the fur that looked silken instead of shaggy.

Fascinated, Cornelia took one tiny step forward and then another. The closer she looked at the creature, the more beautiful she thought it was. She held out her hand in what she hoped wasn't a misplaced show of trust, and the snake head touched the tip of her fingers with its snout. The moment her skin connected with the warm scales, Cornelia felt peace wash over her.

And then she knew.

Tears came to her eyes when she felt the love the creature had for her. A love it shared with all the other beasts in the realm of dreams. Cornelia started to pet the head. She was so overwhelmed, it took her two tries before she was able to speak.

"I love you too. I'm so sorry. I only realize now that you are my children."

The snake hummed softly, a noise Cornelia would have expected coming from a cat. There was more rustling, and when she looked up, she was surrounded by creatures of all kinds. Some looked like the snake-bear she was petting, and others had the body of a horse, the head of an eagle and big leathery wings. There were crossings between snakes and birds, lions and horses, small creatures the size of a housecat and others as big as a house. Cornelia felt her connection to all of them, and she knew they were hers to command and love. She smiled.

"Somebody is invading the dreams of the people in the Valley. Find them and kill them."

The creatures held their heads up as if they were searching for a scent. Some of them vanished in pairs or threes, others alone. The snake-bear nudged Cornelia. She nodded.

"Let's find Sira."

"HEY, LITTLE brother. What are you doing here?"

Canubis entered the sanctuary where Renaldo sat brooding on the ground and stared at the endlessly flowing water.

"I'm trying to think."

Canubis sighed deeply and sat down next to his little brother. He slung his arm around Renaldo's hip and listened to his little brother's sorrow, which was identical to his own.

"It's been three months since Mother brought us here, and so far, nothing has gone as planned. The La'ides were supposed to welcome us, full of gratitude and joy. Instead, we find a people who have partially abandoned the Mothers. They turned their backs on the ones who created them! And those who are still loyal—I can see the disappointment in their eyes whenever they look at us. We were supposed to be their gods, but now we are only demigods who can't even control our powers anymore. They're abandoning us by the dozens, running to that parasitic Good Mother who lures them with sweet promises of a paradise that is gone forever. And just look at that so-called army we have now. We've already lost almost a third of our warriors due to our inexperience, which causes distrust to grow in their ranks. If this goes on, the Good Mother doesn't have to lift a single finger to win."

Renaldo glared heatedly at Canubis.

"You know what the worst part is? I don't mind. It's their fault we are in this sorry state. I've been really looking forward to meeting our people, and now I hate them for being the way they are."

In a soothing gesture, Canubis rubbed his head against Renaldo's shoulder, just like a lion might to reassure its young. "They're not all bad. Some of them are truly loyal, like Dweian and Dria. They deserve our trust. Although I do have to admit I feel my hands itching with murderous intent when I think about the injustice we have to endure because of the La'ides."

"Then how do you do it? Refrain from killing them all, I mean."

A cold smile that made shivers run down Renaldo's back lightened Canubis's features.

"I imagine what kind of god I'm going to be to them once we have eliminated the Good Mother. I'm going to make them pay for everything. The La'ides will cower under our rule, and their cries and pleas will be like music to our ears."

Renaldo snuggled closer to his older brother.

"Sounds tempting. I can already see them cowering."

He hesitated for a moment. There were feelings they both shared, but which had not been said in the open yet. They were still shaken by the loss of their hearts, which made things even more complicated. Renaldo felt this was the time to open up to Canubis.

"I feel so empty inside, brother. Why did Mother do that? It's as if somebody has ripped out my most integral part. It hurts all the time. The pain never stops. How long are we supposed to feel that way?"

"I don't know, Renaldo, I don't know. We have to trust that Mother does know what she's doing and that we will find our hearts soon. Until then, we have to try and make the best of it. I'm fully aware how helpless it sounds, but just sitting here and wallowing in self-pity won't change a thing."

Renaldo furrowed his brows. "I'm not wallowing. Maybe a bit. To be honest, I'm terrified. There's a beast inside me, and it's growing stronger every day. I don't know how long I'll be able to keep it down."

Canubis reared back a bit and grabbed Renaldo's shoulders. His amber eyes pierced Renaldo's insecure gaze. "As long as it's necessary, Renaldo. Because you *are* my little brother, and because you *are* strong. There's no way you'll lose to your nature."

Canubis had spoken with more conviction than he felt and was glad when he heard the sound of approaching footsteps to divert them from this worrisome topic. They left the sanctuary to find Dria hurrying toward them. Her face was full of worry and a hint of fear. Canubis tried his best to force a smile to his lips, knowing the young woman was one of the few who truly worshipped him and Renaldo.

"Dria! Why are you in such a hurry? Has anything happened?"

Dria stopped abruptly in front of them, evading Canubis's gaze.

"Indeed, something has happened, Master. Dweian and I had a vision, one you won't welcome with joy."

"What did you see?"

Canubis didn't even try to keep up the friendly façade anymore. Dria gulped before she started talking so fast, her tongue tripped over some of the words.

"The Mothers appeared to us. Apparently, Ana-Aruna was not satisfied with the severity of the punishment Ana-Isara had given. She decreed that in addition to finding your hearts, you also have to welcome eight so-called Emeris into your ranks before you can regain your power. They will be marked by Ana-Isara herself as part of your family. The Mothers have given us glimpses of what they will be. If you want, I can tell you."

Canubis didn't know how he managed to shake off the rigor Dria's words had caused. His voice was hoarse when he answered the seer, barely able to keep his raging fury under control.

"Later, Dria. You can tell us later. Now please leave us alone. My brother and I have to talk about this in detail."

With a deep curtsey, Dria left, and Canubis pretended not to have seen the utter relief in her eyes. As soon as she was out the doors, Renaldo grabbed a head-high statue of a bird and smashed it on the ground as if it weighed nothing more than a feather.

"I've had enough! I want them to pay. I want them to suffer. There is nothing that will ever make me forgive the La'ides! Nothing!"

Canubis watched in silence as his brother destroyed yet another statue. He did nothing to prevent the deed since it was exactly what he thought had to be done at the moment. It was like a promise between him and Renaldo that they would make their own people pay for what they had done.

From the shadows, Casto witnessed the violent scene, unable to avert his gaze and terrified to his core by the rage the divine brothers emanated. He had thought he'd seen Renaldo's worst side, only to realize that none of the fights they had came even close to the intensity of Renaldo's fury back at the beginning of his life on Ana-Darasa. The bitter irony of the situation was almost enough to cause Casto to giggle. The gods who had been born to redeem their people would now be the ones to speak their verdict. The La'ides were about to pay a high prize for their treason. When Casto thought about it, he could see another parallel to his own life. He, too, had come to Ummana to reclaim what was rightfully his, only to have it handed to him in such a twisted way, he had no problem giving it up in the end, not without taking cruel revenge first.

4. NEW DIRECTIONS

SIC WAS sitting in the tent he shared with Noran, his legs crossed on the soft fur his dark lover had gifted him right before they went on the campaign into the Dark Forest. The revelation that he was able to pump the Echend'dim full of his power to overcome the ancient magic laced with fortune spells woven into the very fabric of the woods had not tipped the scales in their favor, because the enemy was cunning and ruthless in his use of magic, but it had evened the playing field, which made it possible for the Pack to play on its strengths—masterful swordsmanship and perfect interaction between the warriors.

Still, there were more members of the Pack dying than was usual for such a campaign, and Sic was calling more and more of them back. He knew by now why he couldn't determine who would be an Echend'dim before the person died. Their suitability wasn't apparent by outward signs and didn't come from any special circumstances at their births or other romantic notions one would have suspected behind the honor of gaining such a coveted and important role. No, whether somebody became Echend'dim hinged solely on two factors—if Sic got to them early enough after their deaths and if they had the will to live. The stronger the determination to remain on Ana-Darasa, the longer the person stayed available after the initial death, the easier it was for Sic to bring them back. Unfortunately for all of them, the decision whether to stay or leave for the Green Lands was made in death, and apparently none of the warriors knew beforehand into which category they fell.

Canubis had not been overly pleased with this particular information, since it meant he still had to rely on chance when it came to acquiring new Echend'dim, because not even he was coldblooded enough to simply kill all his warriors and then have Sic call them back in the hope most of them would make it. Though he hadn't been as disappointed as Sic had expected. Canubis had explained it easily enough: "I understand the severity of the decision, and I know enough to realize it can only be made between life and death, when one's sight is clear and devoid of any distraction. There may be those who say they want to stay and then realize there's more calling them to the Green Lands than keeping them on Ana-Darasa, and the other way round. And it's only fair those who come to stay with us for eternity get the chance to choose freely. After all, we expect a lot from them."

Sic understood his god's reasoning, it coincided with his own view on the matter, yet he still had trouble accepting it all. Because he didn't just call the Echend'dim back to serve the gods. If that had been all there was to it, he could have accepted the weight of his responsibility more easily. No, he also called them back to serve as an outlet for his own power, a very selfish thing indeed. All his life Sic had been used by others for their personal gain. Suddenly finding himself in a position to do the same, even though the circumstances were different, as Noran and Daran and Lukan never grew tired of pointing out, still made him uneasy. Making the transition from a walking dead man to honored Emeris and feared Luksari had changed Sic in ways he couldn't fully understand. On top of it all, his feelings for Noran were growing each day, and he could sense the man's need to fully connect with him. Noran's pain, caused by the constant rejection from Sic, was palpable whenever they were together, and Sic didn't know how to explain to his former master that he didn't fear him but the severity of the bond they could forge between them. They were light and darkness, forever dancing around each other, always the other's opposite, always occupying a space the other couldn't inhabit at the same time. Sic was almost sure his Luksari light wouldn't swallow Noran's darkness, but the fear remained.

What would happen if he did? Would Noran and he become one in a way neither of them had anticipated nor wanted? And what if they didn't? What did it mean for their commitment to each other if their union wasn't complete? After all, they *were* the exact opposite of each other.

Sic was aware his thoughts were going in circles, focusing on everything that could go wrong. Since the decision he was about to make would once again change his life in ways he never thought possible, he felt he had a right to panic. Sic started expanding his chest in a conscious effort to calm his thoughts and reach deep into himself where the Luksari slumbered. The creature was kind of fickle, only answering Sic's calls when it felt like it, otherwise seemingly content to be a mere onlooker. Sic still hadn't been able to consolidate the Luksari with his own sense of self, even though he knew they were technically the same person—or entity—or being. He simply couldn't tell. Taking deep breath after deep breath, Sic finally felt his tumultuous thoughts stopping their endless spiral into grim scenarios. The Luksari stirred, looked at him through eyes that remembered the universe when it was still one with chaos. Sic shuddered in the face of such unfathomable age, yet he knew he couldn't let his awe get in the way of communicating with this other part of himself.

What do you need?

Sic furrowed his brows. He was pretty sure the Luksari knew. A soft chuckle confirmed his suspicion.

I do know. We are one, after all. See it as your inner voice trying to help you figure out your thoughts.

"You're a bastard. Has anybody ever told you that?"

I am you.

Sic sighed. There was no winning this argument. Could there be a winner if he was having this discussion with himself? Probably not.

"I want to know what I should do about my master." Sic tried to think about his former owner simply as "Noran" as often as possible to better get used to them being equals now, and he was doing a pretty good job of it most of the time, even in his own thoughts. But what he was doing now was profound, reaching so deep into his very being that he felt it necessary to acknowledge what had always been true in some form—Noran was his master, the person who owned his body and heart and soul through one act of such incredible kindness Sic still couldn't fathom it. "I feel the need to complete our connection, forge it into what it was meant to be."

But you're afraid.

"Are you going to hurt him? Consume him?" Since the Luksari was going straight for the jugular, Sic saw no need to hold back either.

I am you. Would you hurt him? Consume him?

"Never."

Then why would I?

"He's darkness. You're light."

He's our balance, the other anchor to this world besides our Zaheerosh. His darkness counters our light, makes it bearable for those around us, contains its cruel sides. We need him. You know that.

"I know I need him for other reasons as well. But I don't want this to be one-sided, us needing and him providing. It's just not fair."

We're providing as well. Our master is in desperate need of balance, something to keep the darkness from consuming his mind again.

"Are you sure?"

Can't you feel it?

Sic could feel it. Could feel how Noran always seemed to be one step away from falling back into the void he'd been trapped in after Arja's betrayal and death. He had always seen his master as a man without fear, but the last year had shown Noran had his own insecurities and inner demons to fight. Only recently had Sic started to believe he could maybe help his master deal with it all. Perhaps it was time for him to become the man Noran needed by his side instead of dreading what would happen if he failed.

Contentment filled Sic, welling up from the place inside him he had come to associate with the Luksari's presence. His other half was happy with his decision, seeing it as something inevitable that was finally coming to pass. And who was he to argue with himself?

AEGID AND Kalad looked up when Daran entered their shared tent. The thief looked exhausted, with deep lines around his mouth and dark shadows under his eyes. His armor was covered in a mixture of blood, dust, and some greenish fluid humans secreted when they received a cut to the gut. Daran reeked of battle and sweat and death, a combination the desert brothers found irresistible. The only thing keeping them from grabbing their husband and ravishing him before he'd had his bath was the forlorn look in his eyes. It called for a different approach.

Kalad stepped forward, effectively stopping Daran's momentum toward the back of the tent where the bathtub was standing. "Let us help you, little thief."

Daran's shoulders slumped, as if the pet name had cut the last string holding him upright. Kalad could feel the tension draining from their lover's body when he finally allowed himself to let go. Aegid stepped next to Kalad, reached for the clasps on Daran's breast shield, and started opening them.

Daran took a deep breath. "Thank you."

Kalad joined Aegid in his efforts to get their husband naked. "Always, little thief."

They made quick work of Daran's armor and clothing, then led him to the bathtub. Once the thief was in the water, his beautiful long black hair fanning out around him, Aegid started a soft massage with the berry shampoo Daran loved so much. Kalad took Daran's sword hand to knead the tension from it. "Do you want to talk about it?"

Daran sighed. "No." He opened his eyes to look at Kalad. "But I should."

Kalad concentrated on Daran's hand, giving their lover time to gather his thoughts. Ever since Sic had started bringing back more and more Echend'dim, Daran's stress had multiplied. Which was understandable, since he was the First of the Eternal Guard, the leader of the Echend'dim. It was a lot of responsibility for a young man who'd been a mere bed slave not too long ago.

"Everything is so sharp." Daran's voice pried Kalad from his musings about the changes their little thief had undergone since they'd found him on the market in Kwarl.

"Sharp?" Aegid's voice was calm, deep, soothing. Together with the magic his hands worked on Daran's scalp, it did the trick of relaxing their thief to the bone.

"I don't know how else to describe it. It's as if everything has become more, even when Lord Sic is not channeling his energy into us. There's always the others in my head, like a distant murmur I can't get rid of, and when I think about tuning them out it feels wrong, but it also feels wrong to have such a connection to somebody who isn't you. And once you've seen the world through magic, it changes everything." He sighed deeply, slipped a bit farther under the water until the underside of his nose was right above the surface.

Kalad and Aegid shared a look. Daran's connection to the other Echend'dim was something they had already discussed at length. What had helped them to grumpily accept it was the fact that their own connection, grown over centuries, was similar in its exclusivity. They didn't keep Daran out, at least not consciously, but behavioral patterns cultivated over several human lifetimes were not easy to shake off. And Daran didn't want them to anyway. His reasoning was that he'd fallen in love with them as a unit, and his understanding of his role in their triad was that of the missing piece completing the pattern. He had different relationships with both of them, the one with Kalad more playful and perverted, the one with Aegid dominated by a mutual interest in art. But those were mere threads, slowly growing and thickening in the process of them getting to know each other's personalities. What bound them together with chains more solid than blue steel was the unconditional love they felt for each other. Everything else was just embellishment.

"You know we've made our peace with you having that connection." Aegid sounded tentative, not sure if this was what Daran wanted or needed to hear.

117

Daran resurfaced enough to be able to answer. "I know. It's still weird. When you took me with you after we first met, I realized quickly that you were my future. I never thought I could have something similar with somebody else."

"Life is full of surprises." Aegid smiled over Daran's head, gently slinging the wet strands around his wrist and tugging. Daran immediately understood and got up without complaint. Kalad watched hungrily as the water traveled down their thief's toned body, caressing the skin in a way Kalad would have been jealous of if the sight hadn't been so alluring. He offered Daran his hand to help him get out of the tub, and Aegid wrapped their husband in a soft towel to get him dry. They boxed Daran in from front and back, giving him their warmth and protection. Daran sighed happily.

"Can we make love tonight?"

The question came out tentative, something Kalad understood. Usually when they had sex, no matter how tame it started, it turned into something feral and wild, due to their predatory, insatiable natures where each of them gave as good as he got. In the beginning, it had been Daran who submitted to Kalad's and Aegid's lust, but since the thief became Echend'dim and accepted his place as the First of the Eternal Guard, his own dominance was coming out to play on a regular basis, proving to the desert brothers that he was truly their equal now. For Daran to show such vulnerability must mean he was truly shaken and in need of their reassurance, something Kalad and Aegid were more than happy to give.

"Of course, little thief." Aegid's voice was like a caress itself, washing over Daran with the promise of safety and comfort. They dried their thief before they took him to the low bed piled high with soft furs and comfortable cushions where they spent their nights. Daran was pliant in their arms, giving himself fully to them, trusting them to take care of him, to love him the way only they could. With hands and lips the desert brothers mapped Daran's body, massaging the places where his muscles had formed hard knots, caressing the spots they knew he enjoyed most. Soon Daran was purring like a cat, arching into their touches, desperate for more skin-on-skin contact to soothe his raging thoughts.

When Aegid oiled his fingers to prepare their thief for penetration, Kalad started stroking both his own and Daran's cock, giving Aegid a show that had his own member straining against the soft fabric of his tunic. Getting Daran ready was both pleasure and torture, and Aegid thanked the goddesses that he was by now used to them, which shortened the process considerably. Not that he didn't want to give his husband all the loving he deserved, but controlling his own urges when Daran was mewling and undulating under his fingers was close to impossible. Aegid was relieved when Daran dug his fingernails into his forearm and pleaded softly, "Take me. Show me who I belong to. Show me that I'm loved."

Aegid looked at Kalad, and they both shuddered at the urgency in Daran's tone. With a soft expression full of love he rarely showed, Kalad leaned over Daran, taking his lips in a deep kiss while Aegid spread their thief's legs, opening him for Kalad's member. Daran groaned softly into Kalad's mouth, took what his husband was giving him, full of gratitude and eagerness. Kalad started moving slowly, tenderly, while Aegid held Daran's shoulders, cushioned their rocking motions with his big body, gave Daran the warmth and solidity he so desperately needed. It was a far cry from their usual rough lovemaking, and yet it was more intense than even their most athletic escapades. This wasn't about dominance or endurance; it didn't matter who led and who followed. Daran needed his husbands—not the two warriors he had bound himself to, not the predators who had stolen him from his home, not the two men who had accepted him as their third—he needed the love of his two anchors in a world that was steadily going crazy around them and was asking more of Daran than he would have ever imagined.

Kalad took his time, denied Daran his orgasm to wind him up more, to prepare him for Aegid, who didn't rush either and slowly, steadily carried Daran to heights the thief never wanted to leave. When he finally came in the loving embrace of his husbands, Daran cried, tears streaming down his face as he accepted the absolute relaxation of his entire body. He was asleep before Kalad and Aegid were done getting comfortable with him between them, and the two desert warriors let him be.

They watched with unconditional love as their thief found his rest, snuggled against both of them.

SIRA WAS trapped. She knew what she was experiencing wasn't real, that it was all just a dream, but she couldn't break free. She was back in the small room at her former master's home, naked and covered in bruises. Soon the men would come. They would take her out of the room and bring her to her master's customers so that they could sample her. Sira tried to remember that she no longer had a master, that Lord Sic had freed her, that she was paid for her services, but the dream wouldn't budge. Tears of anger and despair slithered down her cheeks when she heard the men approach.

A scream tore the air, followed by a heavy *thump*. Sira fixed her gaze on the door. The handle turned and it swung open. In the frame stood Cornelia. To Sira, she looked like an angel, even though she was covered in blood. Behind Cornelia, something big stirred. Screaming, Sira backed into the far corner of the room when she saw three snake heads with blood dripping from their snouts turning toward her. Cornelia smiled at her while she patted one of the heads.

"Don't be afraid, Sira. They are here to help. In fact, they like it when you scratch them between the eyes."

Cornelia held out her hand, and when Sira reluctantly came closer, she showed her the spot. With trembling fingers, Sira started to pet the head and was rewarded with a deep rumble. She could feel her tension slowly dissipate.

"This is nice. They're warm."

Cornelia beamed. "Aren't they cute? No more nightmares for any of us. My children will guard our dreams from now on."

IN THE cave deep down in the sea where she was hiding, the Good Mother screamed in rage. Her carefully crafted nightmares, meant to weaken and even kill the members of the Pack, were destroyed one by one. When she tried to get back into the realm of dreams to enhance them, she could no longer enter. A barrier kept her out, a barrier so strong, it could mean only one thing: the queen of the realm had taken her rightful place. Knowing she could no longer use the dream world to fight against the Pack, the Good Mother retreated to weigh her options.

5. REVELATIONS

CASTO FELT nervous. By now he had gotten used to the mind-numbing flashbacks and confusing memories, often melting into an impenetrable fog only Lys was able to discern. The situation now was different, though. He was inside the temple again, only this time it was all a hazy blur and all the sounds from the world were muffled as if a thick snow had fallen. Something like a veil seemed to cover his eyes and obscure his vision, allowing him to recognize only basic shapes. When the door of the temple opened, Casto cringed at the sudden noise. Two men were dragging Dria inside. For some reason, the three of them were perfectly visible. Dria was fighting against the men's grip with a determined expression on her face. Her belly protruded in front of her like a balloon. During his acquaintance with Cassia, Casto had learned a thing or two about pregnancy and the joys of motherhood. He estimated that Dria would reach her due date in less than a week, given how awkward and unstable her movements were. Her captors pushed her to the ground in front of the fountain. Their faces were full of malicious glee. The bigger one, who sported a brown beard that could only partially hide the broad scar across his face, gave Dria a vicious kick. The other man, smaller and with short red hair, chuckled.

"Slow down, Ja'reh! We don't want this to be over too soon, do we?"

Ja'reh made a clucking sound deep in his throat but retreated.

"You're right, Anon. I was just overwhelmed. Finally being able to get back at the bastard brothers is too good to be true."

Both men watched as Dria slowly sat up. She coughed, holding her swollen belly in a protective gesture.

"How did you manage to step behind time? The last one with that talent was a witch who died about seventy years ago. You are not of her line."

Ja'reh and Anon grinned nastily.

"We don't have to be. The Good Mother has given us access to all the powers once held by the witch clans. As long as we have at least three ancestors with talent, we can tap into the power. Things are changing fast, little seer, and the end of the bastard brothers is close."

Ja'reh looked genuinely pleased with himself. Dria regarded him coldly. How she managed to stay so calm in such a difficult situation was beyond Casto's grasp and made him admire her even more.

"Lord Canubis and Lord Renaldo are the destined masters of Ana-Darasa. No matter what schemes you plan, you will never win against them! Never!"

Anon patted Dria's cheek in a condescending manner.

"Oh, we already have, little seer. Our friends are on their way to bring your brother here. Once we have killed the two of you, the victory will be ours. We have done a lot of research, and we know you and Dweian are the only bond between the bastards and their few followers. With you gone, they will stand alone in no time at all. And since you are the last true seers born to Ana-Darasa, they will also be blind. We're already gathering our troops, and when the time is right, we will not only conquer Quell'renar, we will also wipe the bastards out and pave the way for the Good Mother!"

Dria spat. "All that work for a goddess who can't even walk Ana-Darasa in physical form."

Ja'reh slapped Dria brutally.

"At least she's there to look after us. And we haven't heard of Ana-Isara or Ana-Aruna walking this world anymore either."

"Because they *chose* not to. That alone should tell you where your loyalties should lie. Lord Renaldo and Lord Canubis are our last chance to prove that we're worthy of having gods. People like you only make it easier for the Mothers to toss us aside."

"That's enough! I'm not going to sit here and listen to the rantings of a half-crazed seer who has no clue whatsoever what it means to feel the magic but be unable to use it!"

Ja'reh grabbed Dria and bent her backward over the rim of the fountain pool. Just when he reached for his knife, the door opened again and two women and two men stepped inside, dragging the beat-up and unconscious figure of Dweian between them. One of the women let go and greeted Anon with a kiss on the cheek.

"You've already started?"

"Ja'reh couldn't control himself anymore. How about you, Ann'ria? Did you run into any trouble?"

The woman stepped back. "Not really. Because we were operating behind time, nobody, not even the wolves, could detect us. The seer gave us some trouble, though. He's pretty good at fighting. Who would have thought?"

She smiled nastily.

"Didn't help him. We banged him up pretty badly, but since he's to die anyway, I don't see the harm."

Anon rubbed his hands. "Indeed, there's no harm. Let's prepare our present for the bastards."

He nodded toward Ja'reh, who still held the struggling Dria over the fountain. The man saluted with his knife, then used it to gouge Dria's eyes out. She howled in pain but never stopped fighting back. Ja'reh pushed her into the pool of the fountain, slit her wrists open, and held her under water until her body stopped twitching. Casto stared at the water that was now dirtied by swirls of deep red and felt bile rising in his mouth. He desperately wanted to leave this memory, but he also knew he owed it to the seer siblings to stay and witness their death. Back then, their gods had left them alone, something that would not happen this time. The heart of the Angel of Death was there, and Casto only wished they could know it as well.

Ann'ria beckoned her comrades to bring Dweian to the fountain. Dria's desperate fight had woken him, though he still seemed to be in a daze. His glazed-over gaze couldn't focus on anything particular. Given how badly he had been beaten, it was a wonder he was conscious at all.

"Hurry! Put him into the water!"

Anon sounded nervous, and it took Casto a few moments to understand why. While Dweian and his captors were still clearly visible, Dria's tormented body had become a blur, just like everything around them, which meant she was no longer behind time. The scent of her freshly spilled blood would soon attract the attention of the wolves. Ann'ria flashed out her knife and took Dweian's eyes, just like Ja'reh had taken those of Dria. Then Anon slit Dweian's throat and tossed him into the water next to his sister. Outside the temple, Casto could hear the howling of the wolves, who had finally caught scent of what was going on. The pack rushed into the temple through a side entrance while the group of assassins left through the main door, still safe behind time. The moment the last of them left, Casto's surroundings came back into focus again. There were patches of blood on the ground, the water in the fountain had turned into crimson, and Dweian and Dria's eyes stared blankly at the agitated wolves from the place at the feet of the Mothers' statues, where Anon had placed them as a last mocking farewell to Canubis and Renaldo. Alerted by the wolves' howling, Canubis and Renaldo dashed through the door. They stopped dead in their tracks when they beheld the scene of carnage. For several heartbeats, the two demigods could only stare. When Canubis finally spoke, his voice sounded far off, as if he was reading the words from an internal sheet.

"Go and find whoever did this. Don't kill them. Bring them back here so I can have a talk with them."

The wolves howled once more and ran outside to track down the assassins. Casto knew how futile that attempt was. As long as they stayed behind time, Anon and his gang couldn't be traced. With pity constricting his heart, Casto watched as Renaldo and Canubis fished the corpses of Dweian and Dria out of the water. It was still a deep crimson, which was strange since it was constantly replaced. In face of the tragedy that was still unfolding, Casto decided to ponder this phenomenon later. Canubis and Renaldo sat next to the dead bodies of their most reliable and also most powerful followers.

"We failed to protect them. Seems like we are as useless as many of the La'ides think. Without Dweian and Dria, we won't be able to fight the followers of the Good Mother as we used to."

Renaldo sounded so desperate, Casto felt the urge to soothe him. He had never thought it possible that the strong, unrelenting man with the will of iron he had cursed so many times could have been so helpless and forlorn. It was the first time Casto felt a protective instinct toward his mate, and he didn't like it in the least. Thankfully, Canubis diverted Casto from these unwelcome musings.

"We are not useless, dear brother. We are the Gods of War, the rightful masters of Ana-Darasa and the La'ides. We may be still young, and we may have made some mistakes, but that does not change the fact that they owe us obedience. And we most certainly won't let this challenge go unanswered. The followers of the Good Mother will pay for this shameless deed."

"Well spoken, my son. I'm proud of you."

Out of the shadows between the two statues, Ana-Isara stepped into the light. She looked as haughty and pale as always, and there was a hint of grief in her dark eyes. She knelt between Dweian and Dria and touched their dead, cold bodies lovingly.

"Give me their eyes."

Casto averted his gaze when Canubis picked up the bloody eyeballs and handed them to his mother. The Empress of the Dead bent first over Dria, then over Dweian, and gave them back their eyes. Renaldo stared at Ana-Isara with anger in his gaze.

"Can you give them back to us?"

Ana-Isara looked up. A sad smile played on her red lips.

"You know I can't. I am death, not life. It may console you that Dweian and Dria are in the Green Lands now. They will see eternity in peace under Ana-Aruna's rule. So do not grieve for those who die in your service. They walk under my protection and will never be lost."

She rose to her feet, kissed her sons on the forehead, and left again, dissolving into the shadows like a wisp of smoke. Canubis headed for the temple doors, a determined expression on his face.

"I'll get everything to clean them up and make them presentable. We burn them tomorrow."

NORAN SQUARED his shoulders and tried to steel himself for the sight he was going to get once he entered the tent he shared with his precious mate—the mate who kept rejecting him for reasons Noran failed to understand. If Sic had told him he didn't want to bond with him because of all the horrors Noran had forced on him, he would have still been devastated, but wouldn't have argued Sic's point. Noran *had* been needlessly cruel and mean to his then slave, and not being allowed to even look at Sic would have been a fitting punishment. Things weren't so easy, of course. While Noran was sure Sic had forgiven him fully—his beautiful beloved was generous like that—he couldn't help but suspect there were layers he and Sic hadn't been able to consolidate.

Being able to touch Sic, to love him like he deserved, and yet being denied the deeper bond Noran craved more and more each day was slowly whittling away at Noran's resolve to leave the pacing of their relationship to Sic. He wasn't yet at the point where he was willing to ignore all the promises he had made to his lover and take charge, but the day would be coming, and just knowing it, knowing himself so well, made self-hatred surge inside Noran like a wave of darkness drowning out everything else. The fact that his lover was no longer a powerless slave, no longer helplessly subjected to Noran's whims, didn't alleviate the sense of self-loathing he felt when he even thought about putting more force behind his wishes.

Noran entered the tent expecting to see the usual mask of strained nonchalance on Sic's face he had become accustomed to in the last weeks. With all the new Echend'dim awakening and Lord Renaldo being more or less incapacitated because of losing Casto, there was a lot of pressure on Sic's shoulders, pressure Noran was fully aware he was adding to with his silently reproachful stance. Noran hoped he hadn't yet fully entered the field of passive-aggressive, but he knew he was dangerously close.

Only today Sic's face showed an openness Noran hadn't seen since before they left the Valley. "Master! It's good to see you."

Noran winced internally at the honorific Sic still bestowed on him even though he didn't deserve it in the least. "It's good to see you, too, my love. You seem to be in a good mood." Noran was very careful with his wording, not wanting to aggravate his lover when he seemed to be so at ease. Judging from the way Sic recoiled slightly from him, he hadn't done a great job. "I'm sorry, Sic, I didn't mean—"

"It's fine, Master. I know. I understand. I'm sorry things have been so strained between us these past weeks. And I thank you for your patience. I know how hard it must have been for you."

The tenderness in Sic's voice, the way he apologized for something that wasn't his fault, made Noran wish he were a better liar. But lying to Sic wasn't an option. Not when their relationship had had such a catastrophic start. Absolute openness was the key to building something healthy between them. Openness between him and his lover, as well as toward himself.

"I wasn't patient, my love. We both know it. I'm just grateful you're still willing to see something positive in the way I behaved."

Sic approached Noran with one of his beautiful smiles. "You tried. That's what counts. I'm well aware how hard it was for you to refrain from pressuring me directly. It's also one of the reasons I want to become yours officially."

Noran was so surprised, he grabbed Sic's upper arms in a hold that had to be painful. "You want it to be official?"

Sic simply nodded.

"Why all of a sudden, if you don't mind me asking? You had your reasons, and I respect that."

Sic sighed and snuggled against Noran's chest when he finally loosened his hold. Automatically, Noran slung his arms around his most precious possession. Holding Sic was one of the greatest pleasures of his life.

"I talked to the Luksari. So basically to myself. The reason I didn't want to bond with you until now is because I was afraid what the Luksari might do to you."

Noran stiffened slightly at those words. He would be lying if he claimed he hadn't thought about that same possibility as well. "And now you know it?"

"Yes. I've known all along, I just…. It's hard for me to see the Luksari as myself. There is so much power inside me, I had to compartmentalize it in some way, because I was—am—afraid of it. But that's stupid, because the Luksari is me and vice versa. It's just hard to comprehend. I think I understand better now. The Luksari said we—you and me—are two sides of the same thing, light and darkness, and that I could never consume you the way I feared, because I need you to balance me."

"Oh, Sic." Noran understood now why his precious lover had hesitated to fully commit to him. Not because there were still some unresolved issues between them or because he still harbored resentment against him. Quite the opposite. His wonderful, soft-hearted, forgiving, and generous lover had simply wanted to protect him, like he had done when he had offered his own life to save Noran's in Ummana. Like he had done when he had stolen Casto's jewelry. Sic always tried to protect him. Noran hugged the young man closer, breathed in his familiar scent. "Oh, my sweet beloved. Words can't express how much I love you, how precious you are to me."

Sic melted into his embrace, breathing freely for the first time in weeks. "I'm still afraid of what I'm capable of, Master. The power inside me…." Sic trailed off, trembled slightly in Noran's embrace. Noran kissed the top of Sic's head.

"Don't worry, don't ever worry. No matter how blinding or cruel or powerful your light becomes—my darkness will always be mercy, sweet love of mine. And I swear this to you, I will always be there."

A shudder ran through Sic as he leaned back in Noran's arms. His eyes shone brightly in the soft glow of the candles inside the tent. "Make me yours, my Master, my beloved, my darkness. I need you more than I can say, more than the air I draw into my lungs. I yearn for us to be one, to be truly bonded like only light and darkness can be."

Noran bent forward to catch Sic's lips in a searing kiss. Just before their lips met, Noran saw the Luksari awakening inside Sic, and his own darkness surged in answer to the light he sensed. The shadows that had been suffocating him for so long, that had always seemed to be a burden, took on new meaning now that they finally had the chance to merge with the reason for their existence. Noran no longer fought against the darkness consuming him in a whole new way. Through his power, he saw Sic as he truly was, a blinding, devastatingly beautiful and sometimes cruel force varnished with a kindness that contradicted what lay beneath it. While they kissed, Noran felt his own self expanding, dissolving into darkness, which was drawn to the light Sic was emanating. For a brief moment, Noran was able to get a glimpse of both of them, their forms wavering as if they were nothing but mere mirages in the desert, bound to vanish before a soul could reach them. He felt Sic's hands on his back, sinking into his body, through him, intertwining his light with Noran's darkness, merging the two into a beautiful ribbon of pure power, light and dark combined. Noran still felt physical arousal, he was with the love of his life, after all, but it was merely an addition to an ecstasy so great it would have taken the air from his lungs had he not been in a transcendent state at this moment. Sic was everywhere around him, their very souls starting a dance that would last for all eternity. There were no more secrets between them, no barriers; he could see his beloved, the good and the bad, for even a creature as kind and pure as Sic had darkness inside, and Sic was able to see all of him, his regrets and rage, his selfishness and the determination to own him forever. Sic didn't flinch back, just like Noran did not retreat when the Luksari stared at him with his eons of wisdom and a power that could destroy everything within a heartbeat yet would never do it because it was aware of the loneliness that would follow. *Because this had happened before.* The thought came quickly, like lightning flashing far away in the mountains, there and gone again, explaining everything there was to know about the Luksari.

Darkness and light, light and darkness, united to balance each other. It was the gift the Mothers—or chance, Noran still wasn't sure about that—had bestowed on him. The ability to anchor Sic's Luksari side in this world so it could be utilized for the glory of the Gods of War.

Of course, Noran would never allow anybody, not even his gods, to take advantage of his sweet lover. He embraced Sic with everything he had, with everything he was, and felt his lover's being responding, offering the same, surrounding him with a smile he couldn't see but feel deep in his soul.

THE MAN in the tent cursed. Things were not going as planned. Where the Pack should have been seriously crippled by now, it was becoming stronger instead, the cursed Luksari awakening more and more Echend'dim, whose powers seemed to be growing with each day. Even with the Angel of Death practically incapacitated, the Pack was making headway, and only a few days ago he had felt a surge of rage washing through him, telling him his goddess had faced yet another failure on one of the many battlegrounds against the Gods of War. Time was running out, and he was now desperate enough to use desperate measures. He would have preferred to wait with this particular measure until he could be more certain about a successful outcome, but his time was up and he knew it. He stared at the slave kneeling in front of him, felt the waves of hatred radiating from him. He had the creature under control. He had. With an inward sigh, for he couldn't allow himself to show weakness in front of even somebody as tightly bound as this slave, he opened the chest on the small table to his right and retrieved the one thing that might be able to ensure the Good Mother's victory over the bastard brothers.

"This is *Azashreem*, a shadow dagger. It's the only weapon able to kill the Echend'dim and the Emeris. You will find an Emeris and you will kill them. I don't care which one. And don't waste any time or I'll make you pay."

The man kneeling before him took the dagger, the hatred in his eyes like liquid poison pooling in the dark pupils that—for just a moment—turned into slits. The man reared back in shock. He had the creature under control! His control was absolute! He made a gesture with his hand, murmuring a single word. The slave doubled over in pain; the dagger fell to the ground with a thud. The man smiled coldly. He was still the one calling the shots.

"Out."

The slave made a soft whining sound before he managed to get onto his knees. He grabbed the dagger and left the tent, his upper body still curled around his middle. The man sent a quick prayer to the Good Mother to call her blessing onto this endeavor.

AFTER THE draining experience of becoming one with Noran and his darkness, Sic was exhausted enough to sleep well into the morning. Noran didn't wake him, just reported their bonding to a very happy Canubis and saw to it that they weren't disturbed. Canubis had sent out several patrols to look for more captives, and none of them were expected back before noon. With his soul-bonded lover asleep, Noran lay down next to him again, took Sic's prone form into his arms, and let his eyes close once more.

SIC BLINKED and looked around in Jago's villa in Ummana. It had been some time since he'd been there, because whenever he'd reached for Heljia, she'd been awake. Now she seemed to be sleeping as well, because he could hear her calling for him.

"Uncle Sic! Uncle Sic!"

"I'm here, Heljia!"

She came skidding around the corner, her small, compact body barreling into him before he could manage to catch her. They both staggered before Sic righted himself and swung Heljia up. "I missed you, little one!"

She squealed in delight while he twirled her around, their combined light making the outlines of the structure around them seem even more unreal.

"I missed you, too, Uncle Sic! There was so much happening, and I was afraid and couldn't reach you and Mommy said I couldn't go back to the Valley and everybody there got trapped and I couldn't help."

Sic put her down on her feet. He was used to his little niece being far more mature in the dream world than a two-year-old could be in real life, and what she was telling him was worrying. "You were in danger? The people in the Valley are in danger?"

She took his hand and squeezed it. "I was never in danger. The darkness was too afraid of my light. The monsters knew you would come for them if they harmed me, so they kept their distance. But I couldn't help the others. There was just too much darkness, and my light wasn't enough."

"I'm so sorry, little one. I'm here now. Do you think the darkness is still in the Valley?"

Heljia shrugged. "Probably. It didn't seem as if it wanted to go anywhere anytime soon."

"Then I better have a look." Sic sighed.

"I'm coming with you." Heljia's tone brooked no argument and reminded him so much of Cassia, Sic felt tears choking him.

"I'm not sure that's a good idea, little one. It could be dangerous."

Heljia opened her mouth to protest, but another voice beat her to it. "I'm going to look after her. Together we should be able to protect her."

Sic spun around and saw Noran standing in an almost completely faded doorway, a surprised expression on his face.

"Master! What are you doing here?"

Noran looked around, the shadows surrounding him swirling and dancing with the light emanating from Sic and Heljia. "To be honest, I don't know. I informed Canubis of our joining, and since you were still sleeping, I lay down next to you. I must have fallen asleep as well."

Sic felt a soft tug and looked at the tether between him and his soul-bonded. "I'm sorry, Master, I think I dragged you here unconsciously."

"It's fine, my beloved treasure. I love the idea of you relying on me already. Now tell me, how do we get into the Valley?"

"Oh, that's easy!" Heljia beamed, and the light around her flared. Moments later they stood in front of the main house, where the gods and their Emeris resided.

Noran blinked. "That was fast."

"Show-off," Sic muttered in Heljia's direction. The little girl grinned broadly. She opened her mouth, no doubt to say something sassy and completely inappropriate for a little girl of only two, but a rustling behind them had Sic turning around quickly. Noran was immediately at his side, grabbing Heljia by her upper arm and placing her between them. A strange creature with the torso of a bear and three snake heads, whose scales gleamed golden in the non-sun of the dream, slowly approached them.

"Is this one of the monsters, Heljia?" Sic was alarmed, though not panicking. He could feel no malicious intent from the creature.

"No. This one's nice. Do you think I could ride it? Since Lys isn't here."

Sic eyed the three snake heads. "I'm not sure, little one."

"But I am."

They looked back to the main house, where Cornelia stepped through the door. She was smiling. "It's good to see you again, Heljia. Sic, Noran." She nodded in their direction, then held her hand out. The snake-bear shuffled closer, stretching its three necks until Cornelia could pet them. Sic and Noran stepped aside to make room, while Heljia ducked from under Noran's grip and patted the furry, trunk-like leg of the creature. One head swung around to watch her, and without a hint of fear, Heljia started scratching the scales between the eyes.

"Can I ride you?"

The creature purred, lowering its head until the sturdy neck was the right height for a small girl to climb onto. Heljia didn't hesitate, swung her leg over the neck, and grabbed two protruding scales with her chubby hands. Very carefully, the snake-bear raised its head and made a tentative step forward, looking first at Cornelia and then Sic for confirmation. Heljia's happy laughter echoed through the place, her light flaring with joy. More laughter resounded, and other children appeared, ran toward the creature and Heljia, calling her name.

"She was sorely missed." Cornelia smiled at the scene before them. Other creatures were coming out of the shadows between the houses, joining the games Heljia was initiating.

"I assume the danger is over?" Noran raised a brow.

"It is. Something dark, I think it was the Good Mother, started invading the dreams of the people in the Valley. They got trapped in nightmares and wouldn't wake up. It was terrible, but now they're all hale again." Cornelia shuddered, and Sic gripped her hand. She squeezed it, grateful for the silent affirmation. "Heljia tried to help, but even though she's more mature in the dream world, I couldn't allow her to take such a risk. Besides, she said herself that the darkness was too strong for her, and she couldn't contact you because whenever Heljia was asleep, you were awake."

"The time difference." Noran nodded. Sic stared at his lover.

"Time difference?"

"It's a phenomenon my brother has read about," Cornelia explained. "It's not the same time everywhere on Ana-Darasa, and the farther apart two places are, the bigger the gap between the time. Since the Dark Forest is so far away from Ummana, Heljia was sleeping when you were awake and the other way round."

"I was wondering why I couldn't reach her anymore, but with everything else going on, I had no time to ponder the problem." Sic sounded thoughtful. "It does make sense, though. It also explains why I can't reach Lys either. He's too far away."

"You're able to reach Lys?" Noran's voice was sharp.

"Only in the dream world. It's where he meets with Heljia and me to play. I can't follow him into the real world, though, and since Casto left, I haven't seen him. I tried to contact him, but in the beginning, he wouldn't respond, cloaking himself and Casto like he did with Lord Renaldo, and after the first try, I gave up. I didn't want to put additional pressure on him. I was aware of his presence, though, like an itch at the back of my head. Since we've reached the Dark Forest, I haven't gotten any glimpses of him, which makes me assume we're too far apart."

"Interesting information, but not enough to know where to look for him." Cornelia sighed.

"Be that as it may, tell us about those creatures, Cornelia. You seem to be well acquainted with them." Sic smiled at the Emeris and took his master's hand at the same time. Cornelia raised a brow.

"Just like you two seem to have reached a new level of *acquaintance*."

Sic giggled happily. "My master and I have finally fully bonded. Look." He held up his hand, where streaks of light were intertwining with strands of darkness from Noran, making it look as if they were being sewn together with differently colored strings.

"My congratulations to both of you." Cornelia smiled a bit warily, obviously not sure what to think of it all. Given her own history with rape and what Noran had done to Sic, it wasn't surprising.

"Thank you, Cornelia." Noran bowed his head slightly. "I know you're not happy with me, and I fully understand. I hope time will help me prove to you how sincere I am, how I have changed." He hesitated a moment. "No, changed isn't the right word. There was nothing that needed changing, just redirecting, I guess." The smile he sent Sic's way was so full of love, Sic felt his knees going weak. "My darkness was always looking for the one thing that would balance it. Now that I'm no longer blind, I can finally embrace who I am without hurting others."

Cornelia looked at him for a long time, her expression unreadable. "I understand," she finally said. "It may take me some time to get used to not being wary in your presence, but I can see the change in you. Here in the dream world, many things are clearer than in the real world, and you are more content, more at home in your skin. I like that."

Noran bowed his head again, acknowledging the words as the tentative peace offering they were. Then the three of them stood there, watching the children of the Valley play with Heljia and Cornelia's children.

THE CIRCLE CLOSES

1. ALIGNING

CANUBIS AND Renaldo had just started to wash Dweian and Dria, when the excited howling of the pack interrupted their solemn work. The wolves dragged Anon, Ja'reh, and Ann'ria into the temple. The three assassins tried desperately to free themselves, but the sharp fangs of the predators made it impossible to escape. A cruel smile appeared on Canubis's lips.

"Seems like your precious Good Mother is not even half as powerful as she claims. Or she just doesn't care about her underlings. Either way, I really can't see what is so good about her. It must have been a shock, being thrown back into time at the most inconvenient of moments. Serves you right for abusing magic and ignoring the laws of the Mothers."

Ann'ria spit bloody slime on the floor.

"You may have caught us, bastard, but our mission is still a success. Look at them." She pointed at the corpses of Dweian and Dria. "Your precious seers are gone, killed like sheep by the butcher. You could do nothing to prevent it. You let them down!"

A deep, threatening growl filled the temple, and it took Casto a moment to realize that it was coming from Renaldo. The Angel of Death was close to losing his composure. Canubis shot him a warning look before he concentrated on his prisoners again.

"We may have failed to protect Dweian and Dria, but we will give them a funeral all of the La'ides will remember for a long time. And you will be the main attraction."

He stepped forward, took out his knife, and sliced the Achilles tendons of each of the assassins. Calmly, Canubis watched his writhing, screaming enemies.

"Guard them well. We're going to need them tomorrow."

Even though he could have left the illusion then, Casto stayed and spent the night watching the divine brothers as they held vigil for Dweian and Dria. He used the time to think about a lot of things. Even though he still resented it, Casto started to understand Renaldo better. When it came to hardships, the Barbarian obviously had his share as well. It made Casto wonder whether he would become the same while the centuries went past. He had no illusions that most people who knew him considered him despicable. A willful, stubborn, merciless, and ruthless young man who had the power and resources to get away with his behavior. Except for his freedom, Casto always got what he wanted, one way or another. As Renaldo's heart, he was in a position to lift the game of power to a new level. If they managed to defeat the Good Mother, something Casto had no doubt about, he would be king not only of a city like Ummana but of the world. It was a tempting thought, one that let him almost forget the reason why he had come to Quell'renar in the first place. Leadership always came with a prize, in his case his coveted, precious freedom. Because he had never been truly free, Casto craved it all the more. Being bound to Renaldo by force was bad enough. That he also loved the Barbarian with all his heart made it even more difficult for Casto. It was a dilemma he had yet to solve, and he wasn't looking forward to it in the least.

Until the break of dawn, Canubis and Renaldo barely spoke. On a secret signal, they rose and picked up the corpses of Dweian and Dria. Casto followed them on their way out into the square in front of the temple. The people had prepared two pyres, on which the bodies of the seers were placed. After that, the three assassins were brought forward. Since they could no longer stand, they were held upright by three warriors. The crowd that had gathered to bid Dweian and Dria farewell held their breath when Canubis approached the struggling figure of Anon. His voice resounded loud and clear in the square.

"You dared to lay your hands on our loyal followers. Now you will learn the consequences of doing so. Angering the gods is never wise, but to challenge us in such a blatant manner is beyond stupid. Until now, my brother and I have shown great patience with all of you, and that was thanks to Dweian and Dria, who appealed to us on your behalf more than once."

The amber eyes of Canubis lit up and made him look like a falcon just before it made a kill. There was no doubt that he was not only addressing the assassins but also his own people.

"Your last protection is gone. From today on, there will be no mercy. In case you haven't understood it yet, it is not us who have to prove our worth. It's the La'ides who have to show that they deserve to be led and protected by Renaldo and me. Until we have that proof, none of you is anything but a tool to us. And how useful that tool is depends on our decision alone. Let the death of these heretics mark the beginning of a new time!"

With that, Canubis grabbed his knife and took the eyes of each of the assassins. Then he slit their bellies open horizontally below the navel so that the innards gushed out. Renaldo lit a torch and held it to the pyres, which started to burn immediately. The wolves came forward and began to devour the screaming assassins while they were still alive. The citizens of Quell'renar watched in silent horror as their gods showed their true faces for the first time. Many of them knelt down and started to pray.

Casto kept staring at Renaldo. He had known the Barbarian long enough to be able to read him, even though he was a lot younger in this memory. The Angel of Death, the terrible, fearsome beast that would rule over Ana-Darasa with a fist of iron, had been born the moment the flames started to consume the pyres. The man who had taken Casto's freedom and shackled him with both real chains and love was the same who stood between the flames, unfazed by the heat and hardened in his attitude.

Over the roaring of the fire, Casto heard the ringing of a bell. A man dashed into the square, his face white as linen. He stopped right in front of Canubis and screamed in fear.

"There's an army outside! It's marching toward Quell'renar! The followers of the Good Mother are attacking!"

Panic broke out among the citizens, but Canubis stayed calm.

"How many?"

"About two thousand, perhaps more. They are heavily armed, and they are shielded by magic. I could see the spells!"

Canubis and Renaldo shared a long look. It was the kind of look Casto knew too well. The divine brothers had made a decision, and it wasn't a pleasant one. Renaldo stepped away from the pyres to join his brother.

Canubis smiled. "Are you ready to face the beast?"

"I've always been ready. It's what I am."

Together, the divine brothers left the square to meet the army of the Good Mother. The citizens followed them as if they were under a spell. In front of Quell'renar, Canubis and Renaldo watched the approaching masses of people. A single rider galloped toward them. She stopped a few feet in front of the divine brothers, a condescending smile on her lips.

"If you have come to surrender, I have good news, bastards, at least for your followers. The Good Mother is willing to let those who swear allegiance to her live. Not you two, of course. It will be her pleasure to wipe you from the face of Ana-Darasa."

Canubis looked at the woman. "I was about to say the same. Those of you who decide to abandon the Good Mother will get a fair chance to earn our trust. Those who don't will die."

The woman started laughing hysterically.

"Look around you, bastard! You're outnumbered five to one, and I'm including the old and the children in this estimate. You stand no chance at all."

"That is not for you to decide."

Canubis took out his dagger and threw it so fast, nobody, least of all the female on the horse, had a chance to react. With a *thud* her body hit the ground, and the horse ran away in panic. The Followers who had watched the encounter screamed in rage and started to run toward Canubis, Renaldo, and their few underlings. Renaldo squared his shoulders.

"You better keep your distance."

Canubis shooed the humans back into Quell'renar and watched from a safe distance as Renaldo lifted his arms. Fire broke from the ground in front of and around the advancing army. Renaldo threw his head back and screamed, which made the flames grow higher. All his rage and frustration were in that roar, and with his anger, he fed the flames that consumed not only the army of the Followers down to the last man, as well as their spells and magic, but also scorched the earth and imprinted it with raw magic.

Casto saw what Renaldo did, and he remembered that he had done the same. When Daran had been killed, he had fed the flames under Kwarl with his fury and killed everything alive in the labyrinth. Like Renaldo, he hadn't cared about the lives he had taken. All that had mattered was the force he commanded, the fact that this way, he could soothe his raging heart. At that moment, Casto did not only feel close to Renaldo, he realized for the first time that they were indeed one.

When the fires finally died, Renaldo turned around slowly. His perfect features were an inscrutable mask, and there was no telling what he might think. Canubis nodded at Renaldo in silent recognition of what he had done. The citizens of Quell'renar were on their knees again, frightened to the core by the violence they had just witnessed. Canubis regarded them coldly.

"This is what we are. You better not make the mistake of underestimating us again. Now get back to the square. We owe it to Dweian and Dria to stay with them until the end."

Hastily, the citizens rose to their feet again and followed Canubis and Renaldo back to the temple. Casto stayed behind, unable to pry his gaze from the smoking fields of Quell'renar.

ELUA, BELNOR, and Xi'an looked around the clearing carefully. Just as the wolves had reported, there had been a larger group of people camped out, but they were gone now. Only ashes from cooled fires and a few gnawed bones had been left behind.

"Damn, that's the second time we've been too slow. I really hate these woods! If we could use the horses, this whole damn campaign would be over by now." Elua groaned.

Xi'an let out his frustration by kicking a tree. Belnor looked around. He felt for his brother-in-arms and didn't have the heart to tell him that the frustration he experienced was the very essence of a guerilla war. A soft rustling in the trees made him look up, just in time to see a man jumping down on him. With reflexes honed by years spent on the battlefield, he managed to block the first blow and even get on top of his attacker when they both hit the ground. The man was agile like a cat and evaded Belnor's counterattack by sliding away from him. He then jumped to his feet quickly, spun around as if he wanted to retreat, and threw a dagger at Belnor. The weapon turned into a blur of whooshing steel and sunk into Belnor's chest. Disbelief in his eyes, he reached for the blade that had just taken his life. As he slowly sunk to the ground, Belnor could only watch while the attacker turned his attention to Elua and Xi'an.

Elua already had both her short swords drawn when the stranger lunged for her. She had been too far away to help Belnor, but she was determined to avenge him. Her attacker may have managed to surprise one of them, but now he was at a disadvantage because he had to deal with her and Xi'an, who had his blade at the ready as well. Elua circled her prey, trying to determine where his weak point was. He looked about her age and was roughly one ell and three spans tall. His head was shaved, and his eyes shone green in his fair face. He had a prominent jaw, thin lips, and cheekbones so sharp one could cut themselves on them. The clothes he wore were ragged, as if he didn't care in the least about their utility and just used them to cover himself. His weapons, on the other hand, were sharp and new and well-maintained. She was sure she had seen him before but couldn't remember where. In order to find an opening, Elua executed a feigned attack that was met with a condescending smile. Even when Xi'an joined her, the stranger did not show any weakness. He moved swiftly around her, avoiding Xi'an's sword while blocking her own weapons with his two long daggers. Elua knew this effortless way of fighting from Renaldo, and she realized that they had to be extremely careful with this man. She threw Xi'an a warning glance, which he acknowledged with a small nod. They had been fighting together long enough to be able to anticipate the other's moves. Elua leaped high in the air and somersaulted toward the stranger while Xi'an used the diversion to go for his unprotected back. Instead of evading Elua's attack by stepping sideways, the stranger rolled under her, thus escaping Xi'an's blade. The moment Elua was on her feet again, she felt cold steel penetrate her back. She groaned as white-hot pain slithered through her body, but still she managed to turn sideways and deal out a blow herself. Huffing, she sank to her knees, unable to stay upright. There was blood on her short sword, so she had at least hit the mark. Unfortunately, it seemed as if she had only been able to graze the stranger. He was already back on his feet, going for Xi'an, who had some trouble fighting back because his attacker was unbelievably fast. Somehow he did manage to break through the stranger's defense, though, and give him a wound on his thigh. The man roared in anger. As if this hit had triggered something inside him, he let go of his daggers and jumped at Xi'an bare-handed. Xi'an was momentarily taken by surprise, a fact the attacker used without mercy. His hands closed around Xi'an's neck with a force no ordinary human would have been able to use. Xi'an dropped his sword, and his hands shot up to fend the stranger off, but before Xi'an could reach his arms, the man had broken his neck. Like a rag doll, Xi'an sank to the ground. A speck of blood appeared on the corner of his mouth when his body hit the soft moss. Fueled by anger, Elua managed to get on her feet again, but she was no longer a match for the stranger, and she knew it. Blood was flowing down her back in a thick stream; her grip on her weapons was weak. The stranger sensed that she was no longer a threat and just watched as both her short swords slid from her hands. He approached her slowly, a curious look on his face, like a cat watching a mortally wounded mouse. When he reached Elua, he rammed his dagger into her heart.

His lips were close to her ear. "I'm sorry. I don't have a choice."

CASTO STOOD motionless. He could feel Lys's presence at his back, and he even sensed how the memory slowly faded, but for him, nothing changed.

In front of his inner eye, he still saw the smoldering, blackened earth where the Barbarian's fire had come to life for the first time. Casto didn't know what to make of the whirl of emotions inside his heart. There were too many to choose from, so he clung to the most prominent one. Without turning around, he addressed Lys.

"I don't know who I am anymore. What we just saw—you know I did the same. The exact same thing. For the exact same reasons. Has there ever been a true 'me,' or was it just some kind of snakeskin that has been shed long ago? I was always afraid of losing myself, and now it seems as if there never was a self to lose in the first place. Is this really all I am—Renaldo's heart? A part of him?"

Lys stepped closer and nudged Casto gently on the shoulder.

You're a lot more than just a heart. You know that. And since we're on the topic, what should I say? Before I came here, I was nothing but an idea, a passing thought. Am I really only here because of you?

Casto shuddered. He had never thought about the reasons for Lys's presence in his life. Now that he did, he realized how unfair life was.

"Even if that's the case, I'm still grateful. Though I'm pretty sure I'm not the only reason for your existence. You are the Emperor of the Storms, my brother. You would have come to life one way or another, even without me. I do get your point, though. Even Renaldo and Canubis came to Ana-Darasa for a special reason. None of us had a choice. Still, I resent it. There has to be a deeper meaning to everything I've gone through than just preparing me to be a god's heart."

Lys rubbed his big head on Casto's back.

Perhaps you should try a different view of things. What you have experienced so far may have been solely to harden you for your role as Renaldo's heart. But whatever you are going to do from now on is yours to decide. You may not have absolute control over your fate, but then again, who does? Embrace what you are and use it to your advantage.

"You know me inside and out, brother. Of course you're right."

Casto's features brightened in a way that made Lys shudder. He knew that adventurous gleam all too well.

"I've had enough of memories for the time being. How about you show me how to move in the shadows? It seems like a useful talent."

Lys snickered and turned sideways so that Casto could jump on his back.

As you wish. But I've got to warn you. Learning the skill will bind you to me even more.

"I don't mind, Lys. If it's to you, I don't mind one bit."

"SIC! COME quickly! They have brought Elua, Belnor, and Xi'an in!"

Sic hurried to get out of the tent and follow Noran to the center of the camp. When the three warriors had not returned on time, he had already dreaded the worst. Knowing that his fears had been well-grounded made Sic feel even guiltier, as if he had somehow jinxed them. The three lay on crude biers made of wood. Lukan was bent over Elua's cold body, wailing like a little child. When Sic approached, he reached out for him with his left hand.

"Please, bring her back! Tell her to come back! Just like you did me!"

Sic took Lukan's hand and smiled at him reassuringly. "It's fine, Lukan. Let me have a look."

Aegid and Kalad stepped forward and helped Lukan up so that Sic could kneel next to Elua. His body was already losing its contours, a sign that he had connected with the dead.

"I only hope this works."

Canubis was as tense as the rest of them. It was still a game of luck who Sic could call back. That there was still a spark of life left in those three was a reason for hope.

In the darkness, Sic looked around. He could see Belnor, Xi'an, and Elua wreathed in shadows. Since Belnor was the one who was obscured the most, he turned to him first.

"Do you wish to come back, Belnor?"

Deep in the shadows, there was a faint shimmer, a last attempt to embrace life. Sic smiled. He let the light flow out of his body and destroy the darkness around Belnor. Then he turned to Xi'an, whose spark was a lot stronger. Sic assumed that he had died later than Belnor.

"What about you, Xi'an? Do you also wish to come back?"

The spark flickered in affirmation. Again the light flared and freed yet another Echend'dim. When Sic turned to Elua, his heart sank. There was still a spark, but he could sense it was not there to stay.

"Elua! Please, don't do this to Lukan! Don't!"

A soft breeze, like a gentle caress, touched Sic's cheek. Faintly, already winking out, he could hear Elua's voice.

"Tell Lukan I'm sorry. I'm just too tired."

Sic screamed when Elua's hurt and regret hit him. Then he started to cry, because the love she had for Lukan overwhelmed him. With tearstained eyes and a voice breaking with sorrow, Sic bid Elua goodbye.

"May you enjoy the peace in the Green Lands. I promise you I'll take care of Lukan."

Sic closed his eyes and was back in the real world. He could hear Belnor and Xi'an reporting to Canubis what had happened. Then he felt a brutal grip on his shoulders and stared directly into Lukan's desperate face.

"Why isn't she waking up? Bring her back! Use that cruel light of yours to bring her back!"

Noran stepped forward to pry Lukan from Sic, but the Luksari stopped him with a look. He took Lukan's hands in his and spoke to him as softly as he could.

"I'm really sorry, Lukan. Elua wants you to know that she loves you, but she was too tired. She is with the Mothers now."

"No! No! You can't leave me like that! You promised we'd be together forever! You said I was your destiny! Come back!"

Wailing, Lukan pulled Elua's dead body into his arms, swaying her back and forth as if she were a baby he had to soothe. Aegid and Kalad wanted to go to him, as well as Belnor and Xi'an, but Canubis stopped them all with a glare.

"Leave him alone for now. He needs to grieve."

With that, the Wolf of War turned his back on the crying Echend'dim. Hesitatingly, the others followed his example, the last being Sic, who knew he could do nothing to soothe Lukan's pain and who felt guilty about his inability to bring Elua back. Noran took him in his arms and escorted Sic back to their tent. For the rest of the day, they did not speak while Sic listened to Lukan's cries that were like blows from a whip across his soul.

SILENTLY, LYS appeared behind Casto and sent him to the ground with a quick flick of his head. Casto cursed violently while he rose to his feet again. Lys only snorted.

You weren't paying attention. I wasn't even trying to be careful, and you still didn't hear me coming. You're not focused.

Casto snarled. Of course Lys was right, and that made him even angrier. Merging with the shadows, using them to his own advantage, was harder than he had anticipated, and Casto didn't like it when he failed in something.

"Again. Let's do it again."

Lys nudged Casto playfully on the shoulder to distract him from his anger.

Easy, brother. You won't achieve anything when you're this angry. Breathe in deep and try to feel it once more. Let me guide you.

Casto closed his eyes and allowed Lys to take him along. Becoming one with the shadows was an intimidating yet sensual act. It also meant relinquishing control to a certain extent, something Casto was naturally bad at. In order to travel the shadows, he had to become one with them, allow them to swallow him up. Together with Lys, Casto was able to bear the feeling of no longer being in one place, of losing his footing, but on his own, he just couldn't seem to do it. Almost as if he was afraid. Casto clenched his teeth. He would be damned! He was a warrior and a king, a god's heart even. There was no way he would be afraid of anything!

Lys snickered.

There is no need to be afraid. Your personality is far too powerful to get lost in something as petty as a shadow. Try to enjoy the sensation. If your trysts with Renaldo are any indication, this will be even better than an orgasm.

Casto couldn't help but blush. Ever since he had met Lys, he had gotten used to the fact that their connection prevented any privacy, and Lys was usually tactful enough not to remind him of how completely he was immersed in all the sensations Casto experienced.

"Please don't talk about it!"

Why not? If anything, Renaldo makes you feel really good. And you deserve that.

Casto winced.

"He makes me hate myself. You know how completely I lose myself in him. How his touch makes me ache for more, how I allow him to dominate me, and how much I enjoy his strength. I loathe myself for this weakness!"

That's something I don't understand, brother. You could stop him anytime, but you don't do it. You enjoy yourself. How can you be reluctant about it at the same time? From what I get, you need this.

Casto hesitated. It was so hard to put his feelings into words, and Lys did have a point. Casto reveled in being touched by the Barbarian. There was nothing he craved more in the world than the warmth from Renaldo's skin. He just couldn't forgive the way all of this goodness had been forced on him. Deep down he knew that a part of him would fight the happiness till the day he took his last breath. He was so twisted, it made him wonder if he had gone insane already.

Don't go there, brother. If you were insane, I'd know it. You are brave and strong, with a tendency to tackle problems head-on, which then gets you into serious trouble, but you're not insane.

The absolute conviction ringing in Lys's words helped Casto get his grip back. He inhaled deeply, closed his eyes, and allowed the shadows to take him.

Satisfied, Lys watched as Casto vanished in the darkness. After a moment's time, he followed his brother, eager to teach him even more about the endless possibilities he had at his fingertips.

"EVER SINCE we entered that damn forest, we've been played like fools, and I'm getting sick and tired of it!"

The Wolf of War was in a fury. He hated not having the upper hand, and losing Elua had been the final straw. Canubis was now out for blood.

"Hulda! Even though this whole place is laced with more magic than we've seen in years, I have no choice but to ask you to take the risk. Bring me an enemy who's high up enough to have interesting information. I'm done torturing little lackeys who hardly know their own names."

Hulda bowed to her enraged god, a smile devoid of all humor playing around her sensuous lips.

"As you wish, my lord Canubis. I shall leave right now."

"Do that. And Hulda, I don't care how many you have to kill. Drench the forest ground with blood if you wish to. Just bring me a prisoner worth my attention."

Hulda's elegant fingers put the hood of her black cloak over her head. Her lavender eyes shone like a cat's in the semidarkness. She bowed once more; then she vanished. Canubis leaned back in the sure knowledge that the tables would turn now.

WIDE-EYED, CASTO watched the scene unfolding in front of him. It had taken him over a week before he could summon the determination to go back into the past. With the memory of the burning fields still vivid in his mind, he waited for the aftermath to take place. He was inside the temple again, where Canubis had just approached Renaldo. The Barbarian had a haunted look in his eyes, one Casto recognized too easily.

"Brother, what do you want?"

Canubis stepped closer, regarding Renaldo with a hint of concern.

"We need to talk. About leaving Quell'renar. I've thought about this for some time, and it's just not suitable. Even if we build stronger city walls, this place is just too hard to defend. Not to mention how easily we could get spies or other assassins in here."

Renaldo furrowed a brow, clearly not happy with Canubis's words. When he spoke, sarcasm dripped off every syllable.

"Not to mention that the place is practically uninhabitable since I burned the fields and the harvest with them. Oh, and let's not forget the places where my fire etched raw magic into the very soil. I destroyed the place our mothers created with the La'ides."

Canubis hesitated, knowing there was nothing he could say or do. After all, it was the truth. Renaldo had saved them, but at what price?

"Well, the good news is, the followers of the Good Mother can't live here either. Quell'renar will never see their faces or know their rule. You've seen to that."

Renaldo looked utterly miserable. A lost boy who had no way of coping with the power and responsibility thrown his way. Canubis pulled him into his arms.

"I'm scared, brother. I was out of control out there. I could have killed them all, obliterated the city. And I knew I had to be nonchalant about it because of the lesson we needed to teach our own people. But, brother, I don't think I can do this again. There's a monster inside me, and if I'm not careful, it will devour us all."

Canubis held his trembling brother close. His voice was soothing yet with absolute conviction ringing in it. "You're stronger than that, Renaldo. You are the master of this fire. You will learn to control it, to use it as you please. And our enemies will cower in fear from it, just like they did on the fields. Because this is what you are meant to be, the fire of this world. Besides, I will always be there with you. This is our world, not theirs."

The words seemed to have a soothing effect on Renaldo. He grabbed his brother's biceps for a moment, then pulled out of his embrace, new determination shining in his gray eyes.

"Fine. Let's leave Quell'renar. Any idea where we can find a suitable place to establish a home base?"

"Unfortunately, not yet. I'm sure, though, that something will turn up. Until then, we just wander around and kill every follower of the Good Mother we can get our hands on. Sound good?"

Renaldo beamed. "Sounds fun."

CASTO DIDN'T stay in the illusion to see how the Gods of War left Quell'renar with their people. Instead, he walked out of the city gates and stared at the fields, which had recuperated from the fire more than well. Even though, when he strained his mind, he could still feel the heat the Barbarian had etched into the soil. The fire was indeed a beast. A hungry, uncontrollable beast that would lash out at everybody and everything, with no mind and no feelings except for the rage.

Casto felt Lys's presence at his back, silently offering to shatter the glimpses of what Quell'renar was still throwing at him. Casto shook his head. He wasn't ready to go back yet, and staring at the ever-changing scenery of things that had happened, had been dreamed, or simply could have been soothed him. There were so many emotions burning his chest, Casto didn't know how to sort through them. First there was genuine pity for the Barbarian. Being burdened with such a terrible gift at such a young age simply wasn't fair. It also explained some things about Renaldo Casto had refused to understand until now. Right behind the pity was anger. No, it wasn't just anger, it was fury. Casto was furious with the Mothers who had thrown their *sons* into such a mess and then left them more or less to their own devices. He was furious about the La'ides who had abandoned the Mothers and equally angry with those who had stayed loyal but only halfheartedly. What enraged Casto most was how he felt sympathy for the Barbarian. How he started to revalue their relationship now that he knew so much more than Renaldo had ever revealed to him. He thought he understood why Renaldo had tried to keep those things from him, although it didn't speak well for the kind of relationship they had shared.

Casto's head started to spin. He knew the Barbarian loved him. There was no doubt about that. The question now tugging at his heart and weighing him down was what it was exactly Renaldo loved. The fact that his heart had returned to him? A beautiful warm body that could match his appetite? The control Casto's presence meant over the fire? Or did he indeed love Casto, the person, like he always claimed? And if so, why had Renaldo never spoken of these things when he had tried everything short of torture to unearth Casto's secrets? What irked Casto most was the realization that if he had known about Quell'renar and the things that had happened there sooner, he would have reacted differently on many occasions. Some of the rows he'd had with the Barbarian seemed nothing but shallow in light of the things they could have shared but never did.

For a very long time, Casto simply stood and wondered how he was supposed to sort this complicated mess out.

2. CHANGING OF THE TIDES

BEHIND TIME, Hulda walked through the Dark Forest, all of her senses on high alert. They had already known that the Followers had rigged the woods with more spells than could be wise, but she was still surprised at how deeply the magic was embedded into the very soil. It was like one gigantic trap in which the Pack was caught like a fly in a spider's web. Hulda grinned. The spider would get a nasty surprise very soon. The spells were quite primitive, most of them being protection spells that changed the flow of fate in subtle ways to ensure the bearers' safety. Since they were very basic, it was hard to detect them, but once you knew they were there…. On her way deeper into the forest, Hulda passed dozens, all of them sealed with blood, which meant they could only be destroyed when their caster was killed, a feat she intended to accomplish. When the spells started to thicken, Hulda began to move more carefully. She could feel her prey close by. It was still a shock when she finally found the, or at least one, camp of the Followers—it was set up behind time.

No wonder we couldn't find them, Hulda thought grimly. It was entirely possible that the wolves had passed this very spot without getting so much as a whiff of the inhabitants of the camp. Placed radially around the camp were spells that secured it in the non-space behind time. That they had taken so much effort to hide this camp could only mean that the people in it were important. Hulda crept a little closer, using the shadows of trees as cover. The camp itself was not large—she could only guess how much power it cost to keep the twelve tents hidden all the time. In each tent, Hulda could rather sense than see a source of power. She had found the center of the spider's web. Grimly, the Mother Superior went through her options. She could start killing the spell-wielders right here, although this meant risking losing them all. Canubis had been very clear; he wanted at least one prisoner, and Hulda had yet to determine who that would be. She decided to try a more indirect approach. Stealthily, she sneaked toward the spell closest to her and inspected it. Since it was affiliated with time, she could easily discern the pattern of words that kept it going. Destroying that kind of spell was child's play for *ana regena anoso*. Given the structure of the whole construct, all she had to do was get rid of four of the ten anchoring spells to have the camp out in the real world again. Carefully, almost lovingly, Hulda reached into the heart of the pulsing nest of words in front of her and plucked out the center like a farmer would a vine grape. She used her own power to keep the net going, as not to alert the Followers. Living seemingly in absolute security had made them careless; there were not even guards Hulda had to evade. Like a deadly shadow, she went from one spell to the next until she had disarmed the crucial four. Reaching for her daggers, Hulda let the net collapse.

It was almost anticlimactic to watch as the camp faded from the non-space back into reality. Now she was alone in the gray silence again and could calmly decide whom of the spell-weavers she would take with her. They had finally realized that something was amiss and came running from their tents. Hulda counted five women and seven men, all of them cloaked in the borrowed power only the Good Mother could bestow. Among them was one man of small build and with ambition practically blazing around him, who caught Hulda's eye. She knew then who would be her prey. Before the Followers could organize themselves, Hulda started with the fun part of her mission. She approached two of the females, stepped into time right behind them, sliced their throats with the graceful movements of a dancer, and vanished back into the non-space. The other spell-weavers clustered like nervous sheep. Their terror had a soothing impact on Hulda's own rage. These cowering little maggots were the reason good warriors from the Pack had died. They did not deserve a quick, easy death themselves. Hulda appeared again, grabbed one of the men, and slit his belly open. Screaming, he tried to keep his innards from spilling out while Hulda was already on her next target. With quick movements, she gouged out the eyes of one female and cut the Achilles tendon of another male. The last two women got their hands hacked off, and the four remaining men shared the fate of the first one. Then Hulda stood in front of the small, ambitious leader of the group. He was terrified by the suddenness with which death had descended upon his camp and didn't even raise his hands in self-protection when Hulda hit him with the hilt of one of her daggers. Like a rag doll, he sank to the ground. Hulda focused her attention on the spell-weavers who were still alive. Almost gently she embraced the female with the missing eyes from behind and opened the arteries on both her arms. Whimpering like a child, the woman fell on the soft moss, drenching it with her blood. The one with the hacked-off hands got a kiss from the dagger at the height of her liver and soon fell prey to the internal bleeding. Patiently, Hulda watched while her victims slowly died, their twitching bodies trying desperately to stave off the inevitable. When all of them had taken their last breaths, the Mother Superior of the Sisters of the Night picked up her prisoner and returned to her gods.

"I HAVE good news and bad news."

Noemi looked at the assembled Emeris.

"The good news is that the prisoner Hulda brought back will wake up soon. Which brings me right to the bad news. I have examined him thoroughly and found that he's so laced with spells and power, it's impossible to interrogate him. He wouldn't even feel the pain of torture, and if he did, he would be prevented from speaking by one especially nasty spell. I can probably get rid of them all, but it's going to take me a lot of time, and we'll have to get back to the Valley first. I don't have all the ingredients I'm going to need with me."

Canubis huffed indignantly. His good mood about having such a promising prisoner had evaporated as soon as he heard Noemi's words.

"How about Renaldo's fire? It should burn those spells to a cinder in the blink of an eye."

Aegid had spoken tentatively, knowing what a sore topic he brought up. Renaldo only shook his head.

"The way I am at the moment, I'll probably kill the man before he can utter so much as a single word. I hate to admit it, but I'm nothing more than a liability as long as Casto is gone."

"Damn!" Kalad did not try to hide his frustration. They all shared it, this feeling of not being able to react in a befitting manner to the insults they had been dealt by the Followers throughout the summer. Hulda watched the agitated men with furrowed brows. Canubis glanced at her sharply.

"Hulda, what are you thinking about?"

The killer spoke slowly, as if she was weighing every word before letting it out. "Perhaps there is a way to use Renaldo's fire without losing the prisoner. Canubis, you are in full control of your power, aren't you?"

A moment of stunned silence followed this question, until they all caught on. Canubis shook his head vehemently. "That's absurd, Hulda. I do have full control, but there's no way I'm going to do what you're asking."

"But this may be our only chance, brother."

Renaldo spoke calmly. His face had frozen into a mask, and there was no telling what he truly thought.

"Forget it, Renaldo. You're my brother. I will never use my power of control against you. Never."

"Consider our options, Canubis. We've been running around in circles this entire summer. We still don't know anything about the numbers of the enemy or where they're hiding. Hulda can't scout the entire Dark Forest on her own. I mean, we're lucky she was able to trace that camp, and we really do need a few answers. Of course, we can withdraw now, wait for Noemi to lift all the spells, and then hope the information we're getting is not outdated next spring, though I think that's not what you'd call a successful campaign."

Canubis and Renaldo had locked their gazes, gray and amber drilling into each other. Canubis hissed through clenched teeth, "Leave us alone. All of you."

Like one man, the Emeris rose and hurried to leave the tent. None of them felt an inclination to be present when the two gods discussed a topic as difficult as this one. Even Hulda, who had brought it up, was glad when she was outside in the fresh air.

Inside the tent, Canubis had placed his hands on Renaldo's shoulders. His voice was firm.

"You're my precious little brother, Renaldo. The most important person in my life. Not even Noemi is as close to me as you are. How can you even consider something as ridiculous as me using my power against you?"

Renaldo sighed and leaned his forehead against his brother's chest.

"It's *because* I'm your little brother that I can do it. There's nobody in this world I worship and trust more than I do you. We shared lifetimes on Ana-Darasa. We are destined to walk eternity side by side. If there is one person I will allow to subjugate me, then it's you."

For a long time, the two gods stayed silent, each lost in the same tumultuous emotions, each pondering with a hint of fear the changes their relationship may undergo should they walk this special path. Until now, they had always been equals; their leadership had gone smoothly, for they both knew their strengths and weaknesses and were able to admit them. The question was how they would be able to deal with something as profound as using their powers against each other. It was Canubis who broke the silence.

"I really hate this idea."

"I'm not exactly thrilled either. But we need answers, and we need them now."

Canubis sighed. "Let's get it over with."

THE PRISONER looked up when Canubis and Renaldo entered the tent where he was kept. He was standing upright, his arms stretched out and fastened to two poles on either side. Renaldo scrutinized the man, who was of light, small build with no muscles to speak of and a thin mustache over even thinner lips. His eyes were of a light brown and shone in mockery as he watched the two gods approaching.

"Why are you here? You must know by now that I'm immune to anything you may do to me, and trust me, I'm not going to tell you a single thing just out of charity."

Canubis and Renaldo shared another long look. The prisoner's cocky attitude hardened their resolve. Neither of them could wait to see the condescending worm squirm in agony. Canubis treated the man to a lazy smile.

"Oh, I think you're going to chatter like an old woman in no time at all. No matter how strong the spells you used are, nothing can withstand the fire of my brother."

The prisoner's eyes narrowed. "You're bluffing. We know that without Casto, you're unable to control yourself. If you use your fire, you'll kill me." The mockery in the man's beady eyes deepened. "Must be unbearable for you to be reduced to the state of drawback. All you are at the moment is a beautiful face, and even your bark has lost its vigor."

Renaldo clenched his teeth. He didn't look at Canubis but focused on their prey when he spoke. "Do it. Do it now. I can't stand listening to these insults anymore."

All of a sudden, the tent was filled by an oppressing, aggravating silence. Canubis reached out for Renaldo with his power, and his will swamped the Angel of Death's mind. In that very instant, Renaldo understood how Casto had felt. It was humiliating to lose control so absolutely, to be directed by another person's will. The beast inside Renaldo roared with fury and tried desperately to fight the Wolf of War's command. There was a moment, no longer than it took a heart to beat twice, during which they were perfectly balanced. At this very moment, Renaldo had the chance to gain the upper hand, to subdue his brother instead of yielding to his will. Deliberately, he let it pass. The beast raged. It tore at the chains Canubis slung around it, but there was no escaping the Wolf of War. Grumbling and growling, the beast submitted.

Canubis shuddered. He had always known his little brother was special and dangerous. What he felt now was beyond his imagination. Renaldo was brimming with power, the fire inside him a blaze waiting to be unleashed. Grimly, Canubis gave his orders.

"Renaldo, burn away the spells and the source of power within the prisoner. Do it now."

Pain contorted Renaldo's perfect face when he did what Canubis had commanded him. He felt as if he would be torn at any moment, the wild, untamed fire fighting against the control Canubis executed. Only when he looked at the prisoner did he find a tiny shred of peace. The man's face was contorted in utter horror. Renaldo showed him a beatific smile only slightly tinged by the pain he still endured. Then he let the fire loose. The flames ate away the spells and the source of power within the prisoner's heart. His shrill screams as his protection was destroyed were like a balm to Renaldo's raging emotions. When the spells were all gone, Canubis gave his next command.

"Show this worthless worm the meaning of pain."

Again the beast roared, outraged that it was not allowed to act freely, and again, it finally complied. Thin ropes of fire slithered around the prisoner's body, burning into his flesh, causing him pain beyond imagining. It did not take long until he broke.

"I'll tell you everything. Everything you want to know! Just make the pain stop. I can't bear it!"

Canubis nodded toward Renaldo, who let the fire subside. At the same moment, Canubis's control over him lessened, and he took some deep breaths to get over the shock. He realized that he owed Casto some serious groveling and was determined to give it, if only his mate came back to him. The prisoner had already started blabbering, information flowing from his lips like a current.

"Your entire mission here is part of a scheme. We promised Xe'lien to help her become queen of the East if she lured you into a contract that would keep you occupied here in the Dark Forest for at least three years. The goal was to have you running around in circles, to kill as many of your mercenaries as possible, and to get our hands on at least one Emeris. The Good Mother gave us enough power to accomplish these goals."

"Why would she do that? This would only make sense if she's planning to set us up somewhere else as well."

The man whimpered. "I don't know about the Good Mother's plans. Each of her followers only knows enough to do her bidding. This way, you could never find out too much even if you caught one of us."

Canubis's face darkened, and the man hurried to speak on.

"There is one thing I haven't told you yet. It's something really important."

"Then why don't you spill?"

The prisoner gulped. "I know my life is forfeit, but I don't want to be subjected to your brother's fire again. This last piece of information is my bargain chip. If I tell it to you, you promise to kill me quickly."

Canubis raised an eyebrow. He was surprised that the worm was still able to negotiate.

"Why should I do that? I just have to ask Renaldo to use his fire again."

"But you don't want to, do you? Forcing your brother? You don't lose anything if you grant my request. So why prolong this sad scene any more than necessary?"

Canubis exchanged a quick glance with Renaldo before he returned his attention to the prisoner. "Fine. You have my word. Now spill."

The man breathed a sigh of relief. "Thank you. Before your assassin destroyed our camp, we had just gotten the information that our seers have found your heart. Casto is hiding in Quell'renar. A group of Followers is on their way to take him prisoner."

Renaldo roared. He stared at Canubis, who had taken out one of his daggers.

"Take Ghost and Demon and ride! Get him back here, no matter what it takes." The Wolf of War stared at the prisoner coldly. "I'll take care of matters here."

FROM HIGH up the tree he had chosen as a lookout, Ellewinn watched the Emeris approaching and couldn't believe his luck. The last few weeks he had tried to get close enough to one of them to make use of the shadow dagger the priest of the Good Mother had given him, and here the least intimidating of them just wandered into his arms like a gift from the heavens. Given what he had suffered at the hands of the Followers, especially after one of their secret camps had been eradicated by the assassin witch, Ellewinn felt his heart racing.

It was time to gain his freedom back. He waited till the man was directly beneath him, then dropped from the sky like a deadly shadow. The man didn't even look up when he made a step to the right. With a curse, Ellewinn landed right next to his target, who looked at him with an expression of mild surprise.

"That was quite impressive, dropping out of the tree like that. But it's not very polite to wave a dagger in people's faces."

Taken aback by the bizarreness of the situation, Ellewinn regarded his target more closely. The man was smaller than him, about one ell and two and a half spans, with boring thin hair the color of mud and a face that showed the hardships he had endured. The man was on the lean side, with long, bony fingers and arms that did not seem to possess any strength. The tunic he wore was a little too short and looked as if it consisted solely of patches. His boots were equally worn, as was the scabbard for his sword. The only remarkable thing about the man was a certain curiosity that he emanated like an exotic perfume.

"If you want to kill me, you should really get your act together."

The mockery in the man's voice pried Ellewinn from his trance. His eyes narrowed. "Don't patronize me, old man. This dagger is made from chaos, and it can kill you as easily as I winked out the lives of your mercenaries."

To Ellewinn's surprise, the man wasn't frightened in the least. He even came a little closer to inspect the weapon.

"My, my, looks like the Good Mother has really caught up with us. Made from chaos. That's bad news."

His hand shot forward, the side of it connected with Ellewinn's wrist, and the dagger sailed through the air. It only took Ellewinn a heartbeat to understand that he had just underestimated a dangerous opponent. Just in time, he managed to duck under the dagger the Emeris had aimed at him. Using all his speed, Ellewinn drew his second dagger, unfortunately a normal one, and counterattacked. The man evaded him narrowly, and Ellewinn could hear his clothes rip. They faced each other again, and Ellewinn watched in horror as the long wound on his opponent's chest closed as if it had never existed.

Bantu grinned when he saw the disbelief in his attacker's eyes while the wound healed. This man had been uncomfortably close to killing him, something that did not sit well with his pride. He had decided then that he would teach the warrior a little lesson until he brought up the issue with the shadow dagger. Bantu knew from the prophecies that the Good Mother would find a weapon that could harm even the Echend'dim and Emeris. If this man had really obtained it, he needed to bring him and the dagger to Canubis. Which could be difficult, since the man was a lot faster than Bantu himself, and he had by now lost the advantage of surprise. He tried to distract the man by mocking him.

"What, I thought you knew everything about the Emeris, dagger-wielder. I'm so old, I do heal pretty quickly. So if you want to gain the upper hand, you have to cause some real damage. Come on, put your heart into it!"

Pure fury ignited in the eyes of the other man, and Bantu hoped he would become careless enough to make a mistake. When the man came at him, he realized that he had underestimated the ferocity with which the fighter would react to his banter. Bantu got is hands up in time to meet the blow of the other's body, but he had no chance of balancing them both. They went to the ground, where they rolled around a few times until the attacker managed to gain the upper hand. He pinned Bantu underneath him and reached for the shadow dagger that was lying close. Triumph lit up his features when he raised the dagger with both hands. Bantu tensed, waiting for the final blow, when he suddenly felt himself disintegrating. It was a strange sensation, as if his body was no longer part of reality. The man with the dagger stared with wide eyes at the place Bantu had been, where there was only the moss of the forest floor now. Bantu watched as the man gingerly patted the ground.

"Where are you?"

He sounded almost desperate. Bantu somehow let the countless pieces of himself reassemble behind the man, his second dagger ready in his hand. Bantu found his new talent quite useful.

"I'm here."

The man spun around quickly, only to get hit by the hilt of the dagger full force. With a soft groan, he collapsed. Bantu hurried to bind him and secured the shadow dagger. The thing looked just like a normal blade until the sun shone on it. Instead of reflecting the rays, the steel swallowed them and grew hot in Bantu's hand. Carefully, he wrapped the weapon in a piece of cloth, picked up the stranger, who was not as heavy as Bantu had anticipated given his size, and started back to the camp.

"WHAT HAVE you brought us here, Bantu?"

Canubis glanced curiously at the bundle Bantu had just placed at his feet. The man was tall, at least one and a half ells and two hands. His build resembled that of Renaldo, although the muscles were sturdier. He had very short light brown hair that seemed almost golden and was disrupted by strands of black. The face was broad, with a nose that was a little too long to be attractive and lips so thin they could barely hide the teeth. Still there was an aura of grace surrounding the unconscious man that alerted Canubis. He knew that kind of presence yet couldn't remember where he had felt it before. While the Wolf of War was still musing about the prisoner, Bantu handed him a cloth with a dagger inside. Canubis furrowed his brows.

"What's that?"

Bantu shrugged. "Just take a look."

Canubis unwrapped the weapon and snarled. There was no mistaking this thing.

"*Azashreem*. The Echend'dim's death. And this one was carrying it?"

Bantu nodded. "He called it a shadow dagger, but ultimately, it's the same. I thought you might want to see this."

Canubis patted Bantu on the shoulder.

"Thank you, old friend. This is indeed important." He fixed his gaze on the unconscious man. "We need to find out how many more of these the Followers already have. Take him to Noemi."

"Wait!"

The cry came from Belnor, who had come to see what the commotion was about, together with Xi'an and Lukan. Ever since Elua had chosen to rest in the Green Lands, the two warriors had started to take care of Lukan. Belnor stared intently at Bantu's prisoner.

"It's him. He's the one who killed us. Who killed Elua. There's no doubt about it."

Lukan roared. He drew his dagger with a swift motion, ready to kill the reason for his misery. It was only thanks to Canubis's unrivaled reflexes that he did not succeed. The Wolf of War held Lukan's wrist in an iron grip.

"Hold it, Lukan. I promise you will get your revenge, but first, we need to find out more about the Azashreem. If he doesn't talk, you have my permission to make him do it."

Lukan trembled under Canubis's gaze like a young tree in a storm. Finally he lowered his gaze and pressed his forehead against Canubis's fingers.

"I thank you, my lord."

Canubis let go of Lukan's wrist, glad that the young man had come to his senses again.

"Let's find out what our guest knows."

ELLEWINN EMERGED slowly from the darkness that had consumed him. While his memories flooded back, his body provided him with some unpleasant information. He was shackled to a pole with his arms spread wide. His feet were also bound with chains that fastened him to the ground. Cursing his bad luck, Ellewinn opened his eyes. Three men and a woman were standing in front of him. The most intimidating was the black-haired, amber-eyed predator right in his line of sight, closely followed by the one with the grim features. Ellewinn could feel that this man was barely able to keep his emotions in check. The third man was harmless by comparison. He gave the impression of a friendly dog incapable of harming anybody. The female appeared to be in the same category, but there was something about her that made Ellewinn wary. She definitely was not as innocuous as she seemed. Ellewinn could not see his captor anywhere. The intimidating man spoke first.

"If you're looking for a way out, I've got to disappoint you. You're not going to leave this place alive. Lukan here will see to that."

At the mention of living, Ellewinn groaned. "How long have I been out?"

The black-haired male looked displeased but still answered the question. "For about half a day."

Ellewinn closed his eyes. This was bad, really bad. "Listen, you have to let me go right now. If you don't, it doesn't matter what you do to me, because I'll be dead anyway."

Lukan growled. "Do you really think we'd just let you march out of here after you've killed so many of us?"

Ellewinn winced. He knew he had reached the end of his path, that there was no escaping his fate now, yet he still refused to admit defeat. As long as he could take a breath, there was still hope.

"I didn't do it voluntarily. I was forced by those stupid Followers. They put a seal on me. When I dare to disobey, this wretched thing eats into me like heated iron. I do whatever they tell me to stay alive."

Lukan furrowed his brows. "Somehow, I don't believe you."

The forbidding man glanced at the female. "Noemi?"

She stepped forward and placed her hands on Ellewinn's naked chest. Her eyes lit up in concentration.

"There is something inside him, though I can't tell you what it is exactly. All I can say for sure is that he's laced with magic through and through."

"If what he says is true, then he should be able to feel pain."

Lukan's voice sounded hungry; he was clearly out for blood. Ellewinn locked gazes with the leader, who, after a few moments of consideration, made a dismissive gesture.

"Fine, let's find out. Lukan, you have permission to torture him. But don't kill him yet, do you understand?"

"I do, my lord."

With that, Lukan rammed a dagger into Ellewinn's upper arm and twisted it. Ellewinn screamed as the white-hot slivers of pain raced through his body. The friendly looking man who had kept silent until now took a step forward. His voice was soft, almost inaudible.

"Lukan, please."

It was not Lukan who answered but the leader.

"Leave him alone, Sic. He needs this. And I need answers."

Sic's shoulders slumped, and he retreated a few steps. Lukan glared at Ellewinn.

"How many Azashreem do the Followers have?"

Ellewinn tried to concentrate. If information would get him out of this, he was willing to tell them everything he knew.

"What's an Azashreem?"

A second dagger pierced his arm a little below the first. Before Ellewinn could get his breath back, Lukan was already holding the third. He was just about to ram it into Ellewinn's other arm when Sic interrupted him.

"Wait, Lukan. I think he really doesn't know. Remember what Bantu said? That he called the Azashreem a shadow dagger?"

"You mean the weapon of chaos?"

Ellewinn was glad he had something to talk about. "As far as I know, the dagger I had with me is the only one they had. It takes the Followers a long time to make. They threatened me with death should I lose it." He huffed. "Which is probably the least of their problems now."

Canubis regarded Ellewinn closely. "You're pretty forthcoming for a Follower."

161

"As I said, I'm not one of them. They're forcing me with that cursed seal, and if I don't return to them soon, they're going to kill me for sure."

Canubis seemed torn. He looked at Noemi. "I guess there's nothing you can do?"

"I'm sorry, Canubis. It's the same as with the other man. It would take me a long time to get rid of the magic. Renaldo's fire is the only thing that can just erase a spell as strong as this one."

"My lord, please tell me you're not thinking about letting him go!"

Lukan sounded agitated, and his hands were twitching.

"I'm not sure, Lukan. As far as I'm concerned, he's not lying to us. Could be useful to have a spy."

"If he's telling the truth, he's a worthless spy, since he's controlled by the Followers. It's probably better to kill him right now."

Canubis turned to Ellewinn. "What Lukan says is worth considering. Do you have anything to offer at this point?"

Ellewinn opened his mouth to speak when he suddenly felt a wave of agony overwhelming his body. Compared to this new pain, the daggers in his arm felt almost like a caress. He started to scream and was cut short by another assault. His world shrank down to the rhythm in which his body was subjected to the agony. Oblivious of anything else, Ellewinn collapsed in his chains.

Speechless, Canubis, Lukan, Sic, and Noemi watched as the body of the prisoner twitched on the pole as if it was doing some macabre dance.

"Can't you help him, Noemi?"

Canubis tried to stay calm, although this demonstration of power worried him deeply. His wife spoke in a monotone that showed how shaken she was.

"I'm afraid I can't do anything. This seal is indeed very strong. Even if you were to lend me your strength, I'd only prolong his suffering. I can feel the seal clearly now, and it won't go away until he's dead. Whoever is doing this is enjoying themselves."

"So if he dies, the seal will go away?"

Lukan sounded pensive. His gaze was glued to the shivering body of Ellewinn.

"Yes."

Noemi already knew what Lukan was about to do, and she was grateful for it. Lukan stepped forward and took the prisoner's face in his hands. His voice was calm now, soothing.

"I forgive you for killing Elua. After all, it was not your choice. In return, I'm asking you to forgive me as well. For what I did. For what I'm going to do."

Through the red haze of his pain, Ellewinn stared into the brown eyes of his torturer. He saw regret there, and a love that had turned into misery. He managed a weak smile that morphed into a grimace when the next wave assaulted him. Lukan let go of Ellewinn's face, took the third dagger, and rammed it into his heart with all the strength he possessed.

The twitching stopped immediately. Black tendrils started to appear on Ellewinn's chest. Like a disease they thickened, forming a complicated spell that had bound the man and made him a slave to the Followers. As if forced by an invisible pull, the tendrils started to leak out from the skin. Heavy drops of darkness trickled down to the ground and turned to ashes there. When the last trace of the spell had vanished, Lukan yanked the daggers out of Ellewinn's arms, unshackled him, and placed him gently on the ground. His face was an impenetrable mask that no longer resembled the careless youth he had been until only a few weeks ago.

"So much death and pain. I think I can understand Elua now. It's hard to keep going."

Lukan had muttered those words to himself, not expecting anybody to react. It surprised him when Canubis patted him on the shoulder.

"Staying or leaving, both decisions require all the courage you have. And they both make you stronger."

"Thank you, my lord. I think I understand now."

Canubis wanted to answer Lukan, but at that moment, Sic knelt down beside the dead body of their prisoner. He had the dazed gaze Canubis had learned to recognize as a sign that the Luksari had taken over. Quickly, he yanked Lukan to his feet to give Sic more space.

IN THE world between, Sic stared at the shadows surrounding Ellewinn. Deep inside the gloom, he saw not one, but two sparks glowing, and it took him a moment to realize that they were the slanted eyes of a cat of prey. Carefully, Sic approached the shadows, his gaze glued to the two glinting lights. Slowly, deliberately, a huge feline stepped forward, staring at Sic with the calm, unwavering expression all cats possessed. Sic stretched out his hand and reverently touched the noble head with the soft light brown fur. A purr was his reward.

"I guess that means you wish to come back, am I right?"

The purr deepened. Sic smiled.

"You better close your eyes. My light is pretty intense."

With a snarl, the cat averted its gaze. Sic started to blaze.

CANUBIS, LUKAN, and Noemi watched as the prisoner sat up with a surprised expression on his face. Gingerly, he felt for his chest where the seal had been and then started to smile, albeit not in a friendly way.

Ellewinn couldn't believe it. He was finally free! Like a tide, his memories about the time before he had been captured started coming back to him. Memories so agonizingly sweet, he wondered how he could have forgotten them. The coppery taste of blood in his muzzle when he killed his prey. The crunching sound the bones of the deer made when he brought it down. The ecstasy when his teeth first penetrated the soft skin of his next meal. The sheer joy when he changed his shape from human to cat and back, when the world was all vivid colors and tantalizing smells. Before he could think about it, Ellewinn let the cat take over.

His body stretched as it took on more muscle, his human jaw turning into a muzzle with razor-sharp teeth, his hands and feet becoming paws. Ellewinn let his gaze roam through the tent. There was the black-haired leader, the woman who was also a snake, the man who was wreathed in shadows, the one who had freed him by dealing him the killing blow, and the light bearer. From his feline perspective, they were all perfect predators. Friends. What he needed to find right now were his enemies. He lifted his head and scented the air. Then he started running.

Canubis followed the massive cat of prey outside. Ellewinn in his feline form was pure force and beauty. He didn't resemble any of the cat species on Ana-Darasa, but Canubis had seen his kind before. Only once, shortly after they had arrived in Quell'renar. At that time, he had thought the cat shifters were gone. Apparently, at least one of them had somehow managed to carry on the line. Like the wolves, the shifter cats were bigger and more lethal than their normal, wild counterparts. Ellewinn's coat was of a light brown hue that would make him almost invisible in the forest. He had four sets of impressive claws that could cut through flesh like a sword through water. His massive jaw with the huge teeth could crush a man's skull without apparent effort, and the sheer mass of the cat was more than a little intimidating. Ellewinn was running toward the forest, and Canubis had a clear idea what he was up to. He connected his thoughts with the wolves. *Follow him. We will be behind you. When he starts killing, feel free to join him.* Like silver shadows, the wolves paced after Ellewinn, eager to hunt with such an impressive predator.

ELLEWINN RAN through the forest, following his memories to the place where he had last met with his captors. His heart was full with the thirst for revenge. He could feel rather than hear the wolf pack running after him, but they were not there to chase him. No, they were hunting with him, and strangely enough, he didn't mind. Like all cats, he was a solitary animal, a loner who didn't do well in pack situations. That he didn't mind this strange human-wolf pack hunting with him was another sign of how special they were.

When they came to the rock Ellewinn used as one of his landmarks to not get lost in the Dark Forest, he slowed down. The prey was close, and he had no intention of scaring it away. He crouched on his belly, crawling toward the clearing where the camp had been. They were still there. Ellewinn looked back and saw the wolf pack spreading out, surrounding the camp. Once they had come full circle, one of them let out a short, sharp bark. Nobody would escape them. A little farther into the forest, Ellewinn heard the humans approach, ready to join the fight. They could have the leftovers. He threw his head back and yowled. The sound reverberated through the forest before it was taken up by the wolves, who added their own howling to his challenge. Chaos broke out in the camp. Men and women hastened to get their weapons while they tried to determine where the threat was coming from. Ellewinn didn't hesitate any longer. He lunged out of the tree line, landed on the chest of one of the guards, and bit down on the man's head without mercy. When he heard the satisfying crunch of breaking bones, a red haze obscured his sight, and he went into a blood rage.

WHEN CANUBIS and his men entered the scene, Ellewinn and the pack had already dealt with most of the warriors. The ground was drenched in blood. Canubis lowered his sword to admire Ellewinn. The huge cat shifter had just killed a man with one swipe of his powerful paw and was now pouncing on another who was stupid enough to try and stab the cat with his sword. An enraged roar shook the clearing. Ellewinn brought his front paws down on the man's torso and let his claws slide out. They pierced the writhing body to the ground, giving Ellewinn all the time in the world to bend down and tear the throat out. A sputter and it was over. The cat stepped away from the dead body, looking for its next victim. When there were none left, it turned toward Canubis.

The Wolf of War and the shifter cat stared at each other for a very long time. It was Canubis who finally broke the silence.

"Well fought, *elusi*. Since my Luksari brought you back, you are now officially part of my Eternal Guard, my Echend'dim. I do understand that this may be hard for you, and I will not force you to come with us. Should you decide to trust me and my Pack, I will accept your vows and offer my own in return."

Ellewinn hesitated for a few moments. He wanted to be free. It was all he had been thinking about while the seal had eaten into his flesh, even though he hadn't understood what kind of freedom he had been yearning for. The cat in him recognized that the man in front of him was the ultimate predator on this planet. As such, he felt inclined to submit to him. He also felt that the offer was genuine. The man invited him to join this powerful pack, to be a part of this deadly family. Ellewinn stepped forward and lowered his massive head. The man smiled. "Welcome to the Pack, my friend."

"PLEASE PUT your sword down, Your Highness."

The voice of the man who had spoken was full of derision. Casto slowly turned around, his eyes fixed on the crumpled wall in front of him. From the shadows, ten people appeared, all of them armed with crossbows that were aimed directly at him and Lys. He dropped his sword. The clattering sound when it hit the stone floor echoed through the ruins like a curse. Casto focused on the man who had spoken. He was of average build, perhaps half a head smaller than Casto, with black hair that hung in dirty strands into his plain face. Only his eyes were memorable; they burned with madness.

"How did you find me? This place is quite heavily shielded."

The man snorted. A condescending smile appeared on his face. "No matter how well this place is protected, the Good Mother is with us, and she gave us the power to tear those walls down. Our seers are growing in strength, and finding *you* is not difficult—you're like a beacon in the night."

Casto nodded. He had anticipated as much even before Quell'renar had let him know there were people coming his way. Out of the corner of his eye, he saw movement. The attackers were closing in on him.

"So, what is it going to be? Are you going to kill me?"

Again the man snorted derisively. "Do you take me for a fool? I'm well aware that we can't just kill you. But don't get your hopes up. The Good Mother knows ways to eliminate even the heart of a god. Your days on Ana-Darasa are running out. And once you are gone, the bastards will fall as well. This is almost too good to be true."

"You're right about that one."

Casto had only murmured those words, but nevertheless the man had heard him. His lips thinned.

"What are you talking about?"

Now it was Casto's turn to patronize.

"You made several mistakes today, all of which are going to cost you your life. The first was to come here, and with only ten fighters. That was… unwise. Second, you decided to attack in the late afternoon, probably because you thought it would be easier to creep up on me in the shadows. Clever thinking, but also very, very stupid thinking. Third—" Casto paused for a moment, a cold, menacing glint in his eyes. "—you refrained from killing me on the spot."

One of the fighters had the presence of mind to shoot then and there, but it was already too late. Casto had vanished, and before any of the other Followers could react, the shadows came alive. The man who led the group felt tendrils of darkness slither around his legs. They closed on his wrists and made him unable to move. In the quickly advancing gloom, he could hear the muffled screams of his fellow fighters, all of which cut off quickly. The coppery scent of freshly spilled blood was heavy in the air, and at one point, he thought he heard the gut-wrenching sound of bones breaking under a heavy weight.

Then there was silence, the only sound his own heavy breathing. Desperately, he tried to free himself from the shadows when he suddenly felt the edge of a blade pressing against his larynx. Casto's voice was like a fevered whisper in the man's ear.

"You really should have killed me the moment you caught sight of me. Did you honestly expect me to be such easy prey? I'm almost offended. As you may have realized by now, I'm not only the heart of a god, I'm also a pretty good warrior, and yes, I do have a demon horse who commands the darkness. And you're supposed to be the best the Good Mother can send? Don't make me laugh!"

The blade vanished from the man's throat and Casto stepped into his field of vision. Although it was almost completely dark now, the man could see the blood all over the king's clothes. In the gloom, he looked like a monster from a fairy tale, his blond hair in stark contrast to the gore on his body. Casto fetched ropes from his belongings and returned to his prisoner. While he bound his wrists and secured the rope on a partly crumbled stone arch so that the man's toes were just barely off the ground, he kept on talking.

"I'm grateful to you, though. I'm sure you can tell me some interesting things about your order and the Good Mother."

The man spat. "I'm not going to tell you anything, you conceited bastard! Try your worst. I have learned to endure all kinds of pain."

Casto patted the man's cheek almost lovingly. "I'm sure you have. Me, on the other hand, I was in the hands of a torturer for more than half of my life. Let's put both our knowledge to the test, shall we?"

When he heard the amiable tone, the man realized that Casto was worse than anything he may have imagined. With a shudder, he steeled himself against the hours of pain that were surely awaiting him.

THE SUN rose in splendid glory over the ruins of Quell'renar and was greeted by the screams of the man who was now covered in blood. Casto cleaned the blade of his dagger on the clothes of one of the fallen, his voice dismissive.

"You sure are making this difficult. Why don't you just give in and tell me what I want to know? To be frank, I'm getting bored."

The man spit bloody slime on the floor. His voice was barely audible. "That's your problem. I'm not going to tell you anything. Never."

Casto sighed.

"Seems like I have no choice, then." He approached his victim slowly. "Let's see how well you can withstand fire."

For a moment the man showed real fear; then his features contorted into a display of mockery.

"You're bluffing. Everybody knows you have no control over Renaldo's fire. If you use it, you'll kill me without getting any answers at all."

He stared into Casto's suddenly afflicted face and showed a bloody grin. "You know, it's weighing on your mate a lot, the fact that you haven't mastered his flame yet. It means you're not wholly committed to him. You're making him weak."

Casto's regal features broke into a beatific smile. A giggle escaped his lips while he held up his right hand in front of the man's face. Thin flames broke out on each fingertip, slowly growing in length and heat.

"You mean this fire?"

They both watched as the flames thinned out into ropes of heat that aimed for the man's body.

"Your order has watched me for so long, you took so many pains to find out everything about me, and yet you make such an elementary mistake as underestimating me? Do you honestly want to tell me you never, not even for a heartbeat, thought I could be faking it? I mean, you do know I grew up in Ummana, that I'm the son of one of the most ruthless politicians the Plains have ever seen. Did you really think I would show my trump cards openly when I could hide them so perfectly? I've been able to control the fire for some time now, and no, I didn't tell anybody about it, not even the Barbarian. Why should I, when this little secret could be my saving grace one day? It's your bad luck that you've found out, but don't worry, you won't have to carry this burden for long."

The ropes of flame snaked around the man's torso and slowly started tightening. Casto's voice sounded casual, as if he were making small talk at a banquet.

"You know, the pain you're feeling while this burns into your flesh is nothing compared to the agony you'll experience once the flame touches your soul. If you tell me your secrets now, I may feel inclined to spare you that particular sensation."

Instead of an answer, the man just screamed. Casto allowed the fire to burn for a few moments longer. Then he withdrew the tendrils of heat.

Coughing and panting, the man hung in his ropes, his heart beating so violently, Casto could see it through the shreds of his clothes.

"I'll tell you everything I know. Everything. Just never do that to me again! I'm begging you!"

"Depends on the quality of your answers. Now spill. I want to know where you're hiding your seers, what the Good Mother is planning, and where you have placed your spies."

IN THE early-morning hours, Renaldo felt Casto pull on his fire, which meant he was getting close to his heart. The last days had been pure agony for him, a constant anxiety gnawing at his guts like rats on a fresh corpse while he was riding as he never had before, not even when Lys had carried him to the Mines to retrieve his heart. Back then, the black stallion had done all the work for him, not leaving him any choice. Even though Demon and Ghost were far more than ordinary horses, they weren't sentient manifestations of chaos on Ana-Darasa, and the decision to take a rest now and then had been entirely up to him. All his instincts screamed at him to get to Casto as quickly as possible, while his common sense told him the horses needed to rest to keep going. They were true warrior horses, fighters who would do anything for him and his brother, which also meant their well-being was in his hands. As much as it had pained him, Renaldo had made sure to give them the rest they needed, even though every moment he wasn't moving toward Quell'renar was like a needle piercing his heart. Now he was back in the saddle, and Demon and Ghost were running at full speed again since the ruins of Quell'renar were already visible in the distance. Renaldo cursed. He was obviously too late to save his mate. He only hoped Casto would persevere until he reached the ruins.

An hour later, Renaldo galloped into Quell'renar, his sword at the ready to kill anything that moved. He came upon a scene of pure carnage. The stench of blood and decay was heavy in the air. At the entrance to the temple, he found three bodies that had obviously been trampled by Lys. The skulls were cracked open, and brain matter was smeared on the stones. Inside the walls of the temple, he found more bodies, all of them not only killed but slaughtered. Two more had cracked skulls; the remaining four had their throats slit open. Whatever had happened here, it had been fast and brutal. Some of the corpses were still clinging to their bows. None of them had had the time to draw their swords. Renaldo dismounted Ghost and looked around.

"Casto!"

His voice echoed through the stones, and just when he was about to call for a second time, he got an answer.

"Over here, Barbarian!"

Renaldo raced along the broken pillars until he reached the former sanctuary that was now out in the open since the roof had caved in. Casto stood there, with Lys next to him, and behind the two, the Angel of Death glimpsed a body hanging from a broken arch. He sheathed his sword.

"Seems like I don't have to come to your rescue after all."

Casto shrugged. "As you can see, I'm fine. There was never a need."

"I understand. What happened?"

Casto cast a dismissive glance around. "The followers of the Good Mother were stupid enough to go after me with only ten fighters. Shortly before nightfall. There's no helping some people."

Renaldo bowed to Lys. "Thank you, Lysistratos."

The stallion looked pointedly away. Casto grinned.

"No words of praise for me, Barbarian?"

"You did well. Very well. I'm impressed. Who's your prisoner?"

Casto turned toward the man hanging from the arch. "He's the leader of the group. After some persuading, he had quite the story to tell. Unfortunately, I overdid it. He's dead."

Renaldo gulped. Casto had never been the caring type to begin with, but the casualness with which he reported the death of the unlucky man showed that he had taken on more edges during his time away. It made Renaldo wonder what his mate had done in those almost five months. He decided to leave that thought alone for the time being and to tackle the more important problem, posing the question he didn't dare voice yet had to ask.

"So, are you coming home with me?"

Abruptly, Casto turned away from him. His voice was tense. "I'm covered in blood. I need to wash."

Hesitatingly, Renaldo followed Casto to the fountain that was the center of the sanctuary. He remembered the place very well. It had been here where Ana-Isara had taken his and Canubis's hearts. Renaldo felt his insides constrict. The circle had finally closed.

Casto had taken off his bloody clothes and started to wash himself with vigorous motions. They were alone. Lys had not followed them, something Renaldo was grateful for. Even though Casto was naked in front of him, Renaldo did not view that as an invitation. He knew his mate was not as shallow as that. It was probably bait, to some extent, and a test. Knowing Casto, practically everything was a test. The Angel of Death watched for some time while Casto scrubbed the grime of battle from his skin. He was more tanned than before and looked more haggard. There was a nervous air to him Renaldo couldn't remember from before. When Casto was finally clean, he just stood there, facing the cistern. The wet cloth in his hand dribbled small pinkish drops on the white stone floor. Renaldo decided to take another risk.

"So, are you coming home with me?"

Slowly, Casto turned around. His face was a mask that barely concealed the raging emotions mirrored in his eyes.

"Are you miserable without me?"

Renaldo gulped. "I am miserable. More than you can ever imagine."

"Good. Because without you, I'm barely able to breathe."

Renaldo gaped. He was sure he had just misheard, that his despair was playing cruel tricks on him. Casto flashed him a crooked smile.

"To answer your question, Barbarian, I will come home with you."

When he saw the unbridled joy in Renaldo's face, Casto held up a hand in warning.

"You cannot touch me, Barbarian. That's the condition. You can never touch me without my permission."

Renaldo put his hands behind his back to show that he understood. "I promise I won't."

The derisive smile he got as an answer made him cringe.

"I know what your promises are worth, Barbarian, so don't bother. Just don't touch me."

Gravely, Renaldo nodded. He knew this was part of the punishment Casto exacted, and it was well-deserved. Still the beast inside him raged against the condition. It was furious that the one person who could help it find relief was so close and yet so out of reach. Renaldo gritted his teeth. He had managed to deal with the effects of his forced abstinence for the entire summer, so a few more months until Casto forgave him were nothing, or so he tried to tell himself.

Casto watched the inner turmoil mirrored in the Barbarian's face and enjoyed it. Renaldo looked desperate and tired. He had lost some of his natural arrogance, and the aloof beauty he usually displayed was tainted by an overwhelming sorrow that surrounded him like a halo. Casto was still angry enough to take pleasure from the Barbarian's discomfort and to even push him a little further. He approached Renaldo slowly while running his hands over his body in a seductive manner.

"No matter what, you are not allowed to touch me."

Casto had now reached Renaldo and was standing so close, they both could feel the other's breath on their skin. Casto reached down and opened Renaldo's trousers.

"Even if I were to tease you here, you still cannot touch me."

Sweat broke out on Renaldo's forehead, and his back muscles tensed under the strain of staying in control. Casto chuckled wickedly. He motioned the Barbarian down on his backside and straddled him.

"Even if I were to push you down and use your nice big cock to find my relief, you cannot touch me."

Renaldo's entire body shivered. He gritted his teeth so hard he thought his jaw would break. Having Casto so close, so naked, so alluring, was more than he could bear in his starved state. And yet he did, for if he forced his capricious mate now, he knew he would never get a second chance. Judging from the mocking glint in Casto's eyes, he knew as well, and he reveled in getting his revenge.

Now the king licked his own fingers until they were dripping with saliva before he started loosening himself up. Confronted with such an erotic view, Renaldo felt a red haze obscuring his senses. The beast was roaring, demanding him to take action, to reclaim what was his. The Angel of Death summoned every last ounce of self-control he possessed to withstand temptation. It was almost impossible, especially when Casto started to take him inside his body, slowly sliding down on Renaldo's cock until they were completely joined.

"Even if you are buried deep inside me, you still cannot touch me."

Casto's voice was a feverish whisper yet still demanding. His hips started to move.

"Even if I were to ride you like I'm doing now, you have to keep your hands off."

Renaldo groaned in frustration but complied. Casto bent forward to kiss him on the mouth. Their eyes met.

"Are you suffering, Barbarian?"

"Yes, I am suffering. Badly. But if that's what it takes to have you back in my life, I'll gladly endure it every day."

Casto froze. He could feel Renaldo's honest words pierce through the defensive walls he had built around his heart. Before he knew it, they started to crumble, baring his soul to the man who had wounded it so cruelly. His hurt pride wailed not to give in, not to forgive, but the truth was, Casto was too tired, too lonely to keep on negating what he truly wanted. With tears in his eyes, he kissed Renaldo once more.

"Seems like you found the magic words, Barbarian. Show me what you've got."

Renaldo froze beneath his beloved heart. It took some time until the words finally sunk in. Then a shy smile appeared on his face. His hands reached out tentatively for Casto's face and wiped away the tears.

"My own. My love. Thank you. Thank you so much." He hesitated for a moment. "I would really like to take it slow, to make you feel good. Unfortunately, I don't think I can control myself any longer. It has been so long. I'm starving."

Casto put his own hands over Renaldo's. There was a hint of petulance in his tone.

"Don't worry, I was expecting as much. And now stop talking and start moving."

That was all the invitation Renaldo needed. With a growl he flipped Casto onto his back and thrust in deep. The feeling was so exquisite, he lost his reason then and there. As he poured all his raging emotions, his feelings of regret and loneliness, his longing and his despair as well as the overwhelming love he had for Casto into the king's body and soul, he felt their connection come to life again. It was like a spark that flickered and threatened to die out until Casto accepted it and fed it with his own love and longing. Once more connected on all levels, Renaldo clung to his mate while he took him with long, hard thrusts.

WHEN THEY were finally sated, they sat with their backs leaning on the cistern, enjoying the heat of the sun. Renaldo had his arms slung around Casto's torso, his chin resting on the king's left shoulder.

"It was here where Mother took our hearts. Where she took you."

Casto shuddered. "I know. Lys has shown me."

"How could he do that?"

"I don't really understand either. For him, time is not linear. And Quell'renar wanted me to see as well. It was pretty intense, to say the least. I don't know why, but this place is somehow alive, and it welcomed me. The things I've seen—I always thought you were indifferent, but when I was confronted with the pain on your face after your heart was taken, after *I* was gone, I began to understand."

There was only a slight hint of accusation in Casto's voice, barely tangible, yet Renaldo picked up on it, not sure himself if what he was saying would make things better or worse.

"I never told you, did I? It's not because I don't trust you, surely not. It's just—these things happened a long time ago, and the man I am now has almost nothing to do with the boy I had been. Many of those memories are just painful, and I was glad when time finally dulled them for me. Nevertheless, before I met you, there was always this constant ache in my chest. My thoughts could never really calm down. When you entered my life, I was suddenly too busy to think about anything but your next move. And even though you had me running around in circles, I was truly content for the first time in my life. I wasn't willing to give that up. I couldn't give it up. Besides, I wasn't sure how to do it and even a little afraid how you would react. As much as I was trying to hide, I also wanted to protect you."

Casto placed a hand on Renaldo's arm, enjoying the little tingle it sent through his own body.

"I understand. It still pisses me off, though. You made me share everything with you but didn't let me in on your secrets. I'm also aware there are a lot of them, since you're literally ancient." That got Casto a playful bash on the head, but he continued, seemingly unperturbed, "Yet I still resent that you didn't tell me anything."

"I admit it was a mistake. I'm sorry."

Casto ignored the apology, tightening his grip on Renaldo's arm. He had just remembered something and wanted the Barbarian to know.

"They weren't alone. Dweian and Dria, when they died, they weren't alone. I was there, and I stayed until their very last breath. They were not alone."

Casto felt Renaldo's chest tighten. His voice sounded raw. "Thank you."

Renaldo didn't say more, and for some time they just sat there with the sun warming their bodies. Finally, Casto started talking again, unsure of what he really wanted to say, but also unable to keep the words from stumbling out.

"I saw what you did to the first army of the Good Mother."

Behind Casto, Renaldo tensed. His hold on Casto's body tightened.

"Are you appalled?"

Casto shook his head vehemently.

"Not in the least! Those bastards deserved it." He paused for a moment. "You had no control whatsoever. You destroyed everything."

It was a statement, not an accusation. Renaldo sighed deeply, remembering that particular day and the revelations it had brought.

"You're right. I had no control. When Mother brought us here, we may have been full-fledged gods, but we were also very young. We knew next to nothing about the true extent of our power. Once our hearts were taken, we lost what little control we had as well. When I faced that army, I knew I would annihilate not only the people but also the very ground that was feeding us. It was a calculated risk—well, a move of despair. You saw that army. We stood no chance. It was either my fire or our death."

"Nevertheless, you enjoyed it."

Again Casto was stating a fact. Renaldo kissed him lightly on the neck before he answered.

"Yes, I did. I was angry, frustrated, and full of sorrow over Dweian and Dria's death. I was glad to have something I could vent my anger on. And it felt great, killing them. Sensing their bodies and souls writhing in the heat of my flame, their magic being consumed by my power. I felt so potent, so invincible. It was heady until I realized exactly what I had done."

Casto stroked Renaldo's bare arms soothingly. He didn't know whether it was due to their long time apart or because Renaldo finally shared his thoughts with him, but Casto felt closer to his mate than ever before. It was not the weight of their irrefutable bond, nor was it the mad passion they held for each other. It was something deeper, more meaningful, and also a lot more frightening. Casto had yet to decide if he liked that feeling.

"I understand only too well. In Kwarl, when we lost Daran, I let your fire out, and I didn't care if it caused a catastrophe. All I wanted was to get back at those men, make them pay for what they had done. I embraced the fire."

Renaldo pulled Casto even closer. He chuckled into the king's ear.

"I could tell." He turned serious again. "After that incident, we left Quell'renar, and ever since then, I've worked hard on my self-control. It took me centuries until I was able to use the fire, and it was always a risky thing to do. Only when I met you did I begin to understand that the beast inside me was not only a burden, though I still haven't come to terms with it yet. This summer was a reminder of how desperately I need you—not that it came as a surprise."

Renaldo laughed dryly, without any amusement in his voice. Casto leaned his head against Renaldo's chest, trying to understand all the nuances of what his mate had just revealed to him.

"I think I understand. I love your fire. It's a part of who you are. Of what *I* am. It also scares me to death when I witness what happens when it's let loose. It's a dangerous beast, and I can only guess what it must have been like, trying to tame it without your full strength. I have to admit, I'm a bit intimidated by how strong you must be."

"You're just as strong, my own. You survived where others would have perished. You stayed whole and firm where anybody else would have broken and given up. You and I, we are a lot more similar than I feel comfortable with sometimes."

Casto barked out a laugh. "Are you afraid, Barbarian?"

"Perhaps a bit. Mostly I'm thrilled about our compatibility. It's still strange, though. The only other person so close to me is my brother, and it bothers me how your presence disturbs the status quo. Which is another reason why I kept so much from you. It was my way of keeping you in place."

Casto snorted. "Twisted."

"I know. I'm afraid this is part of who I am."

Casto stroked Renaldo's arm in a reassuring gesture. "I don't really mind. I mean, I can be a merciless, ruthless bastard at times. We are an even match."

"My own!"

Renaldo didn't say any more, just held Casto tight and buried his nose in the wheat-blond hair, a wave of content overwhelming him. After the summer he had had, he was happy to simply sit there in the sun, surrounded by his own twisted history, knowing that what had been forcibly taken had been returned to him.

"SO WE'RE going straight home?"

Casto tried his hardest to keep the giddiness from his voice and failed miserably. He didn't mind too much, though. At the moment, he was simply overjoyed to be with the Barbarian again. Renaldo's smile threatened to cut his face in half. He, too, was in a state of pure bliss. Reestablishing his connection to Casto had done wonders for his temper, and last night had been beyond imagining.

"Going straight home doesn't mean we can't take the time to stop now and then and indulge a little. And having Lys with us means we don't have to worry too much about getting caught in an autumn storm. So anytime you want to slow down, we can do it."

Casto slung his arms around Renaldo's belly and rubbed his head between the broad shoulders. His voice was a seductive purr.

"As long as we only slow our traveling pace down...."

Renaldo laughed out loud. He grabbed Casto, yanked him around, and kissed him deeply.

"And here I thought I wore you out last night!"

Casto grinned against Renaldo's lips. "In case you haven't noticed, I don't wear out easily. Especially not after having been apart from you for so long."

He turned serious.

"I really missed you, Barbarian."

Renaldo squeezed his mate hard. "I missed you too. Let's never do something like this again, shall we? Those past months were torture for me."

"As they were for me. So no, we won't do this again."

Reluctantly, they let go of each other and turned to their horses. It was time to leave Quell'renar. When they rode through the crumbled gates, Casto stopped and looked back. From the moment Renaldo had arrived, the city had stopped showing Casto scenes from the past. It almost felt as if Quell'renar thought its duty was done. Leaving woke mixed feelings in Casto. He was glad to go home, glad that the constant stream of memories and dreams had subsided. He also felt sad. For the past few months, Quell'renar had been his home, and the things he had seen had forged a bond between him and the city that he would never be able to refute. Casto still felt reluctant to think about the changes in his relationship with Renaldo, which were a direct effect of his time in Quell'renar. He would need time to ponder all the things he had learned. Beyond him, Lys shifted and broke the mental connection Casto had built with the fading city.

The Barbarian is waiting.

Casto glanced once more at the crumbling stones, silently saying goodbye, and then he followed Renaldo through the fields toward the border into the real world. Deep in thought, he twirled a strand of Lys's mane around his forefinger.

"Are you angry, Lys?"

Casto didn't have to explain the question. They knew each other too well. Lys shook his massive head.

Not really. I always knew you would go back to him. The only thing I truly resent is that I'm linked to him through you. But that's not your fault, so don't worry about it.

Casto leaned forward to bury his head in Lys's neck. He inhaled the comforting scent of his brother and tried to convey his love without using any words. Lys's answering emotion was like a wave that crashed over them both, drowning them in a feeling of contentment. No matter what happened, they would always be a unit.

Slightly worried, Renaldo tried to watch Casto out of the corner of his eye. He was more than glad they were leaving Quell'renar. The city held no good memories for him, only pain and confusion and anger. The mere thought that Casto had spent almost four months in this cursed place without going mad made him shiver. His mate's inner strength never ceased to amaze him, and he only hoped there wouldn't be an aftermath to Casto's prolonged time at Quell'renar. Renaldo also felt a little awkward around Casto. Now that both their initial urges had been sated, he wasn't sure how to handle the situation. He knew they had a lot of talking to do, and most of it wasn't going to make him happy. Renaldo longed to go back to their old ways and was painfully aware this was not a good idea. Things between them had changed. To what extent remained to be seen.

3. HEADING HOME

FOR THEIR first night away from Quell'renar, they chose a thicket beside the road. During the day Renaldo had managed to kill a couple of wild geese that would make a splendid evening meal. After they had eaten, the two men sat in silence, Casto snuggled under Renaldo's arm, content and sated. It was Renaldo who first broke the silence.

"How did you stay sane in Quell'renar? The place is so laced with magic and memories, any normal person would go crazy in no time."

Casto grabbed Renaldo's right hand and started playing with his fingers.

"In case you haven't noticed, Barbarian, I'm not a normal person. I admit it was scary at first, all those seemingly random scenes, thrown at me in no particular order. But then I realized that Quell'renar was trying to help me. It showed me your origins, your life before you became a barbarian warrior from the North. Which is one reason I forgave you. As it turned out, our lives aren't as different as I've thought."

"Do you think that's a bad thing?"

Casto sighed. "No. Not anymore. It was a difficult concept at first. I was afraid there had never been a 'me' to begin with, given how similar our paths and personalities are. If I'm simply a part of you, like an additional limb which helps you with a certain task, then what was I clinging to so desperately? Everything I endured, everything I did to spite you, every fight we had would have been for naught, because there was no reason to have them in the first place."

Renaldo didn't know what to say. He hugged Casto closer, tried to project a calmness he didn't feel. Everything his heart had just said was valid, was true, and what did that mean for their relationship? He chose his words carefully, like a blind man trying to find his way through a field full of stones and roots about to trip him. "I think we needed those fights. Neither of us is good at expressing feelings that are not anger or rage. If we hadn't fought on a constant basis, we would have parted ways sooner rather than never. And no matter how hard and brutal it was sometimes, the mere thought of possibly losing you makes me want to throw up." Renaldo pressed a kiss to Casto's temple, inhaling his scent at the same time. "The fights have shown us who we are, what we both are capable of. A valuable lesson."

"One you could have intensified by being more open with me." The hint of accusation in Casto's voice wasn't as bad as Renaldo had feared. He didn't make the mistake of not taking it seriously, though.

"Yes, I could have done that. I should have done that. My only excuse for this oversight is the burning wish on my part to leave the past behind."

"I saw your pain." The statement held no judgment but no absolution either.

"When you showed me your pain, I should have shared mine with you as well. I should have realized there can't be a relationship between equals without a certain amount of honesty."

"Are we equals, then?" The sudden vulnerability in Casto's voice cut through Renaldo's heart with blades of blue steel.

"I may not always have acted like it, but yes. Yes, we are equals. I thought you being my heart meant you were mine, and in a sense that's the case, but the past few months have shown me clearly how much I am yours as well. Our dynamic may be difficult sometimes, but I swear to you, I'll never forget again how badly I need you, how dependent I am on you. It humbles me, it makes me cranky, it deeply annoys me, it frightens me. But I'm the Angel of Death, and I do not back down from any challenge thrown at me. Getting used to the facts of our relationship, explaining them to the beast inside me that even now can only think about how it wishes to consume you wholly, is going to be difficult. I'm certain I will slip more than once, and I'm counting on you to not abandon me again but make me see the error of my ways."

"Error of your ways." Casto chuckled. "I promise not to run from you again like a spoiled child with a temper tantrum. I'm not sorry I did it, mind you, because I think it was necessary for both of us, but two grown men with access to powers that can destroy entire cities should probably be more mature." He held up his hand and let a thin stream of fire rise into the air. Renaldo watched this show of perfect control and wasn't surprised. He had seen the corpse of the man Casto had tortured not only with knives but also with fire. Back then, he had been too wrapped up in finally having Casto in front of him again to comment. Now it seemed Casto wanted to show him without putting into words that they truly were one. "When you controlled me so absolutely, I was terrified."

Renaldo raised his index finger, beckoned the fire to him, where it twirled around the digit before he sent it back to Casto as a small ball, which his heart then turned into a disk that he let spin on his palm. "During our campaign in the Dark Forest, Canubis had to subjugate me in order to get necessary information from one of the followers of the Good Mother. I know now firsthand what you endured during the Spring Ceremony. I can't tell you how sorry I am."

"Apology accepted, Barbarian." Casto cocked his head and the disk doubled, the upper one spinning horizontally, the one beneath vertically.

"When did you plan on telling me you had control over my fire?" There was no heat in Renaldo's words, he really wanted to know. With a flick of his wrist, he added two spheres that started orbiting the disks.

"To be honest, I don't know. I found out the day we got Daran back from those bastards. It was a good decision to keep it a secret, as the men who tried to capture me have proven."

"You didn't burn them, though."

"No. Lys may have taught me another neat little trick that came in handy." Renaldo only saw Casto's smile from the side because his heart was still sitting between his legs, but it still sent a shiver down his back. There was something in Casto's eyes, a cold, calculating cruelty Renaldo hadn't seen before. Or at least never so clearly. Somehow, it aroused him to no end, which only drove home the fact how perfectly suited he and his heart were.

"Are you going to tell me?"

Casto leaned back against Renaldo's chest, merging the disks and orbs into one big ball of flame he made pulse in the rhythm of their heartbeats. Renaldo knew they were in sync because he could feel the steady thumping of Casto's heart against his rib cage. Feeling Casto's hesitancy, Renaldo leaned in to kiss his temple. "You don't have to. I hate it when you keep secrets from me, we both know that, but I'm going to learn to accept it and let you have things your way. It's my way of showing my trust."

Casto sighed deeply, and a small smile played around his lips. "You have no idea how much I longed to hear those words from you, Barbarian. *I* didn't know how much I longed to hear them. This feels so good." He turned his torso to kiss Renaldo on the lips. The ball of flame was pulsing even brighter. "Lys taught me how to walk through the shadows. As it turned out, this skill comes in handy when you have to kill eleven men."

Renaldo gazed to the spot where Lys was standing with Ghost and Demon. The black stallion stared right back at him with a mixture of animosity and resignation in his eyes. "Thank you, Lys, for protecting him again." He bowed his head to show his respect. Lys just snorted before he seemed to dissolve in the shadows their campfire and the pulsing ball were creating.

"I'm impressed. You can do that too?"

Casto giggled, the sound making him seem a lot younger and more innocent than he truly was. Not at all like the coldblooded slayer and torturer Renaldo had reunited with in Quell'renar. "Yes, I can. Though it took me a while to get used to giving myself over to the shadows and trust them to do my bidding."

"I can imagine how hard that must have been for you." There was only a hint of sarcasm in Renaldo's voice.

"Now that I have embraced the shadows, it's easier." Casto turned serious. "I have also embraced being your heart." The ball of flame grew, and the pulsing got faster, just like the blood running more quickly through Renaldo's veins when he saw the naked hunger in his lover's gaze. He knew exactly how that hunger felt, because it was his own. Renaldo turned Casto in his arms, pressed him against his chest.

"And I'm your god, your mate, your lover. I'm the air in your lungs and the fire in your body. I'm yours, Casto, yours alone. And your will is my command as much as mine is yours."

Casto breathed heavily against his lips. His whole body shuddered, his hard length pressed against Renaldo's stomach, driving him wild with lust. "As it shall be," he whispered, his hands already searching for the buckle on Renaldo's trousers. Renaldo groaned, fighting the instinct to simply rip Casto's clothes. They didn't have enough spare ones with them, and he didn't want his precious heart to ride naked. On second thought, though.... Renaldo felt cool air caressing his dick, and all thoughts fled his mind when Casto's nimble fingers started stroking him to full hardness. Renaldo wet his fingers with his tongue before he roughly tugged Casto's trousers down and searched for his entrance. His heart whimpered against his lips when he entered him without any finesse because his need was riding him too hard. It didn't take him long to get Casto loose enough to be ready for his cock, and the moment he lowered his heart onto his waiting shaft, savoring the way Casto's inner walls gripped him tightly, the ball of flame descended on them, grew until they were wholly immersed in the flames. Renaldo threw his head back, and Casto latched on to his throat, sucking on it, no doubt leaving a mark. The fire roared around them, growing in heat and intensity as their arousal reached new heights. They moved in absolute sync, so perfectly molded to each other that Renaldo could no longer tell where he ended and Casto began—*as it should be between god and heart.* The thought struck him out of nowhere, a final epiphany after the long and grueling lesson he had endured this summer.

Renaldo couldn't tell how long he melded with his heart or how many orgasms they had before the fire finally started to die down, dripping back into their bodies, becoming a part of their core again. Casto was leaning heavily against him, Renaldo's cock still inside him, his sweaty forehead pressed against Renaldo's shoulder.

"Wow. That was—"

"Yes." Renaldo gently stroked Casto's back, basked in the fact that for the first time ever there wasn't even the tiniest hint of self-loathing and disgust in his heart's voice after their lovemaking. Only love and awe, and Renaldo wanted to shout his happiness to the skies. They sat like that for the longest time, enjoying the closeness that was finally absolute. When Renaldo thought Casto was going to fall asleep, his heart suddenly lifted his head, an inquisitive gleam in his eyes. Renaldo groaned.

"What?" Casto cocked his head.

"When you look at me like that, it's never good."

"I haven't even told you my idea!"

Renaldo simply arched a brow. Casto pouted.

"Fine, I'm not going to suggest we make a little detour to this small village two days ride west of Kwarl, where three of the most powerful seers of the Good Mother are hiding. I'm also not suggesting we could celebrate our newfound bond by killing them all. No, not at all."

"And I owe you an apology, my beloved heart. That's indeed a most wonderful idea. Did you get the information from the man you tortured in Quell'renar?"

"Yes, so I'm sure it's valid."

"I love you, Casto."

Casto's smile was wicked. "You just love to kill followers of the Good Mother."

"Yes. But do you know what I love even more? Killing followers of the Good Mother with my heart at my side."

"I honestly never thought of you as a romantic, but here you are." Casto leaned forward and pressed a kiss to Renaldo's lips.

"Hidden depths, my love, hidden depths." Renaldo chuckled and embraced his heart more fiercely.

"YOU WANT us to do what?" Daran stared at his god, wondering where Canubis got his ideas from. Thanks to Ellewinn and his vengeful cat, they had been able to find and destroy all enemy camps during the last two weeks. Not even the magic spells woven into the forest had been able to protect the followers of the Good Mother from the wrath of the Pack. Now their enemies were all dead, the last scattered runners hunted down by the wolves. Technically their campaign was over, and Daran had looked forward to getting back to the Valley and enjoying some peace and sex with his husbands. Until Canubis had decided there was time for a little detour to Queen Xe'lien's palace.

"I want you and Lukan to lead the Echend'dim to the palace, storm it, kill everybody inside, and bring me Xe'lien's head."

So Daran had heard right. He looked at Lukan and Sic, hoping they would be the voice of reason.

"You would trust us with such an important mission? We are deeply honored, my lord." Lukan was obviously not going to be of any help.

"I think Noran and I should be coming with them." Sic sounded strained, as if he didn't like the idea too much, probably because he wasn't keen on bloodshed and this mission was nothing else.

"Am I the only one who thinks this isn't a good idea?" Daran looked around, not finding any help, not even from his usually overprotective husbands, who appeared to be deeply interested in their fingernails.

"Why are you opposed to this, Daran?"

Canubis's tone was firm but not unkind. He wasn't asking as his god but as his brother-in-arms, which was the reason Daran felt bold enough to voice his concerns.

"Because I may have gotten better at leading, but I have zero experience besieging a castle, and unless Lukan and Sic have taken some secret course without telling me, they don't either. Queen Xe'lien's palace is heavily fortified and well-guarded. I hate to admit it, but I don't think I'm good enough yet to take on such a huge responsibility."

The weight of Aegid's and Kalad's hands on his shoulders grounded Daran while he waited for his god's response. Canubis looked thoughtful for a moment.

"I understand your hesitancy, Daran. And I deeply admire your willingness to admit to a weakness in front of not only me but your fellow Echend'dim." He nodded toward Lukan. "To a certain extent, I share your estimation of the situation. Yes, you have never besieged a castle, and yes, your training wasn't formal. But what you lack in experience and knowledge, you make up for with determination, vigilance, and ingenuity. Not to mention your other powers, which elevate you and the other Echend'dim far above mere mortals the likes of which are guarding Xe'lien's palace."

Daran stared at his hands. He couldn't deny his god's words. They did have all the advantage on their side, he had to admit. Reluctantly he gazed at Canubis. "What if I fail?" It was his biggest concern—disappointing his god again and bringing shame on his husbands. He felt Aegid's hand squeezing his shoulder more tightly, while Kalad leaned in to kiss his forehead. "You won't. You're Lord Daran, First of the Eternal Guard and husband to us. I hate to say this out loud, but you're more than ready to squash somebody like Xe'lien under your heel." Kalad grinned broadly, looking like he didn't have a single care in the world. Only the dark shadow in his eyes betrayed how much he didn't want his beloved husband to go to war without him and Aegid having his back. Daran was grateful for this show of support, which went against everything Kalad—and Aegid—were feeling inside.

"You heard him." Canubis's smile was smug. "And should things really not work out—you have Noran with you. He has seen a siege or two."

Daran looked at Sic's mate and future husband. Noran had come a long way, but he still made the part of Daran that had been a slave for years wary. The man was intimidation personified. Then Sic placed his hand on Noran's forearm, leaning his head against his mate's shoulder, and all of a sudden Noran's entire being seemed to transform into one happy smile. It was the moment Daran realized he could not only work with Noran, rely on his experience and wisdom, but also get his god what he wanted—the head of a queen.

"Fine. We have about a month left before the fall storms set in. We need to start packing now and get on the way tomorrow morning. It should be a week until we reach the palace, and we need to do some spying before we can make any plans. Lukan, please inform the other Echend'dim that we're riding tomorrow."

"Yes, Lord Daran." Lukan bowed, a small smile on his lips. He was slowly getting over Elua's death, though Daran was sure he would have to be there for his friend once they were back in the Valley and no longer distracted by war. He turned to Canubis. "My lord, I need to go pack."

Canubis sent him on his way with a wave of his hand. Aegid, Kalad, Sic, and Noran followed while Wolfstan and Hulda stayed back.

When they were alone, Hulda simply lifted an eyebrow in Canubis's direction. He raised his hands in a defensive gesture. "He's ready. I wouldn't send him if I weren't sure of it."

"I know." The assassin sighed. "And you need to test how well the Echend'dim work together when you're not there, and Daran and Lukan need to learn how to lead. It's just a sobering thought, sending a former bed slave out to besiege a palace and create a bloodbath." Hulda had never been one to mince words, and as a seasoned warrior, she had no problems whatsoever with shedding blood and lots of it. That she was even considering Daran's possible feelings on mass murder was as motherly as she would ever get. Wolfstan placed a hand on his wife's neck, gently stroking the exposed skin.

"Noran will be with them." The simple statement, made in a calm tone, showed that the armorer had forgiven his fellow Emeris fully and taken him back into his good graces. It felt right to Canubis that their tight-knit family was slowly healing and growing. He reached for his cup of wine, swirled the liquid around.

"Renaldo has found Casto."

Both Hulda and Wolfstan looked at him sharply. "You can feel it?" The assassin's voice was crisp, full of hope.

"Yes. He was deeply worried yesterday in the late afternoon, but now he's nothing but content. Casto seems to have forgiven him."

Hulda sighed in relief. "Finally. Are they on their way back to the Valley?"

Canubis furrowed his brows. The link he shared with his twin was getting stronger every day, but the distance was making it more difficult to discern what his brother was up to. "Yes, they are traveling in the direction of the Valley, but they plan on killing somebody first. I'm not sure who, though. They are quite far away, and Renaldo's happiness about having Casto back is blurring everything else. I guess we find out once we're back home."

"Fair enough." Hulda rose from her seat. "I believe we have some packing to do as well." She and Wolfstan left the tent. Canubis stared thoughtfully into his wine. He could feel the upcoming changes in the air, like ripples on an undisturbed lake. The powers the Mothers had spoken about were flowing freely into Ana-Darasa, fueling him and his brother, as well as their Emeris and Echend'dim. War was brewing in the distance, not the puny wars they had fought against mortals throughout the centuries but a divine war, the last one to determine the fate of Ana-Darasa and the La'ides. His blood sang in anticipation of it, as well as in reaction to Renaldo's intent on violence. Things were heading toward the end, and the Wolf of War was determined to be victorious.

"OVER THERE." Casto pointed at the small hut nestled between two large trees. It didn't look like much, certainly not like the hiding place of three powerful seers. He glanced at Renaldo, who watched the place with furrowed brows.

"It's heavily fortified with spells. Probably the reason they don't have any guards. They feel safe." A predatory smile appeared on his face, sending a shiver of lust down Casto's back. "Do you want to do the honors of burning those spells?"

Casto narrowed his eyes. "I'd love to, but I'm not sure I can see them all."

"I'll help you." Renaldo took his hand. "Close your eyes. Focus on me."

Casto did as his husband told him, the act by now familiar since Renaldo had insisted on doing some training with him during their journey back. They were now so in tune with each other that Renaldo could even sense the bond between Casto and Lys, though the stallion blocked him from getting more than just glimpses. It would take time until Lys forgave the Angel of Death, a long time, perhaps eons. It was most definitely a case of like rider, like horse. Through their bond, Casto could see the spells lining the ground and air around the hut clearly. He had been aware of them before, though he wasn't yet experienced enough to truly perceive them.

"What do you think? Can you turn them to ashes?" Renaldo's breath was hot next to his ear, fueling Casto's body with lust and the deep satisfaction of finally being seen as an equal. The grin twisting his features was feral. "Yes, yes, I can."

"Then what are you waiting for, my love?"

Casto needn't be told twice. He sent thin tendrils of his fire out toward the first spell, touching it almost lovingly. The flames caught the magic forced by the Good Mother and fanned out along the runes, quickly eating them up. Casto could have wiped all of the spellwork out with one giant blaze, but he liked the slow domino effect he was creating so much better. When the dancing flames reached the innermost circle around the hut, the door flew open and a hooded figure scanned the area with darting glances. Renaldo and Casto were standing in the shadows of the trees, not really hiding, and it only took the figure a few moments to become aware of them. Spidery fingers reached up to the hood to reveal the face of an older man with thinning white hair that framed his gaunt features in whisps. He tried to draw up to his full height, failing miserably, though it wasn't clear if it was due to old age or fear. "Who are you?" As much as the man tried, he couldn't suppress the quiver of fear in his voice. Casto and Renaldo moved at the same time, both of them enjoying this game with their prey immensely. They slowly emerged from the shadows, no doubt offering a striking and fear-inducing picture. Casto felt like a cat who'd gotten a fat rat cornered. His blood pulsed in his veins, finding a direct connection to his fire, which had meanwhile erased all the spells and was waiting for him to send it to its next target. Next to him he could feel Renaldo, his lover and god so perfectly in sync with him, Casto wondered how it had ever been different.

He smiled at the man. "We're death."

They drew their swords in unison, their fire creating a blazing circle around the hut to keep anybody inside from escaping. Renaldo grabbed the man by the scruff of his hood, yanked him onto both their blades with a brutal twist of his arm. Casto heard cloth ripping, felt tissue giving, the life of the seer gushing to the ground in a wave of blood when Renaldo kicked the body off their swords. A shrill scream pierced the air as something menacing came flying in their direction. They hit it with two blasts of fire, turning the harmful spell to ash before it could reach them. Casto didn't even have to look at Renaldo to know what he wanted to do. While his lover turned right after passing the threshold of the hut, Casto went left, going after a second hooded figure who was trying to hide behind a wooden beam. Another scream told him Renaldo had reached the third seer, and a wet thumping sound made clear the threat had been dealt with permanently. The seer in front of Casto looked at him with huge panicked eyes, making the decision to run the same moment Casto sent out thin ropes of fire to catch them. A pained grunt tore from the lips of the seer when the fire slung around their ankles and brought them down. Immediately, Renaldo was there, grabbing the back of the hood to yank the seer up, revealing the face of a young woman with dark brown hair. She tried to struggle against Renaldo's hold amidst whimpers and agonized groans from the fire eating into her legs.

"Let go!" There was no heat in her demand, her voice already tinged with defeat and a healthy dose of fear. Casto felt a bone-deep satisfaction, seeing their prey squirming like that. Renaldo shook her like a rag doll, his intense gaze drilling into Casto, silently offering him the kill. Casto let the fiery ropes eat their way up the legs of the woman, snaking around her thighs and waist like hungry snakes would with a rat. Her screams pierced the air and didn't let up even when he dimmed the fire down to nothing more than a pleasant warmth, so he slapped her hard to get her out of her hysteric fit. When she stared at him wide-eyed, Casto treated her to his most charming smile. "Hello, little seer, we do have some questions for you."

The woman gulped and squirmed in Renaldo's grip, her eyes darting around the room, looking for an escape that didn't exist. "I'm not going to lie to you, this is the day you die, though how you leave Ana-Darasa is entirely up to you. What do you say, is a little information worth a painless death?"

The sudden stench of urine in the air, overpowering even the copper taste of blood and the more putrid waves of spilled innards, made Casto tsk. "Now that was completely uncalled for. We haven't even started with the real torture, have we, my mate?"

Renaldo chuckled cruelly, tightening his grip on the woman's shoulders. "No, we haven't. So far we've been downright tame. Which we can change immediately, if you wish so."

"P-p-please." Fat tears were rolling down the woman's cheeks.

Casto shook his head. "The time for pleading is long over. You sided with the false goddess against the rightful heirs to this world. There is no mercy for traitors, and frankly, that quick death I've been talking about is quickly drifting out of reach. If I were you, I'd start talking in complete sentences right about now."

The woman gulped several times, no doubt weighing her chances and not liking the outcome. Renaldo raised his sword, the fire climbing along the blade like ivy on a wall. The gesture was enough to make the woman talk. In her haste to spill every tiny bit of information she had, her words came out slurred, but the content was clear.

A little under an hour later, Casto and Renaldo left the burning hut, sheathing their swords after they had consumed the life of the third seer. Some of the things they had learned were worrisome, others as they had already suspected, and then there was the rumor about the army the Good Mother was raising. All of this had to be addressed as soon as they were back in the Valley. When they reached the horses, Renaldo gave Casto a scorching kiss that told him how much his god loved and adored him. Then they jumped on their horses to make their way home.

4. DETOUR

"IMPRESSIVE." LUKAN let his gaze wander over the impossibly high walls of Queen Xe'lien's castle. On their one-week travel to their destination, they had discussed trying to sneak close enough to execute a surprise attack, but Noran had patiently explained to them that surprise attacks on castles never worked and that the chances of Xe'lien not knowing about their approach were close to zero. Case in point, the catapults mounted on top of her walls. Daran sighed. "Impressive indeed." He looked around at his fellow Echend'dim and Sic and Noran. Sic wouldn't be of any help concerning strategies, so it was Noran Daran put his hopes in. "What do you think, Lord Noran?"

Noran shrugged. "The usual method would be to besiege the castle until the occupants are too weak to offer any resistance. Unfortunately, we don't have that much time. We need to find another way in."

"Why don't we climb the walls?" Ellewinn's tone suggested he couldn't understand why Daran hadn't thought of this before.

"Because even though we're no ordinary humans anymore, we aren't cats either. The only one who could climb those walls is you, and once they see you, they're going to kill you. And even if you should make it to the top, you'd be alone." Lukan shook his head. "We won't do that."

Ellewinn pouted but seemed to see reason. Daran stared at the walls, and an idea started forming in his mind. "If you climb those walls, would you do it as a human or a cat?"

Ellewinn shrugged. "Doesn't matter. I can do both." He extended his hand and let his claws slip free. Lukan and the others gasped in shock. Even though Ellewinn was now part of the Eternal Guard and their brother-in-arms, there hadn't been much time to really get to know him. The bond they shared with him was as strong as that with the other Echend'dim, but politeness had kept them from prying too much. Ellewinn had endured unspeakable things none of the others wanted to force him to relive just to sate their curiosity.

"I guess it makes no difference." Daran contemplated first Ellewinn, then Lukan and the other Echend'dim. "I think this could work. We create a diversion at the western wall, some attempt at storming it to keep their attention away from the main gate. Ellewinn climbs the wall next to the guard tower closest to the main gate. He sneaks down and opens the gate for us. Before they can redirect their forces, we're through the gate and start the bloodbath our god is asking for. We don't even need a signal because we're linked. As soon as Ellewinn reaches the gate to open it, we'll know, which allows for a seamless operation. What do you think?" Daran looked around, stopped his gaze at Noran, whose lips slowly broadened to a bright smile.

"And you thought you can't take a castle. It's a solid plan, and even if they keep enough guards at the gate to make your entry difficult, Sic can fortify you with his power so you make it through."

"Speaking of Sic." Belnor nodded respectfully in the smith's direction. "Why don't you just level the whole castle with your power?" The question carried no challenge or mean undertone, just genuine interest why the most powerful weapon in their arsenal wouldn't be used.

"Because Lord Canubis tasked his Echend'dim to destroy Xe'lien." Daran smiled weakly. "Sic is only here as a courtesy, so to speak. He won't always be, and we need to learn to act as a unit, on our own. I need to learn to give orders, to listen to counsel, to make decisions and live with the outcome. We all need to learn to rely on each other and the powers we've been given. Lord Canubis was right to send us here. We are the arm that wields his sword, so to speak, and we need to be firm and secure in our actions."

Belnor raised his hands in a placating gesture. "All right, I get it. I was just asking."

"And rightfully so. It's always good to consider all your options, and if this weren't a training, I would definitely give Sic a more prominent role." Noran nodded toward Belnor, acknowledging his question as valid.

"Lord Noran is right. We always have to think of everything." Daran smiled. "So let's try to find the holes in my plan."

They went through every possible scenario regarding Daran's idea and finally decided to simply do it. Late in the afternoon, when the sun was already low on the horizon, making it more difficult to see, a group of Echend'dim started an attack on the western wall of the castle, sending burning arrows and small barrels with tar against the unyielding stone. As predicted, the guards on the wall sounded the alarm and congregated where the attack was happening.

From the shadows of the woods surrounding the castle, Daran watched the western wall looming in the flickering light of small and ineffective fires.

He kept track of Ellewinn's progress through their bond, knowing the elusi had already reached the top of the wall. There was a brief moment where Ellewinn was faced with four opponents, but a quick surge of power from Sic took care of them. Ellewinn went down on the inside of the wall, and as soon as he reached the mechanism to open the gate, Daran gave the signal. He and his men ran toward the gate, which opened so perfectly, they didn't have to slow down for even a moment. The loud bang of the gate hitting the ground alerted the castle's guards to this new threat, but it was already too late. They were inside the enemy's territory now, swarming the palace ground and killing everybody in their sight. Ellewinn appeared next to Daran in his cat form, swiping his deadly claws right and left, protecting Daran's flank. It was a strange sensation, being connected to the cat, the animal's senses adding another surreal layer to Daran's already distorted perception. In its entirety, it made him faster and sharper; nothing could get past him anymore. Sic's power was flowing freely into him, strengthening the bond he had with his brethren, letting him know what was going on everywhere without breaking his concentration. They made their way through the palace, leaving behind nothing but blood and death, just like their god had asked them to do.

The traitorous queen tried to keep them out of the throne room, her most formidable warriors shielding her, but it was of no use. When they all lay slaughtered at Daran's feet, Xe'lien tried to negotiate, then she begged, and in the end she lost her head in a swift movement of Daran's sword. To his own surprise, Daran felt no pity or mercy for her. She had tried to betray his gods, his people, and she paid the price for her hubris. Her blood was nothing more than a stain on his clothes, one he would get rid of before they started their journey home to the Valley. Xe'lien's head was put in a wooden box for transport, her castle ransacked and then burned to the ground.

Sic and Noran watched from the forest, witnessed the strength and unity of the Echend'dim. When it was time to ride, Daran guided his horse next to Sic's. For some time, they just rode next to each other, not saying anything. Noran kept in the background, leaving the two friends to whatever they had to hash out.

You're not happy. Daran spoke in Sic's head, because saying those words aloud would have hurt too much. *Do you hate me now?*

Sic's love for him washed over Daran before the words could reach him. *No! Never! I do not hate you, nor do I hate what you did for our gods.*

I know it's necessary, I know it's inevitable, and I know she had it coming. I just think it's such a waste of precious life. Do you understand?

I do. And I resent myself a bit for not feeling more strongly about her death. If anything, I see it as insignificant, and doesn't that make me a bad person?

Another surge of warmth rushed through Daran, assuring him that he was still capable of emotion. *No. I don't think so. You have to protect yourself. We all have to. We live in a world where mercy has little room, and in order to protect the ones we love, we have to choose our path. The fact that neither of us is human anymore doesn't make it easier.*

What do we do, then? I hate to see you sad. You've had enough of that to last for more than a hundred lifetimes.

A smile appeared on Sic's lips; it was still tentative, but it was there. "We protect our bond. We stay close and we stay brothers. We will be support and protection for each other."

Daran felt a heavy weight sliding off his shoulders. This was a promise he would gladly give. "We will. Forever."

"Forever."

The two friends looked at each other, the severity of that one word no longer crushing them.

"CANUBIS, THEY'RE here!" Kalad was grinning from ear to ear when he announced the arrival of Renaldo and Casto, not caring that he had just ripped open the door to Canubis's quarters to disturb him and Noemi during their lunch. Canubis was inclined to forgive him because he himself was hardly able to contain his giddiness. He'd felt his brother's approach ever since they had made their way back from the Dark Forest, and once he had the Pack safely settled in the Valley, the connection to Renaldo had become clearer every day. His brother and Casto had killed somebody on their way home and then taken their sweet time, probably to enjoy each other a bit longer, because once they came back to the Valley, the mundane struggles of their daily lives and chores would start to interfere again. Canubis could relate, and since he knew they were on their way, he had no problem giving them that reprieve. His brother had earned it. For that reason, he rose from the table without chastising one of his oldest Emeris. With a broad smile, Noemi followed suit, she, too, eager to greet her brother-in-law and his capricious husband. As much as it galled Canubis to admit it, he had missed Casto, though he would never, ever say so out loud.

The three of them made their way to the entrance of the main building, where Aegid, Hulda, Wolfstan, Bantu, and Cornelia were already gathered. Canubis acknowledged Cornelia with a slight bow of his head, still a bit rattled by how close the Good Mother had been to killing everybody in the Valley while he was away. Knowing that from now on his people had another line of defense, the protection of ana regena raktol, the queen of nightmares, soothed the anger he felt about the attack from the Good Mother. Before he could delve deeper into how much he hated that stupid bitch, the clopping of hooves announced the arrival of his brother and Casto.

When the three horses appeared around the corner in the path, Canubis felt the air leave his lungs. He had expected to find the usual picture, his brother happy to have his heart back, Casto grumpy because he had again made a concession he hadn't really wanted to give. Instead, he saw a unit, two flames that were finally burning in accordance, the power lying within it directed by two wills that acted as one. Not even he and Noemi were that close, and in a way it made sense. Everything his brother and Casto did was to the extreme; it was the nature of the fire, the nature of the beast inside Renaldo. After countless battles, after years of outright war with short ceasefires, the Angel of Death and the King of Ummana had finally found peace in each other. It was so beautiful in its lethality, Canubis wanted to weep tears of joy. Instead, he simply opened his arms and embraced them both once they got off their horses. "Welcome home, both of you. I'm so glad."

"As am I, brother. As am I." Renaldo hugged him back fiercely, conveying with his whole being how happy he was. Casto said nothing, but he did snuggle into Canubis's arms, like an alley cat finally accepting touch. They stood there for a while, until Noemi broke into their circle, snatching Casto from Canubis. She slung her arms around Casto's waist, laughing and crying at the same time. "I missed you so much! Life isn't the same when you're not there to glare at everything!"

"I missed you too. Though not your disgustingly positive outlook on life." The laughter in Casto's voice was like the sweet chime of bells. He was indeed like a cat, making people happy just by emitting a pleasing sound.

After they had all welcomed Renaldo and Casto, and three stable boys had taken the horses, they went back to Canubis's quarters to talk about everything that had happened. With wine in hand, Canubis gave a short report on how the campaign had ended and that they were awaiting Daran's return with the Echend'dim in roughly a week. Then Cornelia filled them in about the attack of the Good Mother and how it had all culminated in her taking her rightful place as the queen of the dream realm. She regarded Casto with a strange look in her eyes. "When I talked to Heljia, she told me she plays with Lys when she visits the Valley. She was sad that he wasn't there when you were—away."

Casto furrowed his brows, his eyes getting that faraway look when he was conversing with his ride. Suddenly a smile appeared on his lips. "He does, and he loves it. He just never told me about it because, apparently, I'm too boring to play properly and he loves having Heljia and Sic to himself. Something to do with Luksari power and chaos. I'm not sure if I should be offended."

Renaldo leaned into Casto and gave him a loving kiss on his temple. "Let them have their fun. We have our own, my heart."

Casto shrugged. "You're right. We don't need them." He still pouted and then arched a brow when he saw everybody in the room staring at them. "What?"

"Renaldo just kissed you." Kalad sounded awed, with just enough mischief strewn in to make clear he was teasing.

"And?"

"You never let him kiss you just like that. There's always some eye rolling or huffing or hissing involved, usually all of it. Which makes me wonder who you are and what you have done to Casto."

Casto narrowed his eyes while the others were snickering. He didn't respond with one of his scathing comments, though. A thin thread of flame shot out from his index finger, reaching Kalad faster than anybody could react, and wrapped around his throat. It was obviously not hot enough to do any damage, for Kalad simply lifted a brow in Casto's direction, but he had the assembled Emeris gasping in utter surprise. Renaldo sat next to Casto, his chest swelling in visible pride.

"You were saying?" Casto's voice sounded deceptively sweet, a tone they all had come to associate with impending doom.

Kalad, always quick with his thinking, managed to hide his surprise. "Wow, I take it back. You're still your lethal, insufferable, arrogant self. Sorry for assuming otherwise."

"Ass." The fire vanished, not having singed a hair on Kalad's body.

"So you've finally managed to tame my brother's fire." Canubis smiled until he saw the look his brother and Casto shared. "What?"

"Well, I've had control over the fire since Daran was kidnapped. I just didn't tell anybody. Tactics."

Canubis opened his mouth to tell his wayward brother-in-law what exactly he thought of his so-called tactics when Renaldo chimed in. "I hate to admit it, but it was a wise move on his part. The Followers who tried to take him prisoner in Quell'renar believed the same, and they paid with their lives for their wrong assumption. To be honest, we have discussed keeping it a secret for longer, but we realized we probably wouldn't be able to do it now that we've reached this new level of unity."

"You were thinking of deceiving us? Of deceiving me?" Canubis couldn't believe it.

Casto shrugged. "I wouldn't call it deceiving. Think more of it along the lines of storing knowledge until it's useful."

"Semantics, and you know it." Canubis felt anger welling inside him.

"He's right, Canubis. It's a clever move." Hulda sounded entirely too admiring for Canubis's taste. "Think about it, my god." The use of his title did little to calm the Wolf of War. "Making your enemy believe you are weaker than you really are. I don't like being kept in the dark, but in this case, Casto made the right call. By keeping such vital information to himself, he had an ace up his sleeve nobody could have predicted. Apparently it saved his life, and I do agree it would be advantageous to keep it secret. We should try and keep it inside these walls and among the people present. Unless you think the Followers were able to tell anybody your secret?"

Casto shook his head. "The only one who saw me using it died too fast to blab about anything but the things I wanted to know."

Canubis looked around. None of the Emeris seemed to be angry about not having known. His own irritation probably stemmed from the fact that it was his own brother keeping things from him.

"I didn't know about it until he told me in Quell'renar." Renaldo had picked up on Canubis's anger.

"And you weren't angry with him?"

Renaldo shrugged, glancing lovingly at his heart. "It's his nature. It's how he grew up, how he survived to become my heart. I wasn't happy, mind you. Though knowing that my feelings regarding the matter didn't even factor into Casto's decision-making somehow helped. He saw an opportunity to gain the upper hand and was pragmatic enough to take it. End of story."

Canubis mulled his brother's words over. Renaldo was right, of course. Having somebody in their ranks who could strategize like that, who could think of outcomes that only existed in potentia, somebody who could look into the future and make his decisions based on estimations was very valuable indeed. He sighed, looked directly at Casto, who didn't flinch or show any other signs of distress at having angered his god. With sudden clarity, Canubis realized what else was valuable to have—somebody who made his decisions without any regard whatsoever to the sensitivities of two Gods of War.

"I don't like it, but Hulda and Renaldo are right. The way your mind works is too precious to stifle it with demands you're going to ignore anyway. I'm going to trust you to have the best for the Pack in mind when you do the things you do."

For a long moment, Casto held Canubis's gaze. The things Canubis saw in those deep spheres—the determination, the ruthlessness, the lethality, and the absolute focus on the ultimate goal—they gave him hope. He had to stop seeing Casto as an amusing distraction for his brother, a nuisance that shook Renaldo's life—and therefore that of everybody in the Valley—up. The King of Ummana had long surpassed such petty descriptions. He was an ally, a part of the family, the heart of his brother. It was time Canubis recognized Casto's role. The silent understanding between them solidified, and Casto nodded.

"I promise."

All of a sudden, the atmosphere in the room relaxed, making everybody breathe a sigh of relief. It was Wolfstan who got the conversation back on track.

"What happened after you left Quell'renar?"

Renaldo grinned. "You mean aside from hot sex?"

Kalad made a hooting sound. "No, tell us about the sex. What could be more important?"

Hulda just shook her head with a smile. "I think we all know very well how *hot* your sex is. Just try not to burn anything when you're going at it in your bed. What we really want to know is who you killed."

"Yeah, that too." Kalad threw his hands in the air.

"Fine. My gorgeous husband had gotten some interesting information from one of his attackers in Quell'renar about three seers hiding close to Kwarl. We decided to take a look. As it turned out, the information was good. There were three seers, hidden by powerful magic. Casto burned their protection away, and we killed two of them and questioned the third."

"And what did you find out?" Noemi sounded worried. Since the Mothers had left Ana-Darasa, she had started taking on more of Canubis's burdens to help him with all the massive changes going on, not only with himself but also within the Pack. Canubis tried to shield her from the worst, though as the only true nurturer they had in their ranks, it was only natural for her to feel the strain more heavily.

"Not much we haven't known before, or at least suspected. The three were the most powerful seers of the Good Mother, and she had infused them with her strength to get an edge in the upcoming war. Luckily for us, forced visions are even less reliable than naturally occurring ones, and even though they did eventually find Casto, it did them no good. Now that the three are dead, the Good Mother has lost her eye into the future. The only truly worrying information was that of an army the Good Mother is amassing somewhere beyond the sea. The seer blabbered something about darkness taking the light from the Echend'dim. It was all very cryptic, because she didn't really understand it herself."

"Azashreem," Bantu murmured.

Casto stared at him. "What does that mean?"

"The death of the Echend'dim. Daggers made of chaos to kill the light. Actually, we brought one back from the Dark Forest. I can show you later."

"Just one?" As always, Casto came right to the point.

"Yes, only one, and we were led to believe there weren't more—yet. I haven't had the time to properly examine the dagger, so I can't give you any details. What I do know from earlier studies and from a quick examination is that the dagger is not made of a metal known on Ana-Darasa, which is probably the reason our enemies only had this one weapon. No matter where or how she's getting them, it has to cost the Good Mother; otherwise she would have given more of them to her followers. Which is the only good news regarding those blades."

"Is there a way to find out how she gets them and to prevent her from doing it?" Casto looked thoughtful.

"I could try to find out. No promises, though. This is old knowledge. Very old." Bantu took a sip of his wine. "Perhaps we could ask the Luksari once Sic is back. Or even Lys? I already asked Sar'reff, but with Lys being absent for so long, he has slipped back to not talking at all."

If he took Bantu's words as an accusation, Casto didn't show it. "We can ask Lys tomorrow. Now I want to get rid of the journey's grime. If this was all, Lord Canubis?"

The way Casto asked made perfectly clear he thought there was nothing else to discuss, and Canubis, still full of joy about having his brother back, simply nodded. "Go and wash up." He wrinkled his nose, unable to not land that little blow. "You certainly need it."

Instead of getting angry as he usually would have, Casto just laughed. "Your own fault for dragging us into this meeting right after we arrived. Are you coming, Barbarian?"

Renaldo got up, smiling broadly. "I'm here, my love."

Together, the Angel of Death and the King of Ummana left Canubis's chambers.

THE NEXT morning, Bantu met with Casto at the stables. His god's heart was breathtaking, as usual, but not having seen Casto for so long, Bantu found himself staring like everybody had done in the beginning, when Renaldo had just found Casto. The king didn't give an indication that he noticed Bantu's rudeness, though Bantu was sure he knew. Nothing escaped Casto's sharp eyes, and he stored every scrap of information in his vault-like mind until it was of use.

"Good morning, Casto. You look rested."

"Good morning, Bantu. It was a pleasant night." The king grinned broadly. His ability to adapt to every attitude he was confronted with was another thing Bantu wasn't sure he admired or feared. "Do you have the dagger with you?"

Bantu nodded and reached into the leather bag he was carrying around his right shoulder. The Azashreem was wrapped tightly in a cloth to prevent it from doing any harm. Bantu wasn't sure what damage the weapon could do exactly, and decided to err on the side of caution. Casto's approach was a little less careful; he took off the cloth in an almost impatient move and held the dagger at the hilt, staring at the blade with narrowed eyes.

"It feels familiar, but in an odd way. Lys?"

Bantu couldn't suppress a gasp when Lys suddenly appeared right next to Casto, his huge head with the intelligent eyes forming out of the shadows created by the roof of the stables. A demon horse indeed. Never one to be impolite, even when he was deeply rattled, Bantu inclined his head slightly. As far as he understood, Lys was royalty, similar to the Gods of War, and deserved this show of respect. "Good morning, Lysistratos."

He got a soft whinny in return; then Lys focused on the dagger. He nudged it with his soft nose, which caused the blade to make a strange sound and quiver in Casto's hand. Small tendrils of darkness floated from the blade in Lys's direction, only to be pulled back into the weapon almost violently.

Casto sighed. "This is bad."

"Does this mean Lys knows what exactly the Azashreem is?" Bantu knew his voice sounded a bit too eager for the severity of the situation, but whenever there was something new to learn, he couldn't help but be excited.

Casto looked at him with a mixture of amusement and exasperation. "Yes. It's basically forced chaos. In order to create a weapon like this, you need to reach into the realm of chaos and steal a small part of it. Doing so when you're not part of chaos like Lys or Sar'reff are requires a lot of power. Then you need even more power to seal the bit of chaos into a blade that has to be made of a special alloy, containing blue steel and molten stone. Once the chaos is inside the blade, it somehow merges with the alloy and creates something new and unknown on Ana-Darasa. The chaos inside the blade tries to escape because the alloy is order, but also acts like some kind of chains. When you stab a human with the blade, nothing happens. They simply die of a mortal wound. But when the weapon comes in contact with magic...." Casto shrugged. "Lys says chaos and magic were not one but kind of, like, mixed before the Mothers introduced order to the universe. They are drawn to each other, and because chaos can't leave the dagger, the magic is pulled into it, which in turn kills the vessel holding the magic. In this case the Echend'dim and Emeris. Though Lys says this dagger isn't built strong enough to withstand a lot of magic. If I were to stab you with it, it would probably break before it could suck all the magic out of you. You would survive. As would any Echend'dim, as long as Sic pours enough magic into them to shatter the alloy."

"Are you saying this is not as bad as we feared?" There was a trace of hope in Bantu's voice. One Casto shattered immediately by shaking his head.

"No, I'm saying this particular dagger is not as dangerous as the Followers might have hoped. Chances are this is some kind of test project, and if I were the Good Mother, I would be very busy making a lot more of these, experimenting with the alloy and trying to trap even bigger bits of chaos inside them. If she's truly amassing an army, I'll bet you Renaldo's biggest blue diamond she's doing everything in her power to have as many of her soldiers as possible carry such a weapon. Lys says the only way to destroy such a weapon is to free the chaos, so we need to find out how to release it from the alloy. A task I gladly put in your capable hands, since my knowledge of chemistry is limited to the workings of certain poisons." Casto shrugged. "If you need more information, Lys says you're welcome to ask him." The king turned to the huge horse, touching the soft nose with an expression full of love. Bantu, who had lived long enough to know a dismissal when he saw one, started wrapping the dagger back into the cloth.

"I'm going to inform Canubis, and then I'll be in the library. Thank you, Lys, Casto."

Lys snorted, and Casto waved his hand. "This concerns us all, and frankly, I'm glad you're the one doing the research. I have full trust in your abilities."

Before the last Spring Ceremony, Bantu would have suspected the king of mocking him. Now he could feel the sincerity coming from Casto. As surprising as it was, Bantu enjoyed being acknowledged by the capricious king whose character was so very different from Bantu's own. Bantu watched as Casto jumped onto Lys's back with graceful movements. The stallion reared, turned on his hind legs, and started to run, quickly becoming nothing more than a small dot on the path to the forest surrounding the houses of the Pack.

"FINALLY HOME." Daran breathed in relief when he saw the narrow passageway into the Valley. The guards standing there waved at them excitedly, and the howling of the wolves told the entire Valley they were back.

"Yes, home." Lukan's voice was heavy with grief, and Daran didn't hesitate to put his hand on his friend's arm in a soothing gesture. As Daran had predicted, with the end of their mission, Lukan's emotions had shed the tight lid the young warrior had had on them. Facing his sorrow over losing Elua was hard for Lukan, even though Daran, Sic, and the other Echend'dim did their best to help him. Through their bond, they all could feel the grief and devastation swamping Lukan in waves, and they made sure somebody was always there to show him he wasn't alone. Sic, who was riding next to them, smiled at Lukan.

"I've talked to Noran, and since he's moved in with me, his quarters are free. We want you and Ellewinn to have them until you decide what you want to do with Elua's house."

The unshed tears in Lukan's eyes when he looked at Sic almost broke Daran's heart. He felt a twinge of guilt, thinking he was coming home to his two husbands while all Lukan had left was an empty house filled with memories of happy times. "Thank you, Sic. This means a lot to me. I really couldn't stand being in the house at the moment. I don't want my grief to taint the good times Elua and I had there. When I make my peace with her death, I'll decide what to do with it."

"Take as much time as you need." A single tear slid down Sic's cheek, reminding Daran that Sic still felt guilty about not having been able to convince Elua to come back as Echend'dim. "It wasn't your fault, Sic. Elua was a grown woman, and she made her decision. There was nothing you could have said or done to change her mind."

Daran looked at Lukan, who sighed. "Yes, she was stubborn like that." The Echend'dim closed his eyes for a moment. "After you brought me back from the dead, our relationship started to change. I think deep down, Elua had made peace with dying in battle long before she met me. She was stoic like that. And when I was suddenly Echend'dim—well, she accepted it, was happy for me, but even then, she never liked to talk about how wonderful things would be once she was Echend'dim as well. I thought it was because she didn't want to jinx it, but now I'm sure it was because she knew she didn't want eternity. On a certain level, I can understand it. There are days I wish I'd just given in to the peace the shadows were offering." When Lukan saw Sic's eyes widening, he hastened to add, "Those are rare, though. Mostly I'm glad to be here to see how things are going to play out. Elua was an integral part of me, and she always will be. She showed me a life I would have never dared dream of while I lived with my parents. And I love her enough to respect her decision, even though there are days when I hate her for leaving me. It's going to take time, but I will make my peace with the way things have gone. And I thank you for your help and support. Without you, this would be a lot more difficult."

Both Sic and Daran smiled at Lukan, and a soft yowl to the right informed them Ellewinn had heard their conversation and was expressing his support as well. To everybody's surprise, Lukan and Ellewinn had formed a stable friendship. Daran suspected it had to do with the fact that Lukan had killed Ellewinn to free him of the seal, though he didn't dig deeper. This was between the two men, and if they had managed to overcome their differences in such an amicable way, Daran was glad to leave the subject alone.

An imperious whinny echoed through the ravine, and both Sic and Daran smiled broadly. "Casto," they said in unison. Noran, who was riding behind Sic, made a face, while Ellewinn shifted into his human form so fast, his entire body blurred for a moment. With an elegant jump, he landed behind Lukan's saddle, his eyes lively with curiosity. Lukan had obviously gotten used to occasionally having a very naked cat shifter at his back and didn't even flinch anymore. Ellewinn had heard countless stories about the king on their way to the Valley and now couldn't wait to meet him for the first time. The whinny sounded anew, followed by the clomping of hooves beating the hard ground in a quick staccato. Then Lys came around the bend, his long black mane and tail trailing him like a banner, with Casto's wheat-blond hair setting a stunning counterpoint.

Ellewinn watched the approach of the man he had heard so much about. The mixed feelings he had gotten from his new brothers-in-arms about the man—from utter love, admiration, and devotion to annoyance and even anger, all paired with respect, either grumpily or wholeheartedly—had made his curiosity overflow in the last few days. Sic and Daran jumped from their horses, as did the king even before his ride had come to a halt. The three men embraced, laughing and joking, sharing words of love and endearment. Ellewinn took the time to watch the black stallion Casto had ridden. When the others had told him Lys was not a horse but a creature of chaos, Ellewinn hadn't believed it. Now he saw with his own eyes how right they had been. His cat yowled softly in his head, happy about being part of a pack with such a powerful creature in it. To Ellewinn's surprise, the cat had taken well to being part of a group, mostly because they were dangerous predators and hunting with them was fun and bloody, as the siege of Xe'lien's castle had shown. And now he was in the presence of yet another top predator. Ellewinn wasn't fooled by Casto's beauty or the way the expression in his clear blue eyes had softened when he had embraced Sic and Daran. Where Canubis was power personified and the other Emeris and the wolves were excellent hunters who knew death intimately, Casto was something else. Ellewinn had no doubt the man could be a wolf or even a cat when it came to dealing death. But that was not all he was. There was a snake in him, too, one who would patiently wait for its prey to step into the embrace of its deadly slings or until it could inject its lethal venom into the bloodstream of whomever it wanted gone. Casto was the kind of predator who could adapt and wait and either be quick or patient, always regarding the situation. He was a miracle who deserved Ellewinn's admiration. Lukan's laughter pried him from his musings.

"Don't get too enamored, my friend. Casto belongs to Renaldo."

Ellewinn huffed. "I'm aware. I was just looking."

"That's what we all do. Practically all the time."

Casto was done hugging his friends and had made a step backward. "It's so good to see you again."

"Yes, it is. Where are my husbands?" Daran's voice was full of longing.

Casto laughed, the sound pleasant even though there was a hint of cruelty in it, indicating yet another layer to his complicated personality.

"Last I saw of them, they were trying to look dignified and suppress their eagerness to finally get their hands on you. They've been insufferable the last few days."

"Why didn't they come with you?"

"I was already at the stables when the wolves announced your return. I jumped on Lys and came here while their horses were still grazing. And because it was clear I would beat them getting to you, I think they decided to wait." Again Casto's laughter filled the air around them, pleasing and cruel at the same time.

"You're such an ass." Daran went back to Rajan and got into the saddle. "My poor husbands!"

Sic giggled while he, too, climbed back onto his horse. "Then let's not make them wait any longer."

Casto huffed. "You're no fun at all." He winked at Lukan and Ellewinn before he turned around and jumped back onto the black stallion, who wore neither saddle nor bridle. The way Casto was one with the horse even before he reached it told Ellewinn everything he needed to know about his skills as a rider.

"I'm going to tell them you're here."

"You just want to rub it in you greeted us first!" Daran was laughing outright, the sound more carefree than Ellewinn had ever heard him. It seemed Casto was bringing out the playful side in his friends.

"And if?" The stunning blond shrugged, his eyes sparkling with mischief.

"I wish you fun, of course." Daran nudged Rajan with his heels, and the horse started walking again.

Casto lifted his hand in farewell, and the black stallion darted away. He was out of sight before Ellewinn had time to fully grasp he had been there at all. He jumped down from the horse Lukan was riding, shaking his head like his cat did when it got wet. Lukan's chuckling reached his ears, the quality so different from what Casto's laughter had been.

"Don't worry, Ellewinn. Casto has that impact on people. You will get used to it—or not, since I'm not sure if Casto is somebody you could ever truly get used to."

"You can't. Even when you think you've finally figured him out, he does something that leaves you with your jaw touching the ground. It's one of the reasons he's so much fun to be around."

The soft smile playing around Sic's mouth told Ellewinn there was a lot more to Sic's relationship with Casto than simple entertainment, and one look at Noran's scowling face was enough to convince Ellewinn that whatever kept Sic and Casto close was frowned upon by Noran. This was one of the reasons Ellewinn preferred solitude, not having to deal with such complicated things as relationships and human interaction—though since most of the members of the Pack weren't exactly human, Ellewinn wasn't sure if his usual rules applied. He shifted back into his cat form, following the lead of Daran toward a future that might not be what he and his cat had once envisioned for themselves, but which promised to be a lot more interesting than he could have ever hoped for.

5. PREPARATIONS

QUEEN ANESHA was sitting in her private rooms, reading over the latest reports from her spies and basking in the wonderful feeling of having her worst enemies taken care of and her lesser enemies cowering in fear. It was such a good thing to have the upper hand. She looked over at Aktan, who was playing with Regulon, bumping the little boy on his knees, which had the baby squealing with joy. Against her better judgment—Anesha knew better than to let emotions get in the way of anything—she felt a surge of warmth spreading through her chest where she assumed most people had a heart, and for a moment, she allowed herself to enjoy the feeling. Deep down she knew she didn't want Regulon to grow up to become like her and her brother—twisted and cold and deadly, incapable of seeing anything but enemies or opportunities, sometimes both, wherever they went—but she also knew there was no way around it. If she wanted her precious boy to not only survive but also to thrive, he had to become like her. There was always somebody out to get them, always an enemy to stay one step ahead of, as Erac and those three smiths had proven. Their deaths had made all the predators sniffing around the throne of Ummana more than wary, had caused many to retreat into the safety of their lairs with their tails tucked between their legs, but they wouldn't stay there. At the slightest whiff of weakness, they would be back, trying to tear chunks out of her and her family. Just by being his mother, Anesha had condemned Regulon to a life full of danger and backstabbing and lying, and yet, looking at his beautiful chubby face contorted in sheer joy, she couldn't bring herself to regret having him brought to the world. It would be her duty to see to his well-being and safety, and if she had to kill every single one of her enemies to do it, she wouldn't lose any sleep because of it.

With a smile that reached her eyes, Anesha got up to join her child and his father on the lounge.

IN THE darkness of her hiding spot beneath the sea, the Good Mother was fuming. She had lost her best seers, and putting more of her power into the few she had left was an exercise in futility, since they would never be powerful enough to be of any use to her. She had felt it when they died on the blades of Renaldo and his heart, and she had wanted to scream in rage when she felt the fire destroying all the power she had given to them. When she had learned Casto had been in Quell'renar, she had hoped the cursed place would drive him into madness. Instead, the stupid heart had again shown more resilience than she had given him credit for. Not even she dared to enter the ancient city where she had faced her first defeat at the hands of the bastards, and Casto had lived there for a prolonged time, seemingly unharmed by the ancient magic, the memories and illusions and dreams that haunted the place, interwoven like freshly spun wool and impossible to distinguish from reality. She stared at the ten long daggers in front of her. Trapping chaos inside them was unbearably difficult and costing her more power than she could afford. But if she wanted to have a chance against the bastard brothers, she needed more of these weapons. Again she cursed the creature of chaos that had sided with the brothers. By any rights, the Emperor of the Storms should have been her ally; instead he did the bidding of one of the hearts. And if all of that wasn't enough, the Good Mother could feel Ana-Darasa rejecting her more and more since the Creator Goddesses had left. The planet had long chosen her masters, and it wasn't the Good Mother. She gritted her teeth, remembering how difficult it had been to bend the magic in the Dark Forest to her will. It had required so much blood, and in the end, all she had managed was small-scale magic, not nearly enough to deter the brothers for more than a summer, where she had hoped to engage them for at least three years. All of her careful plans were failing one after the other, dissolving into ashes where she had hoped they would bring a turning of the tides. She narrowed her eyes. Not all was lost yet. This planet and its pathetic inhabitants were all she had left, the only anchor keeping her from being scattered throughout a universe she had had no hand in creating. Hatred, deep and dark, bubbled up inside her, fueled her power and determination. Ana-Darasa would be hers; there was no other option. She concentrated on the daggers again, reaching for the veil separating the order of this world from the realm of chaos. It was painful and draining and terrible, tearing it open and dragging bits of chaos into a place where they didn't belong. Yet the Good Mother kept on doing it, left with no other choice.

IN THE dream world, Noran stood next to Cornelia and watched as Heljia and Sic climbed onto Lys's broad back, ready to have a race with a few of

Cornelia's children. One of the snake-bears nudged Heljia's butt when she couldn't quite get her foot over Lys's back, and the stallion snorted his thanks. Then they all got ready before they raced off into the direction of the woods, which flickered slightly, the only indication that they weren't real. Or not in a way people usually defined realness. Neither Sic nor Heljia or Lys seemed perturbed by it. Noran looked at Cornelia, who was petting a smaller creature that looked like a snake with a cat's head. She seemed content.

"Stop staring, Noran. I'm fine." Cornelia looked up at him, her eyes piercing him with a newfound sharpness she usually only showed here in her realm where she was queen.

"I'm sorry. It's all just new for me." He stared into the distance, where Lys vanished in the shadows of the woods, the creatures he was racing howling in mock outrage. Here in the dream world, feelings were much easier to decipher, and Noran liked it—mostly.

"You have come a long way, Noran." Cornelia's voice was soft; she clearly didn't want to pry if it was uncomfortable for him.

"I have. I can't say it was a nice journey, but I'm glad I am where I am." Again he stared in the direction of the forest, but the three troublemakers were gone.

"They'll be back." Cornelia sounded amused, as if she knew exactly what he was thinking. "Lys has taken them out of the dream world and into the shadows to annoy my children. They love these games."

"You trust Lys?" It was something Noran had often contemplated. He knew his feelings toward the stallion were tainted by his difficult relationship with Casto, and he still couldn't shake the unease whenever Sic interacted with this creature that might look like a horse but was something else entirely. Cornelia shrugged.

"I'm pretty sure it doesn't make a difference, because should Lys decide to act against us, I don't think there's anything you or I could do to stop him. I'm not arrogant enough to think I understand a creature born from chaos, but I have gotten enough glimpses of his powers here in my realm to know there's a lot more to him than I think even Casto knows. What I also know is that Lys is irrefutably bonded with Casto. The bond is clearly visible even here, even when Casto is refusing to join their games. I can see his fire pulsing around Lys like a cloak, merging with the chaos." A smirk appeared on her face. "I can also sense Renaldo there, even though neither Lys nor our fiery god want to acknowledge it. I wonder how many centuries it will take until these two make their peace with each other."

"Probably as many as it will take until Casto forgives me." Noran sounded more wistful than he wanted. Of course, Cornelia picked up on it immediately and touched his arm, something she hadn't done in so long, Noran couldn't remember the last time. It was another sign he was on the right path, back into the arms of his family of gods and Emeris.

"I'm not sure Casto's forgiveness is something you should be aiming for. I fear it's too frustrating."

Noran shrugged. "It is. I can't exactly blame him for it either. It's just…." He threw his hands up in frustration. "A part of me wants him to forgive me, for my own peace of mind. Another part of me knows I don't deserve it, not yet. And another part feels I shouldn't be groveling for something from someone I don't even like. Even if I had been my old self when we met, I just know I would have had problems with Casto. He's the kind of person I can barely tolerate."

"And he's your husband's best friend." Cornelia sounded thoughtful.

"He is." A bright light in the distance told him Lys was bringing Sic and Heljia back.

"It is a dilemma. I grant you that. Perhaps you just have to concentrate on what you have in common with our difficult king." Pointedly, Cornelia looked in the direction of the light. Sic and Heljia were like beacons in the translucent state of their surroundings.

"Sic." Noran said the name like an endearment, because to him, it was. His beautiful husband was everything good and bright in Noran's world— even if the light could be cruel sometimes.

"Yes, Sic. I believe he's not only the link between the Echend'dim and our gods, but also the link to many more relationships within the Pack. Maybe even between you and Casto."

As much as it galled Noran, he knew Cornelia was right. His relationship with Casto had always involved Sic. Perhaps it was time to let his sweet Luksari's magic do its work and for him to stop fighting against something he wanted, no matter how much he resented it at the same time. Cornelia's laughter was accompanied by a short peck on his cheek, her words softly spoken, for Lys was approaching them fast.

"Just let it happen. I don't think you have much of a choice, anyway."

Looking into the flushed, happy face of his lover, Noran knew he would do anything to please Sic. Even if it meant making nice with the insufferable Casto.

"HOW IS Lukan doing?" Aegid looked up into Daran's face. Their beautiful husband had just come back from a visit with the young warrior. His cheeks were flushed from the cold outside, a cold Aegid and Kalad did their best to avoid at all costs. Now that the Valley was once again buried under layers upon layers of snow, the desert brothers were mostly holed up in their rooms, using Daran as their link to the outside world.

"He's doing better. He still has these moments of incredible sadness now and then, but all in all, the good memories are predominant. Training together definitely puts him in a good mood, and Ellewinn is a great help as well."

"And how are you doing?" Kalad had gotten up from the mountain of pillows and blankets on the ground in front of the fireplace to pull Daran into his embrace.

"I'm good. I think I've almost gotten used to having a link to so many different people, and I'm finally able to ignore them to the point where it feels as if they aren't even there while still being with me."

Aegid had gotten up as well and embraced both his husbands. Daran's link to the other Echend'dim had put a strain on their relationship where Aegid and Kalad had to get used to sudden flares of jealousy whenever they realized Daran was sharing something with an Echend'dim they weren't privy to and Daran overcoming the guilt he felt over having a strong connection to somebody who wasn't his husbands. Ultimately it had strengthened their bond and taught them to communicate clearly and promptly whenever problems bobbed up, but there had been days when all that had kept them from going for each other's throats had been the amazing sex they shared. Aegid had the suspicion this was all part of growing as a unit, and he was just glad that the worst was behind them. He and Kalad had learned to accept that Daran now had a whole slew of brothers and sisters he was close to. Once Daran had stopped seeing his connection to the other Echend'dim as a burden, Aegid and Kalad had also given up their resentment against it. Now they were back to their usual rhythm, which meant sex was going to happen for the rest of the day and well into the night. Spending winter with Daran was way better than enduring it on their own,

Aegid thought to himself while he watched Kalad helping their gorgeous husband out of his clothes. Aegid reached for Daran's long braid, his fingers itching to grab it and yank Daran toward him. And why should he deny himself when they all wanted it with the same eagerness?

IT WAS the night of the Spring Ceremony, and Lys stood in the shadows cast by the moons hitting the branches of the naked trees in the forest. This particular night had always been difficult for him, not only because his beloved anchor was forced into doing something he then enjoyed and at the same time resented simply for enjoying it—Casto had always been complicated, one of his best traits in Lys's eyes—but also because of the sheer power flooding the Valley. Lys was chaos, and the power the disciples of the Mothers and the Gods of War offered their gods was difficult to handle. Magic was more than even the Gods of War could grasp, and its connection to chaos not as clear-cut as even the Mothers had believed. Lys knew there was no sense in explaining these things to anybody, because in the end, they didn't make a difference, at least not to the Gods of War and their followers. Only the Luksari understood the mechanisms behind it all, and there was a reason these creatures usually faded quickly from solid beings back into raw magic held together by memories and dreams. What Sic had accomplished was rare and exciting and not without complications, though Lys could feel the Luksari had it all under control. And if he ever slipped—Lys would be there to protect his anchor, his brother, his soul. Perhaps even Renaldo, because as much as Lys wanted to resent it, he knew Casto needed the fiery god as much as Renaldo needed Casto. It was funny, really, from a certain perspective.

Lys snorted. This night was different, he could feel it in his bones, which was why he had retreated into the shadows. He could sense the blood being drawn, the members of the Pack renewing their vows. Deliberately, Lys opened his connection to Casto wide, knowing he had to be a part of this, more so than usual. The power slamming into him like a fist was a shock nevertheless. He could feel his anchor, could feel Casto's rising lust, which was just the conduit for the much more important things going on. Lys found it amusing how even the Gods of War didn't understand the deeper meaning behind their lust and sexual appetites. Oh, they did see how being connected to Noemi and Casto made it easier for them to bear their power, but they lacked the knowledge of why and how and, most importantly, *where*. Lys felt himself dissolving into the shadows, drawing from the energy flooding his bond with Casto. Even power that was channeled through a heart and siphoned back into the gods needed an additional outlet. The excess had to go *somewhere*, as it always had and always would. And *somewhere* was chaos. And Lys was the king of his realm, chaos personified. He took what his beloved anchor gave him, reveled in the wild sex Casto and Renaldo shared, the intense heat of their fire reaching him even in the shadows. Wave after wave crashed into Lys, each one bigger than the one before, and then suddenly, like a tsunami breaking over him, Lys was there, the link between him and Casto no longer unconscious and simply a given. Surrounded by flames and shadows, Lys, Casto, and Renaldo formed a triangle, staring at each other in utter surprise. Lys couldn't remember something like this ever happening. Chaos was meant to feed quietly, taking out of magic what made it unstable, not in the way the Mothers or Gods of War thought, but in the way that kept everything from constantly blowing up and reforming again. Renaldo was the first to speak, though no words left his lips.

I can feel you.

You always could. I just didn't let you. Lys snorted.

Why now? Casto made a step forward, shadows and fire dancing around him, the energy Renaldo was feeding him pulsing inside his body, reaching out to Lys. And Lys understood.

Because you accepted us both. You're perfectly balanced now. He looked at Renaldo, then at the fire and shadows connecting them. *A perfect link.*

Renaldo furrowed his brows, looking between Lys and Casto, staring at the lines between all three of them. He let out a curse, and the fire flared, raced into Casto, where it was welcomed, taken in, changed, elevated, sent both ways, back to the Angel of Death and to the Emperor of the Storms. Renaldo and Lys both groaned, the purity of what was being given too great to be taken silently. And then Lys felt it, another connection taking root, one he had rejected and suppressed until now, because never before had chaos been linked to a representative of order. When his shadows reached Renaldo's fire, it was a tentative meeting at first, both powers not used to being entangled after such a long time apart. Then there was another pulsing, a flare full of hope coming from Casto, who tried to push the connection between the two focal points in his life. Unable to deny his anchor anything, Lys let it happen, just as Renaldo, who could never say no to his heart.

The circle closed, the final piece slotted into place. Ana-Darasa may belong to the Gods of War, but now chaos was back as part of Creation, as it had always been. The Mothers had never been able to see beyond the destruction chaos caused and had stifled the universe they created by banning it, not understanding the consequences of doing so. Or perhaps they had understood and done it anyway, hoping to create something different. Nobody could truly understand the motivation of the Creators. With Casto as the link between Renaldo and Lys, magic would be able to come back, creating a new order for which the Gods of War would stipulate the rules and laws. A new world indeed. Just as it had been promised in the Prophecies.

Lys stared at Renaldo, who slowly bowed. The understanding in the god's eyes was all Lys needed to bow his head as well. Renaldo reached out, his fire dancing around his fingertips. Lys stepped forward, allowing his shadows to merge with the fire. It was a living creature, magic, returning to the world like a small sapling breaking free from the soil after centuries of drought.

Casto stepped right into the heart of it, absorbed it like a stone would the heat of the sun. He smiled, delighted and evil at the same time, his mind undoubtedly already going in a thousand different directions, scheming and weighing their options, and Lys loved him even more for it, because the things they would be able to do....

Renaldo, too, stared at Casto, full of love and devotion now that he finally understood how utterly misplaced his arrogance had been. Casto was the heart of it all, the center around which chaos and magic would spin in their endless dance, feeding each other, growing stronger and stronger until time became nothing but a passing fancy, something no longer needed for them. Opposite sides of a coin, very much like the Luksari and Noran, though not the same, because even though the Luksari was magic, it was a different kind, one that had taken on shape, just like the darkness inside of Noran was no longer chaos and shadows, but something formed to match the Luksari. Lys marveled at how everything became clear, how all the little threads of the tapestry suddenly formed a picture he could interpret.

The circle had closed.

And of course his anchor was immune to the weight of the moment.

You think we can keep this under wraps?

XENIA MELZER was born and raised in a small village in the South of Bavaria. As one of nature's true chocoholics, she's always in search of the perfect chocolate experience. So far, she's had about a dozen truly remarkable ones. Despite having been in close proximity to the mountains all her life, she has never understood why so many people think snow sports are fun. There are neither chocolate nor horses involved and it's cold by definition, so where's the sense? She does not like beer either and has never been to the Oktoberfest—no quality chocolate there.

Even though her mind is preoccupied with various stories most of the time, Xenia has managed to get through school and university with surprisingly good grades. Right after school she met her one true love who showed her that reality is capable of producing some truly amazing love stories itself.

While she was having her two children, she started writing down the most persistent stories in her head as a way of relieving mommy-related stress symptoms. As it turned out, the stress relief has now become a source of the same, albeit a positive one.

When she's not writing, she translates other authors' manuscripts to German, enjoys riding and running, spending time with her kids, and dancing with her husband.

Website: www.xeniamelzer.com
Email: info@xeniamelzer.com

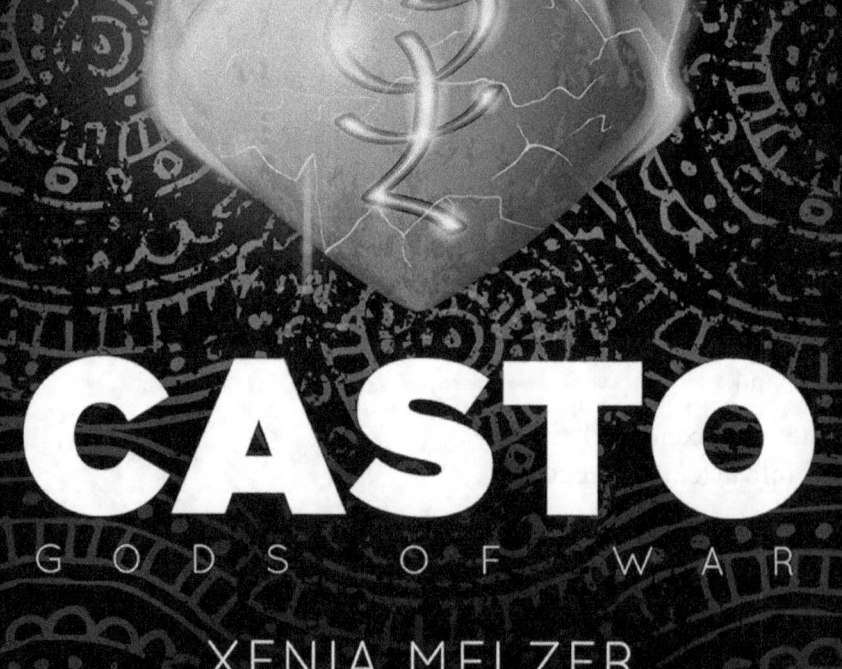

CASTO

GODS OF WAR

XENIA MELZER

Gods of War: Book I

All is fair in love and war. Renaldo has lived happily by that proverb
his entire life. But he has finally met his match, and he's about to discover
how unfair love and war can be.

When demigod and warlord Lord Renaldo takes a beautiful stranger
captive during an ambush, he is delighted to have found a distraction that
will keep him entertained during the upcoming siege. Little does he know,
Casto is keeping more than just one secret from him. Slowly, Renaldo
gets sucked into a turbulent roller-coaster relationship with his mysterious
prisoner, one that begins with hatred and soon spirals into a whirlwind of
conflicting emotions. And when it seems that things can get no worse, an
old enemy stirs right in the heart of his home.

Determined to keep Casto by his side, Renaldo has to find a balance
between the capricious young man and his own destiny as a ruler and god
to his people.

www.dsppublications.com

LOVE
AND THE
STUBBORN
GODS OF WAR: BOOK II

XENIA MELZER

Gods of War: Book II

All is fair in love and war. By now, Renaldo has found out the hard way how utterly stupid this statement is once you've met your match. And Casto won't give an inch in their ongoing war for love.

After a tumultuous start to their relationship, Renaldo and Casto seem to have finally reached calmer waters. But just when Renaldo starts getting comfortable and thinks he can relax, things get out of hand again. His old enemy, the Good Mother, is dangerously close to defeating the divine brothers by reaching out to what is most dear to him. Casto still clinging to his stubborn pride is all the plotters need to drive him and Renaldo apart. Burdened by the secrets of his past, Casto fights with everything he's got not only to save his life, but also to secure his future happiness. Facing the destruction of everything they have built together, Renaldo and Casto must choose between pride and love.

www.dsppublications.com

For more
great fiction
from

DSP PUBLICATIONS

visit us online.
WWW.DSPPUBLICATIONS.COM

www.ingramcontent.com/pod-product-compliance
Lightning Source LLC
Chambersburg PA
CBHW070107260626
47160CB00004B/1351